ENEMIES

ENEMIES
A Saga of the Great Lakes Wilderness

William J. Seno

PRAIRIE OAK PRESS
Madison, Wisconsin

First edition, first printing
Copyright © 1993 by William J. Seno

All rights reserved. No part of this publication may be reproduced or transmitted in any form or by any means, electronic or mechanical, including photocopy, recording, or any information storage or retrieval system, without permission in writing from the publisher.

Prairie Oak Press
2577 University Avenue
Madison, Wisconsin 53705

Typeset by KC Graphics, Inc., Madison, Wisconsin
Cover design and illustration: Mike Laier, Blue Mounds, Wisconsin
Printed in the United States of America by BookCrafters, Chelsea, Michigan

Library of Congress Cataloging-in-Publication Data

Seno, William Joseph
   Enemies: a novel / by William J. Seno : based on Travels and adventures in Canada and the Indian territories by Alexander Henry and the journals of explorers who encountered the North American wilderness.
     p.   cm.
   ISBN 1-879483-10-6 (alk. paper) : $10.95
   I. Henry, Alexander, 1739–1824—Fiction. 2. Indians of North America—Great Lakes Region—Fiction. 3. United States—History—French and Indian War, 1755–1763—Fiction. 4. Canada—History—To 1763 (New France)—Fiction. 5. Great Lakes Region—History—Fiction. I. Henry, Alexander, 1739–1824. Travels and adventures in Canada and the Indian territories. II. Title.
PS3569.E622E53   1992
818'.54—dc20   92-24434
                                                                                CIP

For Leah

Preface

First a confession: In writing *Enemies*, I have shamelessly lifted details, passages, episodes, and a plot from old books by long-dead authors.

The plot of *Enemies* is based on the true story of Alexander Henry, a would-be fur trader who embarked for the Great Lakes wilderness at the close of the French and Indian War. Details of Chippewa life are drawn from the observations of Johann Kohl, an ethnologist who lived among the Chippewas in 1855. Certain passages are based on the journals and memoirs of explorers of the Great Lakes region—Radisson, Hennepin, Allouez, Dablon, Marquette, Perrot, Catlin, and Pond.

The sources to which I have referred in writing *Enemies* are identified in the back of this book.

In defense of my good intentions, I can only argue that my many acts of literary theft have resulted in this book's greatest strength—its authenticity.

1

My countrymen made history on the morning of September 9, 1760, when they hoisted the Cross of Saint George over the walled city of Montreal.

Fifteen thousand British soldiers greeted their flag with jubilant huzzas. They knew they had reached the end of five years of bloody warfare. They knew they were victors. New France was utterly defeated, and all Canada lay in British hands. But while the soldiers thought only of returning home, my thoughts turned to schemes for profiting from Britain's new domain. I intended to partake in the spoils of this war.

In the days that followed, I made up my mind to journey to the far reaches of France's fallen empire, there to engage in the fur trade, a lucrative field of endeavor suddenly thrown open to British enterprise. I began to think of myself as bold and even courageous. Like bold men before me, I intended to seize upon a pivotal moment in history to build my fortune.

(As events unfolded, however, it became clear that my plans were every bit as foolish as they were courageous. The war had hardly ended; wounds were fresh; the wilderness was alive with enemies. As for myself, I knew nothing of the fur trade; I spoke no Indian languages; I had never paddled a canoe or even walked on snowshoes. At the tender age of eighteen, I knew nothing of the dangers that would soon confront me.)

Fortunately I recognized my shortcomings, and I sought the advice of Englishmen and Frenchmen alike—anyone who might share with me his knowledge of the fur trade. I was not surprised when the French angrily refused to discuss the matter with me, nor was I particularly concerned when certain Englishmen warned me of grave dangers in the Canadian wilderness.

The most dire warnings came from none other than Sir Thomas Gage, governor-general of Montreal. I had requested an audience with General Gage to obtain the license required to engage in the fur trade. When I arrived for my meeting with the general, I found him bent over papers at his desk.

"Your Excellency, thank you for seeing me on short notice. I am Alexander Henry, formerly of East Jersey. I served with the army of General Amherst in its campaign against Montreal. I am here to request a license to engage in the fur trade on the Upper Lakes."

General Gage stopped writing and looked up. "No Englishman would be safe in the Upper Country," he stated conclusively, as he motioned for me to be seated.

A raw-boned, sad-eyed man, General Gage seemed out of place in his office. His scarlet dress coat hung loosely from his angular shoulders; his powdered wig perched atop his head like a silly bit of decoration. He seemed far better suited to sit astride a horse than to sit behind a desk.

The general spoke to me in a fatherly manner. "Son, you must not presume that the war is won, simply because Governor Vaudreuil, sitting here in Montreal, proclaimed that he surrendered Canada to us. I admit that the governor's surrender sounded quite proper to my English ears. But Vaudreuil does not have the only say in the matter. Canada is teeming with savages and border French, and I assure you, they will not share the governor's notions of peace and surrender." General Gage drummed a finger on the desk top. "I assure you, they will kill any Englishman they lay their hands on."

The general's warnings seemed gross exaggerations to me, for I had already spoken with a number of Frenchmen, none of whom had threatened me with the slightest harm. I considered

General Gage to be something of a hypocrite—this man who had ordered hundreds, perhaps thousands, of soldiers to their deaths, but who now refused me the simple freedom to risk my own life.

"Your Excellency, I have been assured that the Indians of the Upper Country will deal peaceably with an English trader."

At this the general spat on the floor and leaned across his desk to thrust his face at mine. "Did you ever hear the scream of an Indian who wants your hair?"

I was too startled to answer.

"There's no hatred in the scream, no anger in it. Only a simple thirst for blood."

I paused to collect my wits. "Sir, if it is my hair at stake, then I request the liberty to risk it."

General Gage leaned back in his chair, chuckled, and smiled broadly. "Lad, you remind me of General Braddock. The old man was every bit as confident as you are, and every bit as foolish. He thought he had only to march his grand army up to the gates of Fort Duquesne, and the French would meekly throw out their guns and surrender. But his blind confidence cost Braddock his life; it cost the lives of a thousand British soldiers; and it cost me this shattered arm."

General Gage let his left arm drop on the desk before me. This seemed a strange turn for our conversation to take.

"In the spring of 1755 General Braddock arrived at the Hampton docks, at the head of two regiments of British regulars. I commanded the 44th Foot. We were the largest army ever to land on American soil, and ah, but we made a grand sight—row after row of freshly equipped British regulars, all turned out in smart, new uniforms. We had come to settle matters with the French.

"Old Braddock was a brave man, mind you, a rugged veteran of the Coldstream Guard. He once made a fine commander, when he led his troops on the open battlefields of Austria and Scotland. But in this country, in this godforsaken wilderness, he was no more than a dangerous old fool. He had far too high an opinion of himself and his regulars, and too low an opinion of the colonials. Although he recruited five hundred Virginians, it was only against his better judgment, for he considered them too slothful for military service. He ordered that the Virginians be used as little as possible, if fighting should start.

"As for the Indians, they were quite beneath Braddock's contempt. Several bands of Iroquois came to us that spring, all dressed up in their battle outfits, all besmeared with paint. They volunteered to join us in fighting their old enemies, the French. We welcomed them properly, with fife and drum and cannonade, and they, in turn, entertained us with war dances, which were droll affairs in which they demonstrated how they killed enemies and took scalps. I rather enjoyed their show, but Braddock looked upon the Indians as simpleminded brutes. He sent them away without so much as a proper goodbye.

"But the old fool should have listened to the Iroquois. He should have enlisted them, if only as scouts, for they could have warned us of the trouble he was marching us into. As things happened, our only scouts were an engineer and a hundred axe men, who cut a road through the forest for the army to follow. Our grand army was an enormous snake of red and blue uniforms, four miles long, twelve feet wide; cannons and supply wagons in tow; packhorses and cattle bringing up the rear. Our long, thin army crawled across the mountains and through the forests of Virginia and Pennsylvania, following the sound of chopping axes and falling trees. It took us all of a day to move just three miles.

"Braddock's plan was to seize Fort Duquesne, then drive the French out of the Valley of the Ohio. He thought he could surprise the French, for Britain had not yet issued a declaration of war. But Braddock's grand army crept so slowly through the forest that the French must have known it was coming from a long way off.

"At noon on a hot day in mid-July we arrived at the fords of the Monongahela, just a few miles above the French fort. I remember the day as if it were yesterday. The sky was cloudless. I was leading an advance party across a wooded ravine when I looked up and saw the strangest sight of my life. A lone man came bounding toward us through the shadows of the trees. He was dressed like an Indian, but he wore the tall hat and the high collar of a French officer. To this day I don't know if the queer fellow was French or Indian. For all I know, he may have been the devil, for he surely did the devil's work. He spotted us, stopped in his tracks, turned slowly, picked his tall hat from atop his head, and waved it grandly through the air."

General Gage swung his right arm through the still air of his office.

"The woods exploded with gunfire. Musket balls came flying at us like a storm of hail. The air was alive with hideous screams, like nothing I had ever heard before. I wheeled my column about and ordered the enemy's fire returned, but my men could not see the enemy. They saw only puffs of smoke floating among the trees. The brave fellows fired a volley into the trees and advanced, all the while shouting 'God save the King.' But their shouts were no match for the horrible screams of the enemy.

"As my column advanced, I caught glimpses of savages and French moving from tree to tree, along both our flanks, and I realized that we were fighting our way into a trap. Soon there were enemy guns behind every tree, to our right and to our left, pouring a deadly cross-fire into our ranks. I ordered my men to fall back, but as they did so, the main force of Braddock's army came rushing forward. Our two forces came together, and all was chaos. Our men were falling everywhere.

"Old Braddock had no notion of how to fight this blind sort of fight. The maneuvers he once learned on the battlefields of Europe were of no use to him here. He ordered his artillery to open fire, but the cannons did nothing but knock the tops off a few trees. He ordered his infantry to form ranks, but without knowing the direction of the enemy's fire, the soldiers did nothing but huddle like sheep in a few large masses. The battlefield became their slaughter pen."

General Gage slowly wrung his hands, as he told his story.

"At least the Virginians understood this sort of fight. They scattered about, took shelter behind trees, and one by one, they began to return fire. But old Braddock would not brook their actions. The old fool thought the Virginians were cowards to hide as they did. He charged madly about on his horse, cursing the Virginians, thrashing at them with his sword, ordering them to form ranks. Those who followed his orders were again exposed to the deadly fire of the enemy. The ground soon was covered with our dead and wounded.

"Braddock was a man possessed, galloping about the battlefield on his charger. Four horses were shot out from under him. At last he ordered a retreat, but at the instant he did so, a ball pierced his chest. He fell to the ground and lay there, bleeding from his mouth, gasping for air. He ordered me to leave his body behind, but I countermanded his order. I had two Virginians bear him off the field.

"I took command of the army, as it fell into a headlong retreat. I ordered the Virginians to cover our rear, and they did so as best they could. As for the wounded, I had no choice. I left them behind, on the field of battle. Only God knows what became of them."

General Gage stared at the top of his desk, and wrung his hands.

"We managed to haul Braddock away with us. Four men bore the old man on a litter, for he could not bear the pain of riding a horse. Three days later, as we stopped for a rest, Braddock raised himself up on an elbow, lifted a hand in the air, and proclaimed to the trees that surrounded us, 'We shall know better how to deal with them another time.'

"But the old man was mightily mistaken. In a few minutes he was dead. We buried him on the spot. The supreme commander of His Majesty's forces in North America was buried beneath a wagon track, so the enemy would not find his body.

"All told, we lost a thousand men and sixty-five officers that day on the Monongahela."

General Gage rubbed his forehead, and spoke in a hushed but angry voice. "The screams of those Indians are still fresh in my ears. They will haunt me till I die."

I observed a respectful moment of silence.

"Sir," I finally offered, "the Indians of the Upper Country may not be so hostile as the Indians who fought you."

The general looked up and fairly shouted at me. "Lord in Heaven, man! Who do you think ambushed us on the Monongahela? They were Ottawas, Chippewas, Hurons, Potawatomis—Upper Indians the lot of them. And their war chief was a half-breed soldier who commanded the fort at Michilimackinac—a man named Langlade. For all I know, he's up there still, waiting for more Englishmen to kill."

The general raised a finger before my face. "I tell you, Michilimackinac is the very heart of enemy country."

I sat in silence, not knowing how to advance my argument.

General Gage sought to conclude our conversation with an official ruling. "Son, there is no peace with the Upper Indians. You would lose your life if you were to venture among them. I deny you your license." He turned his attention back to the papers on his desk.

I persisted.

"Sir, I have been informed that you recently granted permission to one Henry Bostwick, an Englishman, to leave for the Upper Lakes. I have been told that he embarked with a number of canoes, all loaded with trade goods. Sir, I consider it neither proper nor fair for you to have favored him in this manner."

My brash impudence angered the general, who rose abruptly to his feet, as if to strike me. But he paused. Leaning over me, scowling, he spoke with measured words.

"So, Mister Henry. So be it. In the name of His Majesty, King George, I hereby grant you a license to engage in the fur trade at Michilimackinac."

The grant of license had the ring of a death sentence.

General Gage ordered his clerk to draft the appropriate document. As we waited for the clerk to finish his task, the general stared into my eyes. I saw the general's expression gradually soften, the scowl slowly leave his face. The clerk handed the document to the general, who signed it without reading it and handed it to me.

"Son, I fear that you will soon have reason to remember my warning."

2

Why did I risk my life as I did? Was I courageous, as I thought at the time? Was I foolish, as others suggested? Was I ambitious? Was I greedy?

With hindsight, I suspect that my desire to enter the fur trade was born out of little more than a sense of bitter recklessness.

As a boy growing up in East Jersey, I had heard tales of the fabled fur traders—men who turned their backs on civilization to live among the Indians, who amassed fortunes by bartering for animal skins in the depths of the wilderness. Such tales had fired my young imagination.

But the greatest influence on my young mind was the heartfelt faith of my family. We belonged to the Religious Society of Friends, more commonly known as the Quakers. We were devout, peaceful, and prayerful. We never ate a meal without first entering into the silence of thanksgiving. We never began a day without first gathering together to hear my mother read a chapter from her Bible, after which we sat together in a reverent hush. During our times of silent prayer, I felt that something real and vital was taking place among us; I felt that each of us was moving toward a still place of communion with God. And when one of us was inspired to break the sacred silence, the words came so simply, so clearly, that it seemed as though God himself was among us.

In the year 1755 war broke out between France and England. I was thirteen, and my brother was seventeen. But there was never any thought of either of us going off to fight in the war, for my family believed that killing was not God's way.

In the next few years, however, my faith in God was to be severely tested, and finally destroyed. First, my father fell victim to a mysterious illness that sapped his strength and weakened his mind. We prayed fervently for him, but he only grew worse. With each week that passed, he became weaker and thinner, till eventually he could hardly move. I, a boy of fifteen, had to carry my father's frail body about in my arms. At times when I held him, it seemed that I could feel the life draining from his body. He gradually lost the ability to speak, and near the end, he did nothing but stare blankly into space. My father could neither see us nor hear us, yet I managed to convince myself that he was seeing God.

Several months after my father's death, a sudden illness befell my mother. She suffered from a high fever and congestion of the lungs, and by the second day of her illness, she was having great trouble breathing. Day and night I knelt on the floor beside her bed and prayed, constantly tortured by the sound of her every desperate gasp for air. Her breathing came harder and harder, till at last she became delirious and cried out for her own mother, who was long dead. In my frantic prayers at her bedside, I imagined that my mother and I were adrift in a boat on the sea. A storm was raging all about us. But the comforting words from the Gospel of Mark spoke to my heart:

And there arose a great storm of wind, and the waves beat into the ship, so that it was now full. And Jesus was in the hinder part of the ship, asleep on a pillow: and they awoke him, and said unto him, 'Master, carest thou not that we perish?' And he arose and rebuked the wind, and said unto the sea, 'Peace, be still.' And the wind ceased, and there was a great calm. And he said unto them, 'Why are ye so fearful? how is it that ye have no faith?'

But all my faith and all my prayers did nothing to help my mother. Death took her away from me. And when she died, I was relieved that her suffering was at an end. But I did not thank God—for I no longer believed in God.

In the days that followed my mother's burial, my brother and I continued our family's practice of praying together. We continued to sit in silence, our heads bowed. But I no longer felt the living silence of the Lord—I felt only the empty silence of death. I shared my feelings with my brother, who was greatly alarmed by my doubts. He insisted on reading to me from the Gospel of John, repeating to me the promises Jesus once made for our salvation and our eternal life. I told my brother that I no longer believed in the promises of Jesus. I said that my thinking was more in keeping with the lamentations of Job:

My days are swifter than a weaver's shuttle, and are spent without hope.
O remember that my life is wind: mine eye shall no more see good.
The eye of him that hath seen me shall see me no more: thine eyes are upon me, and I am not.
As the cloud is consumed and vanisheth away: so he that goeth down to the grave shall come up no more.
He shall return no more to his house, neither shall his place know him any more.
Therefore I will not refrain my mouth; I will speak in the anguish of my spirit; I will complain in the bitterness of my soul.

3

The new life I chose for myself was as far removed from the Quaker faith as it could possibly be. I became a part of the bloody war being waged for North America. In the summer of 1760 I joined the army of General Amherst, not as a soldier but as a merchant, supplying the needs of the army. I spent a large part of my inheritance to purchase medical supplies and munitions at Albany. I then joined the British army at Oswego, as it prepared to cross Lake Ontario and attack the French at Fort Lévis.

The attack on the fort lasted for some five days in mid-August. I arrived on the scene just in time to witness the surviving French soldiers surrender their fort. The log stockade of the fort lay in splinters, after taking a pounding from the cannons of British ships, which lay at anchor in the river. The battle provided me with an opportunity to sell medical supplies at a good profit.

Following the capture of Fort Lévis, General Amherst swiftly carried his army against Montreal—the last bastion of French power in all of Canada. General Amherst's army was joined at Montreal by a second army, commanded by General Murray, and a third, commanded by Colonel Haviland. More than fifteen thousand British soldiers and a thousand Iroquois warriors were assembled before the walls of Montreal—while the city was defended by just two thousand French regulars and militia. In the face of such overwhelming odds, Governor Vaudreuil negotiated a peace, in which he surrendered all Canada to the King of England.

So the war ended. For me it had been a short war, uneventful, and rather profitable. The only real violence I had witnessed was the flogging of a British soldier for insubordination. Yet the war left me strangely unsatisfied and hungry for new adventures.

Thinking to avail myself of the newly opened market in Canadian furs, I hastened to Albany to procure a supply of trade goods, which I intended to carry to Montreal. But the winter came on swiftly, and I found I was only able to return to Fort Lévis. I stayed there through the early part of the winter, during which time I busied myself selling merchandise to the garrison at a good profit.

With the arrival of the new year (the favored season for traveling over the snow) I made ready to go down to Montreal. My journey was to be through a country thick with forests, varied only by the broad surface of the frozen river and inhabited only by Indians and wild beasts. I hired as my guide a Frenchman named Jean Baptiste Bodoine, a seasoned veteran of the wilderness. Monsieur Bodoine arrived for the start of our journey with a keg of brandy strapped to his back. He was a slight man. In his hooded robe of beaver skins he looked for all the world like an Esquimo. His hair was speckled with gray, but his beard, which he wore in the old French style, was as black as the night. He handed me a pair of snowshoes—an article of equipment I had never before used. I strapped the snowshoes to my feet, took one successful step, and with my second step, I toppled into the snow. My fall in the snow drew hearty laughter from Bodoine, who stood at a distance and offered me no help whatsoever, other than gleeful advice on where to place my hands and feet. After much clumsy effort on my part, I managed to regain my feet, and off we went, across the frozen, snow-covered surface of the River Saint Lawrence. I moved tentatively and tried to keep my feet beneath me, but my slow pace raised the ire of Bodoine, who lashed at me with his tongue. All day long I struggled with my snowshoes, and by the time the winter sun started to set, I was utterly exhausted.

After three days of such toilsome travel, Bodoine and I finally reached Isle de Perrot, a large island situated on a wide expanse of the river, just above Montreal. Here Bodoine proposed nothing less than to spend the night with a band of Indians, who he said were camped nearby. These particular Indians, he said, were Abenaquis, so-called settled Indians, who had fought for the French in the recent war. At first I refused to visit their camp, concerned as I was that they had not yet given up their habit of fighting Englishmen. Bodoine, however, said he personally knew the Abenaquis of this camp, and he assured me that I had nothing to fear from them. The thought of shelter, rest, and a warm fire finally persuaded me to set aside my concerns and follow Bodoine.

We arrived at the Abenaqui camp at nightfall. The camp consisted of four long, arched lodges, each covered with birchbark, all of them deserted. Bodoine directed me to one of the lodges, but he warned me against eating any food I might find there, as this would be considered bad manners by the Abenaquis. Within the lodge I found eight or ten fireplaces and the skins and blankets of many Indians. I built a fire for myself, covered myself with a blanket, and fell fast asleep.

Little did I know that, as I was sleeping, the Abenaquis returned home and were invited by Bodoine to sample his brandy.

Sometime during the night I was rudely aroused from my sleep by a sharp kick to my chest and a howl of anger. I opened my eyes to see a bald Indian with a red face standing over me. He was holding a knife in one hand, and he was struggling with several other Indians, who seemed to be trying to hold him away from me. Perceiving the danger I was in, I started to rise to my feet, just as the red-faced Indian broke free and lunged at me with his knife. I raised my arm to parry his thrust, and his knife stabbed through the flesh of my hand. The other Indians managed to pull the madman off me, and an Indian woman grasped me by the arm and quickly guided me out of the lodge. Once outside, she made urgent signs that I flee the place. I looked about for Bodoine, but he was nowhere to be seen. Without his direction I was at a loss as to where to go. I realized that I could not retreat to another lodge, for I heard howls and shouts of anger coming from all the lodges. I could not speak a word of the woman's language, but when I repeated the name "Bodoine," she understood my meaning. She made signs to assure me that she would look for my guide, if I would stay hidden behind a tree. I seated myself in a snowdrift behind a large tree, and from my hiding place I watched the Indians as they ran from lodge to lodge, as if to quell the disturbance. I had no coat with me, and the bitter cold quickly penetrated my body and set me to shivering. Fortunately, the cold also congealed the blood in my wound and stopped the bleeding.

After an hour of such misery, I heard Bodoine calling my name. I went to him and was surprised to find him quite drunk. It now became clear to me that my guide had shared his keg of brandy with the Abenaquis, and that his generosity had resulted in the wild drunkenness which nearly cost me my life.

I showed Bodoine my wound and demanded that we depart immediately. He retrieved our snowshoes and coats, and we set off along a beaten path that entered a deep wood. But no sooner were we a few hundred feet from the Indian camp than the drunken Frenchman began to sing. I ordered him to be silent, but he only laughed and sang all the louder. I was forced to follow his infernal noise through the stillness of the night, all the while fearing that my Indian attacker would catch up with me. I wondered how Bodoine could be so careless with my life, and I began to suspect that he had shared his brandy with the Indians in hopes that they might kill me.

At daybreak we reached the easternmost point of Isle de Perrot. Before us stretched the frozen surface of a wide expanse of the River Saint Lawrence, known as Lac de Saint Louis. Through the cloudy atmosphere I could barely make out the distant shore of Isle de Montreal. I was all for pressing on across the ice, in order to place as much distance as possible between myself and the Abenaquis. My greatest desire was to arrive at Montreal before nightfall. Bodoine, however, insisted on halting and encamping on this point of land, arguing that he thought a storm was coming on, and he feared we might be caught by a blizzard while out on the ice.

Bodoine's newfound caution infuriated me. "You were not so cautious when you gave your brandy to the Abenaquis," I charged. "Was it stupidity on your part, or did you hope they would kill me?"

Bodoine, still somewhat intoxicated, responded to my question with a dull look of surprise, which slowly broadened into a toothy, squinting grin. "It must have been my stupidity, monsieur, for surely I did not wish to see you dead." He cocked his head to one side. "Why, monsieur, would a Frenchman wish to see an Englishman dead?"

I seized the Frenchman by the front of his coat and tossed him into the snow. "Henceforth, sir, I will not be needing your services," I declared, standing over him. "You are dismissed. I will fare better without you." I threw a handful of coins into the snow at his feet. "You are paid."

We exchanged looks of heartfelt hatred.

I turned toward the lake to complete the last leg of my journey. I had taken but a few steps when the clap of a gunshot resounded in my ears. I turned to look back at Bodoine, who was holding a smoking pistol.

"Englishman," Bodoine shouted, "I need not bother with killing you. You will kill yourself soon enough." He let out a high-pitched laugh of derision, which rang through the cold air.

I started off across the lake, moving at a furious pace, angry and eager to escape the sound of the Frenchman's laughter. But I quickly discovered that my snowshoes did not glide properly over the deep snowdrifts on the lake. The snowshoes were forever sinking and sticking, as if in wool. My progress was exceedingly slow. I plowed through drift after drift, into the teeth of a stiff wind. I grew warm from exertion, and I loosened my coat and pulled off my cap. The sound of Bodoine's evil laughter gradually was replaced by the sound of the wind whistling past my ears.

I paid but scant attention to the ragged, gray clouds that hurried over my head, but after an hour or two, cold rain began falling from the sky. The rain changed to sleet, then to needles of ice, that stung at my face. Snowdrifts dragged at my feet. The wind worked with all its force to impede my progress. My clothing was drenched with perspiration and sleet. I felt my legs weaken, and a general fatigue settle over my body.

Perhaps I could have better endured my fatigue if I could only have seen myself advancing across the ice—but such was not the case. I could no longer see the distant shoreline through the falling ice. Ahead of me I saw only a gloomy sky and snowdrifts without end, piled like dunes of sand across a white desert. I directed my path by the direction of the wind, and used my nose as a keel. When I felt one cheek grow colder than the other, I turned my face back into the wind. The falling ice changed to flakes of snow, which came swirling at my eyes, dizzying me.

To regain my strength, I stopped for a few minutes and turned my back to the wind. My inactivity, however, only served to chill me. My coat froze into a shell of ice, and my body began to shake violently.

I resumed my struggle onward, and after a time my shaking stopped, but I realized that I could no longer feel the pain in my wounded hand. My hands and feet were numb from the cold. Slipping and stumbling, I began to steer a zigzag course among the drifts in a vain effort to avoid the deepest of them. My head grew heavy; my thoughts confused. I lost any sense of time or place. My legs stomped clumsily onward, as if by themselves, so excited by overexertion that they could not stop. I no longer saw the snow falling before my face—I saw only a dull gleam of light.

Finally I bid my legs to stop, and I fell over on my side in the snow. I felt neither cold nor pain—only profound weariness. I shut my eyes, and the faces of my dead father and mother appeared before me, still and expressionless as gravestones. I knew that I was about to die. I rolled over on my back and opened my eyes for one last time. Black snowflakes swirled across a white sky. I closed my eyes.

"You will kill yourself soon enough."

What? I raised myself on one elbow and looked about. It was Bodoine's voice. Had the Frenchman followed me onto the ice? His derisive laughter echoed softly through the blizzard. His voice came from somewhere above me, somewhere outside the storm. It seemed as though the wretch was watching me die, and he was laughing at me.

I raised myself to my knees. I regained my feet. I turned my face into the wind. My legs moved forward.

4

I was saved from death in the snow by a Frenchman named Leduc, who found me thrashing about in the woods near his cabin on Isle de Montreal. The kind old gentleman led me to his cabin, dressed my wounded hand, and put me to bed. (Or so he told me later, for I have no recollection of these events.) He patiently nursed me back to health with a steady diet of broth. As he did so, I shared with him my plans to enter the fur trade. I asked him if he knew of a trustworthy guide who could assist me. He suggested a Canadian by the name of Etienne Campion, a reliable man, he said, who spoke a little English, and who had years of experience in the fur trade.

Two days later, having recovered my strength, I set off to visit Campion, whom I found staying at a boarding house in Montreal. I expected to meet a seasoned, older man, but Campion was in his early thirties. He was short and powerfully built, and he sported a red beard and a shock of red hair.

"Monsieur Campion," I began, "I am Alexander Henry. Monsieur Leduc has suggested that you might be so kind as to offer me your advice, for I am considering a new venture in the fur trade. To that end, I have obtained the necessary license from the governor-general. I am prepared to pay you for whatever advice you might see fit to offer me."

I did not broach the subject of hiring Campion as my guide.

Campion clearly was skeptical. He sat across a table from me, stroking his beard and offering no advice. "Canada is a dangerous place for a fair-headed English boy," he observed.

Hesitantly at first, I proceeded to elaborate on my plans, but I quickly exhausted my meager knowledge of the fur trade, and an awkward silence ensued.

Campion finally asked me about my role in the recent war.

"I supplied General Amherst's army with goods during the last months of the war," I said. "In truth, I have endured greater dangers since the war ended."

"And what dangers have you endured?"

"My guide for the journey here, a man named Bodoine, led me to a camp of Abenaquis on Isle de Perrot. I narrowly escaped their camp with my life."

"I know the man," Campion said. "You are better off without him. In point of fact, monsieur, you will be better off if you forget all your ideas of the fur trade. The Canadian wilderness is a dangerous place, even for a man who knows the country. If you had trouble making the short journey here from Fort Lèvis, you most certainly will not survive a long voyage into the wilderness."

Campion proceeded to list for me the hardships and dangers I was likely to encounter in the wilderness. His speech was intended to discourage me, but it had quite the opposite effect on Campion himself. As he spoke of cold and hunger, of vast distances and dangerous waters, he warmed to his subject. Soon he was expounding on the rewards of the fur trade, as he paced back and forth across the room, gesturing grandly with his arms, a silver cross swinging from side to side across his chest. It was readily apparent to me that Campion had broad knowledge of the wilderness, the fur trade, and the Indian nations that supported the trade.

"Monsieur Henry," he said, rapping his fist on the table, "if I knew an Englishman of some means, an Englishman in whom I could trust, and who could trust in me . . . he and I together could acquire great wealth in the Indian trade. I believe the successful trading companies of the future will be partnerships of Frenchmen and Englishmen. And the first such partnership to apply itself to the Upper Country will secure a large part of the fur trade for many years to come."

Campion's energy seemed boundless. It shone forth in his optimism, his ambition, and his curiosity. When he spoke, his eyes sparkled, his voice rose and fell with inflection, his hands and arms moved without stopping. When he listened, he concentrated intently on the many levels of meaning he seemed to gather from even the simplest of my comments.

I informed Campion that I had the necessary means to finance a trading voyage, and I stated with certainty that I intended to employ men to carry trade goods into the country that surrounded the Upper Lakes.

At this Campion stomped his foot to express his approval. "The Upper Country," he proclaimed, "is a region richer in furs than any other part of the earth." He pointed to me, grinned, and winked slyly. "You, monsieur, have a shrewd sense for this business. You know that the war has halted the fur trade for five long years, and you understand what this means. It means the Indians are in desperate need of merchandise. It means the Upper Country is full of beaver. It means the Indians will sell furs cheaply and will buy merchandise dearly. Never before, monsieur, have I seen such an opportunity for profit."

It was now my turn to play the skeptic. "What of hostile Indians?" I asked.

Campion paused thoughtfully before replying. "The Indians of the Upper Country are fierce fighters, it is true. And for many years they have been told to hate the English. But they are, for the most part, honorable men. I believe that if you visit them in peace, they will welcome you in peace."

I was about to offer Campion employment as my guide, when he broached a rather different subject. He walked up to me, clapped his hands on my shoulders, and made me an offer in the form of an announcement: "You and I, Monsieur Henry, we will be partners." He embraced me with a bearlike hug.

His proclamation startled me. "What do you propose?" I asked.

"I will act as your guide and your liaison with the Indians. You, of course, will be the *bourgeois*, the sole owner of merchandise, canoes, and peltries. When the first year's enterprise is complete and accounted for, we will share in the profits. You will receive two thirds; I one third. If no profits are to be had, I will receive nothing."

I was astonished at Campion's bold proposal. Yet his charisma, his spirit, and what I believed to be his trustworthiness soon won me over. I agreed to his proposal. He was to contribute his expertise to our venture; I was to contribute my inheritance.

I offered Campion my hand in agreement, but before he took it, he raised a finger to make one further point. "It must be understood, monsieur, that you are to have the final say in all matters concerning business, but that I will have the final say in all matters concerning the safety of the voyage."

To this I readily agreed, and we struck hands.

5

The summer was too far advanced to begin a long voyage into the wilderness, so Campion and I decided to spend the winter in Montreal. We planned, when spring arrived, to embark for the Upper Lakes, a vast territory the French knew as *Le Pays d'en Haut*—"the Upper Country."

No trade goods were to be found in Montreal at the time, so Campion and I journeyed to Albany to buy merchandise from the English and Dutch merchants there. At first Campion suggested that I do all the bartering with my countrymen, but once the trading began, he could not resist entering into negotiations. Most of the merchants were eager to deal with us, but one, an old English gun seller, angrily refused to speak with Campion. He pulled me aside to warn me. "Lad, that Frenchman will strip you of your wealth. He will lead you to your death. He will dance on your grave."

The shops at Albany were stacked to the rafters with a wide array of merchandise suited for the Indian trade: packets of twist and carrot tobacco, kegs of rum and high wine, muskets, bags of ball and shot, bars of lead, bullet molds, gunpowder, flints, nests of brass kettles, iron spear points, hoe and axe heads, hatchets, knives, chisels, stroud blankets, calico and worsted cloth, boxes of needles and thread, silk ribbons, awls, combs, scissors, looking glasses, clay pipes, hawk bells, vermilion, gorgets and arm bands of brass and silver, prayer sticks, crosses, amulets in the shapes of animals, beads of colored glass, and cylindrical beads made from sea shells, known by the Indians as *wampum*. Campion advised me to purchase the items that he said were most needed by the Indians—particularly guns and ammunition.

Returning to Montreal with our trade goods, Campion hired a crew of French canoe men, known as *voyageurs*. These men were generally unkempt and rowdy, but they all seemed proud of their calling, as if they belonged to a superior class of nobles. They followed Campion's orders to the letter, and they worked like beavers.

I soon noticed that all the voyageurs whom Campion hired were short. I stood a full head above many of them. I asked Campion why this was so, and he said he employed only short men because long legs would take up too much cargo space within the canoes. What the voyageurs lacked in height, however, they more than made up for in strength. Their shoulders and necks were thickly muscled. They walked with light yet purposeful steps. One man in particular caught my eye. He was an older fellow named Porlier, who strongly favored one leg. Yet the man had adjusted so well to his affliction that he moved about with remarkable power, and even grace.

The canoe men dressed gaudily. All wore shirts of brightly colored calico. Some wore red sashes about their waists, and some wore handkerchiefs on their heads. Some wore worsted pants, while others preferred deerskin leggings. (I was the only one dressed as a proper English gentleman—in waistcoat, topcoat, breeches, stockings, and buckled shoes.)

Campion immediately set the men to work building canoes. Their first task was to take to the woods, in search of materials. Within a few hours the men returned with everything they needed to build the canoes: sheets of birchbark, sticks of cedar, sacks full of pine tar, and the sinewy roots of the spruce tree, known as *wattap*. With these simple materials in hand, they sat themselves down in a clearing and applied their craft.

Each canoe was to be built by the crew of men that would eventually paddle it, and all the men took great pride in their creations. They boasted of the swift lines their canoes would take, and they criticized the sloppy craftsmanship of the other crews. Before the canoe frames were half built, the voyageurs were issuing challenges to one another to race and were wagering on which canoe would be the fastest.

Sticks of cedar, delicately thin and light, were bent and notched to serve as ribs, splints, gunwales, and bars. As the sticks were bound together with cords of wattap, the frames of the canoes began to take shape. Small sheets of birchbark, a quarter inch thick, were laid over the frames, which looked for all the world like gigantic shoes being fashioned by cobblers. The birchbark was sewn onto the frames, again with wattap, and the pine tar was melted and gummed into the cracks and the holes, to prevent leaks. Not a single nail was used in the entire assembly, and each canoe seemed to hold the very life of the forest—the lightness of the birch, the strength of the cedar, the aromatic sap of the pine, the sinews of the spruce. As a final act, a sort of christening, the voyageurs painted festoons of red, green, yellow, and black along the sides of the canoes. On the high prows and sterns they painted fanciful patterns or the silhouettes of animals—in one case a bear, in another a moose. One canoe was adorned with the *fleur-de-lis* of France.

When the canoes were finished, fully decorated, and hung from trees to dry, I felt rather proud of my little fleet. Each canoe was more than thirty feet long and five feet wide. The French had names for these large trade canoes, calling them *canots du maître* or *canots de Montréal*. Campion called them *les grandes dames* of the Northwest trade, and he explained to me their virtues. "The canoe is a most practical vessel, invented by the northern Indians. We French have improved upon the Indian design in just one way—we have made the canoe larger. A Montreal canoe can float all of four tons of merchandise; yet it can be carried on the shoulders of just four men. The canoe is light because it has no keel; but it is also fragile. In rapids it flies downstream like an arrow, and if it strikes a rock, it is damaged or destroyed. Even so, a canoe can be repaired or rebuilt anywhere in the wilderness, so long as there is birchbark, wattap, and pine tar nearby. Thus the Montreal canoe is the perfect vessel for the fur trade."

Campion explained to me in great detail the geography of the voyage we were about to begin, as well as the decisions we would face along the way. Michilimackinac, our destination, was a trading post guarded by an old French fort, strategically located on a broad strait of water that joins Lake Michigan with Lake Huron. The fort was the center of trade for a large part of the Canadian wilderness.

Campion said our voyage to Michilimackinac could proceed by one of two trade routes. One followed Lake Ontario, Lake Erie, and Lake Huron. Campion said this route was a good one for supply boats and bateaux, but he did not favor it for canoes because of its greater distance and high waves on the lakes, which often roll and swell like the ocean.

A second route ascended the Ottawa River, known by the French as *La Grande Rivière*, toward the west, eventually nearing a small river that flows into Lake Huron at Georgian Bay. From there the route followed a chain of islands along the north coast of Lake Huron, to reach Michilimackinac. The chief problem with the Ottawa River trade route was the presence of many rapids and falls, which forced voyageurs to carry canoes and cargo overland on their backs, in some places across long distances, or up and down steep and rocky terrain. The carrying places were known as *portages* and were considered the most grueling, most dangerous part of a voyageur's job. Nevertheless, Campion said he favored the Ottawa River route, as had French voyageurs for more than a hundred years before him.

Following Campion's advice, I decided that our voyage should proceed by the Ottawa River trade route.

On August 4, 1761, we embarked on our voyage to the Upper Country. We launched our canoes at the head of the rapids at Lachine, just above Montreal. My little fleet numbered nine vessels, manned by seventy-four voyageurs, Campion, and myself. Each canoe carried eight or nine men, sixty-five pieces of cargo, several hundredweight of food, two oil cloths, a sail, an axe, a tow line, and a large sponge for bailing water. I was worried when I first saw my canoes laden with all this cargo, for the vessels rode so low in the water that the gunwales were just six inches above the waterline. I thought that the canoes would surely capsize and that all my property would be lost.

Campion placed skilled men in the stern and the bow of each canoe. A steersman, or *gouvernail*, stood at the stern and steered the craft with a long paddle. A foreman, or *avant*, sat in the bow and watched the water ahead, looking for shallows or rocks and signaling with his arms where the gouvernail should steer the canoe. The avant also helped guide the canoe through rapids, using a setting pole in going upstream or a long paddle in going down. The middlemen, or *milieux*, sat side by side on low seats in the middle of the canoe and used their paddles to propel the canoe through the water. Three canoes made up a brigade, and each brigade had its own guide, who acted as leader. The guide paid the men their wages and answered to me, the owner, or bourgeois, for any theft or loss. I engaged the men to transport my trade goods from Montreal to Michilimackinac, then to carry my newly acquired peltries and skins back to Montreal on the return trip. For this service I paid each middleman one hundred fifty livres, and each endman three hundred livres. Campion, who advised me regarding these rules, said they had been established under the French government.

The only food we provided for the men was maize, or Indian corn, and pork lard for flavoring. The corn was prepared by first being boiled in strong lye. Then the husks were removed and the grain was mashed and dried. In the process the grain became soft and friable like rice. I provided for each man a quart of Indian corn for each day of the voyage, and Campion reckoned that a bushel of corn and two pounds of lard could feed a man for a month. We took no other food with us, not even bread or salt, for we had no room for such luxuries within the canoes. Every inch of space was reserved for the cargo we had to transport across the wilderness.

When I questioned whether the men could survive on such a spare diet, Campion assured me that they could. "Canadians are the only men on earth who would agree to such meager fare over such a long period of hard labor," he said. "Their willingness to do so will forever secure for them and their employers a monopoly in the fur trade."

In a short time we arrived at the Sault de Sainte Anne, a stretch of rushing water above Isle de Montreal. (It is only after passing these rapids that a voyage to the Upper Country can be said to have properly begun.) On the bank of the sault stood a small wooden chapel, where the men went to confession and offered up their prayers to Saint Anne, the patron saint of all Canadians in their travels by water. Hard on the heels of the confessions and prayers, however, Campion observed a second custom. He gave to each man a jug of rum, which was intended to last them the duration of the voyage. The men then proceeded to observe a custom of their own, and drank all of the rum on the spot. Sainte Anne and the priest were no sooner dismissed than a scene of wild drinking ensued, in which the men surpassed even drunken Indians in singing, fighting, and savage gestures.

Yet early the next morning, well before dawn, the men dutifully awoke, ate their breakfasts of Indian corn, reloaded the canoes, and pushed off. They dug the red blades of their paddles into the water and struck up a canoe song about soldiers returning from war:

> *Nous étions trois capitaines,*
> *Nous étions trois capitaines,*
> *De la guerre revenant,*
>   *Brave, brave,*

De la guerre revenant,
  Bravement.

All that morning we traversed Lac des Deux-Montagnes, a wide stretch of water at the mouth of the Ottawa River. As bourgeois of the voyage, I escaped the chore of paddling, but my long legs were so cramped amidst the cargo in the canoe that they soon became stiff and numb. I longed to walk again on dry land.

At midday we saw Indians approaching us from across the water, their three small canoes gliding as swiftly and effortlessly over the water as birds glide through the air. They told us they were settled Indians, returning down river to their village near Montreal. I bought from them maple sugar and a few beaver skins, in exchange for sundry trade goods. They asked me for rum, but I refused to sell them any. They behaved in a civil manner toward me, but before they left, they asked the voyageurs if I was English. When told that I was, one of the Indians snorted and said, "The English are mad in their pursuit of the beaver. They risk their lives for it." He pointed to me and said, "The Upper Indians will kill him."

By sunset of the first day we reached the Longue Sault, a stretch of wild, rushing water on the Ottawa River. As the men set up camp at the foot of the rapids, I noticed several old stakes planted in the ground. One stake had a second stake tied to it in the shape of a cross. I looked more closely and saw that all the stakes had once been crosses, and all but one had fallen apart from decay. I asked Campion about the moldering crosses, and he confirmed my suspicion, saying that they marked an old graveyard.

"Each cross marks the grave of a voyageur who drowned in these rapids," Campion said. "You can see for yourself, monsieur, that no one has drowned here recently. For as long as the war has lasted, the French have been too busy dying elsewhere."

That night the men sat about their fires and traded tales of the wilderness. At one point Campion called the men together.

"My friends," Campion said, "as patriotic Frenchmen, it is fitting that we spend a few moments to remember the heroic deeds of Adam Dollard and his followers." Campion pointed to the ground beneath his feet. "One hundred years ago on this spot, Adam Dollard and his brave men sacrificed their lives that New France might live. They came to this lonely place with the same spirit that once inspired the Crusaders to depart for the Holy Land. They trusted in God to preserve their lives—yet they were fully prepared to die. Dollard and his men came here to fight the Iroquois.

"The year was 1660. All New France was suffering under the scourge of the Six Nations of the Iroquois, who carried their bloody hatchets to the very walls of Montreal and Quebec. The Iroquois approached like foxes, attacked like lions, and departed like birds. They were everywhere. They were nowhere. No Frenchman was safe from them.

"In May of that year a Mohegan warrior was captured by the Algonquins. After he was tortured for a time, the Mohegan revealed a frightful secret—the Iroquois were gathering in large numbers above and below Montreal. They planned to overrun Montreal, then fall upon Trois Rivières and Quebec. They intended to destroy the entire colony.

"Terror seized the people. Omens of disaster appeared from out of nowhere. Thunder resounded from cloudless skies. A comet in the form of a blazing canoe crossed the heavens. The women and children of Montreal huddled in fear behind the thick walls of the city hospital.

"In the panic that prevailed, the young commandant of the Montreal garrison stepped forward. He was Adam Dollard, Sieur des Ormeaux. He proposed a plan that was bold to desperation. He inspired sixteen Frenchmen—farmers, traders, artisans, and soldiers—to follow him to war against the Iroquois hordes. The seventeen men struck hands and pledged to one another that they would fight to the death. They wrote their wills, confessed their sins, received the sacraments, and departed.

"The Frenchmen reached this place in early May. On this very spot they found a circular fort of stakes, built by the Indians. Here the Frenchmen waited for their enemies to appear.

"The next day a scout brought word that a single canoe of Iroquois was on its way downriver. The French set an ambush at the foot of these rapids, and they killed all the Iroquois in the canoe but one, who managed to escape and warn his people of the trap. Several hours later, a chorus of screams from the head of the rapids announced to the French that the enemy had arrived. An army of Iroquois warriors, two hundred strong, swept down the Longue Sault upon them, and the French hastily retreated within their fort.

"The Iroquois did not hesitate. They broke apart the canoes of the French and, setting the birchbark ablaze, they ran at the fort and tried to set it on fire. The Iroquois were driven back by sharp volleys from the French, who were heavily armed with muskets and musketoons loaded with scraps of iron and lead. As the Iroquois fell back, they left one of their principal chiefs dead on the ground. Dollard, wishing to fix the attention of the Iroquois, ordered two Frenchmen to rush out under cover of fire and hack off the head of the slain chief. The French set the chief's head atop a pole above the fort. Seeing the impaled head of their leader, the Iroquois were beside themselves with rage. Time and again the Iroquois attacked the fort, and time and again they left their dead behind them on the ground.

"For five days and five nights the Iroquois worried the French with gunfire and howled threats of an attack. Within the small fort, the French fought by turns, and prayed. The French grew weak from hunger and thirst and want of sleep. They dug a hole in the ground, and from it they drank mud.

"Early on the sixth day the French heard excited yells and war cries, which told them that the Iroquois had been joined by reinforcements. The French looked out their loopholes and made the sign of the cross, for they saw their own deaths approaching. They saw hundreds of Iroquois warriors, leaping from side to side behind wooden shields, howling like wolves, snarling like wildcats. Of a sudden the Iroquois rushed upon the fort and reached its walls. They swarmed about the fort like angry hornets. Crouching beneath the loopholes, the savages hacked furiously at the palisade with their hatchets. Dollard pressed powder and scrap into a musketoon, and he plugged its muzzle to make of it a grenade. Lighting the fuse, he and his men tried to throw it over the palisade, but the musketoon fell back upon the French and exploded. In the confusion that followed, the Iroquois gained the loopholes, thrust their muskets into the fort, and fired upon the French. The savages opened a breach in the stockade, and Dollard and his men sprang to defend it. Swords and hatchets in hand, the Frenchmen and the Iroquois threw themselves upon one another.

"The Frenchmen fought to their deaths.

"The victorious Iroquois buried their dead and attended to their wounded, who were many. Then they cut off the heads of the dead Frenchmen and set the heads atop posts planted there, along the riverbank. They did this to honor the courage of their slain enemies. As darkness covered the earth, the Iroquois built large fires and danced about the severed heads to celebrate their victory. Suddenly the impaled head of Adam Dollard moved its eyes, looked down upon the Iroquois, and shouted at them in their own tongue. The severed head threatened a fiery vengeance upon the Iroquois, that would rain down upon them from out of the sky. The terror-stricken Iroquois fled in panic from the place, and they gave up their plans to attack Montreal.

"In this way," Campion concluded, "a handful of brave Frenchmen saved all of New France." Campion then knelt on the ground and led the voyageurs in a short prayer in memory of Adam Dollard.

I lay awake that night, listening to the rush of water down the Longue Sault. I imagined that I could hear boulders beneath the water tumbling over one another, and even that I could feel the pounding surge of the water through the ground on which I lay. The very earth seemed to be moving beneath me. I was eager to encounter the Canadian wilderness, to see for myself what truth lay behind the fantastic stories and the dire warnings I had heard. I wondered if the wilderness had been tamed by a century of contact with the French—or if I was about to experience the same savagery that once confronted Adam Dollard.

The next day, however, was not a day of adventure, but rather a day of drudgery. I was awakened before dawn by the sound of the men eating breakfast. By the time I arose, some of them were already loading cargo onto their backs, in the manner employed by Indian women. One piece of cargo was set on the shoulders and was suspended from a band that passed across the forehead. A second piece was placed upon the first, where it lay against the hollow of the neck and supported the head. Each piece weighed ninety pounds, and each man carried two pieces at a time. One stalwart fellow got up from breakfast and nonchalantly swung three pieces onto his back. All day long he shuttled back and forth across the portage, carrying three pieces at a time. For his intrepid service he received no extra pay; his only reward was bragging rights, which he exercised freely.

All along the portage we were attacked fiercely by mosquitoes and sand flies—tiny demons so insidious and so pervasive that we could not escape their pestiferous stings. To keep them off me, Campion suggested that I build a fire, over which I stood and smoked myself like meat. Meanwhile the men had to carry their loads through thick clouds of the insects, and their sufferings were dreadful. In the ardent heat of the day, streams of blood commingled with sweat ran down their chests from exposed faces and necks. Yet no man shrank from his duty; all were animated and eager to get on with the job. When one young voyageur groaned and showed signs of fatigue and pain, the older men scoffed at him and treated him with contempt. (I could not help noticing that they chided the young man most vehemently when they passed me and my fire. I suspected that some of their taunts were truly directed at me.)

Throughout the course of our voyage, the irrepressible Campion served as chief choirmaster and storyteller. During the day he led the men in ribald canoe songs, all of which they knew by heart. Around the campfire at night, he told countless tales of the wilderness. The voyageurs themselves were forever boasting of their heroic exploits. Each man bragged of his strength, his courage in battle, or the women he had known.

One evening Campion asked me to recall my own experiences in the recent war. I had seen no fighting in the war, so I told the men of my efforts to move long boats full of military supplies down a series of rapids on the River Saint Lawrence. I had been responsible for three long boats, all of which had capsized in the strong current. I had managed to save my life only by clinging to the bottom of a submerged boat, like a rat clinging to a sunken log, till I was rescued from the water by an aide-de-camp. The British army lost dozens of supply boats to the rapids that day. As I recalled the clumsy misfortunes of the British army, the voyageurs laughed boisterously. But when I added that a hundred British soldiers drowned in the treacherous waters, the men fell silent.

Some fifty miles above the Longue Sault we stopped at a cataract of water that falls into the river from a ledge of rock forty feet high and a thousand feet wide. This lovely sheet of falling water gave the place its name—*Sault de Rideau*, or "Curtain Fall." We stopped here to rest, and most of the voyageurs lit their clay pipes to relax for a moment. A few of the younger men, however, ventured out along a ledge of rock that ran beneath the fall. At times the men were entirely hidden behind the curtain of water; at times they thrust their heads through the water, and shouted and laughed like children. I marveled at the simple delight they took in the falling water.

Often during the voyage I wondered what the men thought of me. I suspected that they hated me for being English, although they never showed it. I knew they felt contempt for me, as I was young and inexperienced, and I did no work. Yet most of the men were faithful to their code of honor and proved entirely loyal to me, their bourgeois. I sometimes thought of helping them with their work, but Campion advised against it.

He said it would be highly improper for a bourgeois to join in the work of voyageurs.

I recall one particularly awkward scene that occurred at a landfall. The riverbank was rocky, so before the canoes struck land, the voyageurs stepped into the water to ease the canoes onto the shore. I was about to step into the water myself, when one of the older Canadians abruptly hoisted me onto his back and carried me ashore. I was astonished. At first I thought his actions were a joke, played at my expense, but when I saw that none of the other men were laughing, I decided to quietly accept the ride. I later asked Campion about the incident. He said it was a custom among voyageurs to serve their bourgeois in such a fashion. I instructed Campion to inform the men that I did not want such courtesies paid me in the future.

The Ottawa River displays great variety over its three-hundred-mile course above Montreal. In places its waters spread calmly across broad lakes, where the voyageurs often raced their canoes. In other places the waters rush impetuously down falls and over rapids. In places the banks of the river are high bluffs. In others the land is flat. Tall forests of pine and maple grow in some places. Open, flower-strewn meadows, which the French call *prairies*, stretch along the riverbank in other places

By mid-August we reached a narrow channel of water that Campion claimed was so deep that the longest rope could not touch its bottom. Here, along the north bank of the river, ran a high ridge of stone that dropped sheer to the water's edge, and which returned magnificent echoes to our canoe songs. A point of this ridge rose almost eight hundred feet above the water and was known as *L'Oiseau* or "the Bird." At the foot of this cliff it was customary for voyageurs to baptize young men who were making their first voyage. Campion performed the ceremony by ordering all the novices (myself excepted) to leap into the water, while he made the sign of the cross over their heads and uttered a few pious words. Those who could not swim were kept afloat with setting poles.

Several days later we reached the mouth of the *Rivière du Moine*, where we spotted a small camp of northern Indians called Maskegons. I traded several articles to them for skins. When they realized I was an Englishman, they asked if the English were in possession of the country below. I informed them that the English now ruled all of Canada. They eagerly asked if English traders would be coming into their country. They said their families would starve if they could not buy ammunition and other necessities. I told them that English traders would soon be supplying all their needs.

Finally, late in August, we left the Ottawa River to enter a stream that the French call *Rivière Petite* and the Indians call *Matawa Sipi*. The banks of the River Petite were continuous cliffs, without enough soil to bury a dead body. Along the river I saw Indian graves where bodies had been laid upon bare rock and covered with stones. I saw Indian paintings on the sides of cliffs, and in one cliff I saw the opening of a cave, which inspired fantastic stories among the voyageurs.

Soon we left River Petite and entered a series of swamps, known as *Les Portages à la Vase*, or "Carrying Places through the Mud." The swamps spread across a height of land that separated the waters flowing toward the Ottawa River from the waters flowing toward Lake Huron. The portages across the swamps marked the point in our voyage where the men would no longer have to paddle upstream. The men observed the milestone with a joyful ceremony of heaving their setting poles into the air and leaving the poles behind.

I soon learned that Les Portages à la Vase were most aptly named. The ground was wet and boggy, and in places it quaked under our feet and gave way beneath us, so that we were mired hip-deep in mud. We watched with envy the clean and elegant grouses, which lifted their legs so daintily that they seemed to fairly trip across the top of the swamp, while we clumsy humans had to sound the depths of the swamp with our feet. Campion blamed the beaver for our troubles, complaining that the industrious animal had built dams that had submerged the ground over which we had to pass. We clambered through the mud of two portages, but at the third portage we broke apart a beaver dam, which let off so much water that we were able to float our canoes down a small stream. It was a curious thing to see the Northwest trade carried on a stream so narrow that a man could leap across it.

At length our efforts brought us to a more substantial stream, which bore our canoes into a large lake called *Nipisingue*, and known by the Indians as Lake of the Sorcerers. This lake was pleasing to the eye, the spirit, and the belly. Its shores were covered with meadows, all ablaze with golden flowers, and in the meadows I saw bears, beavers, and *o'tic-a'tic* or "caribou." The waters of the lake abounded in bass, sturgeons, and a monstrous, evil-looking sort of pike called *masquinonge*. In two hours we caught as many fish as we could eat.

On the lake we met several canoes of Indians called Nipisingues, who were surprised to see an Englishman in their country. They predicted that I would be killed by the Indians at Michilimackinac.

We left Lake Nipisingue and entered *Rivière des Francais*, which falls swiftly westward, over dangerous rapids, toward Lake Huron. A few of our men were eager to "run" their canoes down some of the rapids, both for the challenge of it and as a way to avoid the back-breaking work of carrying around. I left it up to Campion to decide which rapids could safely be descended in canoes. In places where he allowed the canoes to run the rapids, the steersman and foreman in each canoe used their long paddles to maneuver the vessel past dangerous boulders. In other places Campion ordered that the canoes be partially emptied and lowered down the rapids with ropes. At the most dangerous rapids he insisted that all cargo and all canoes be carried around.

At the first set of rapids we encountered, one of our canoes was damaged when it struck a boulder. We managed to pull all the men and most of the cargo from the water, and we repaired the canoe in a short time, but the steersman of the canoe, the crippled Porlier, was humiliated by the accident. He quickly became the brunt of jokes and insults from the other men. Even his own middlemen derided him, claiming that henceforth they would refuse to serve in his canoe, for they wished dearly to live.

That night Porlier stayed off to himself, away from the campfires where the men were laughing at his expense.

The next day we came to a dangerous fall of water, known as *Sault de Parisienne*. It was a narrow, steeply inclined shoot of water, which Campion said required extraordinary skill to descend, for at the foot of the fall lay two submerged rocks, one after the other but on opposite sides, so that a canoe had to be turned sharply across a high ridge of water to avoid both rocks. Campion forbade any attempt to run the Sault de Parisienne.

As the men were carrying their loads around the sault, we heard sudden shouts of glee coming from the head of the fall. Looking up, we saw Porlier's canoe, occupied only by Porlier and his foreman, heading straight into the rushing water. Both men were bent over their paddles and were hollering, whistling, and enjoying themselves immensely. Campion and I could do nothing but watch as the current swept the fragile vessel downstream.

It took little more than an instant for Porlier and the foreman to maneuver the canoe deftly down the shoot of water, past the treacherous rocks, and into a quiet pool at the foot of the falls. This feat was performed to the clamorous cheers of the other voyageurs. But when the cheering subsided, Campion sternly ordered Porlier and the foreman out of their honored positions at the stern and the bow. He took from them their long paddles, and he handed them short paddles. He informed them that their positions henceforth were to be in the center of the canoe, among the middlemen. There they were to stay for the duration of the voyage.

His sudden demotion made Porlier the brunt of still more jokes, but having proven himself at the Sault de Parisienne, he seemed to enjoy the jokes as much as anyone.

It was late on the afternoon of September 3, 1761, when I first saw the flat blue line of Lake Huron on the distant horizon. The great lake stretched across the edge of the earth like a vast ocean.

That evening we set up camp on a lovely spot of prairie on the lakeshore, where the men gummed the canoes, and I watched the sun set into the lake. The men were in high spirits, for all portages now lay behind them. All that remained of their voyage was to cross the billows of the great lake that lay before them. The men stayed up much of the night, singing and dancing.

We embarked on Lake Huron early the next morning. As we set off, I thought the tall waves, which ran high from the south, would surely sink us. But my canoes rode on the water with the ease of seabirds.

Later that day, as the lake grew calm and the sun shone brightly, I looked beneath me and saw huge boulders laying at the bottom of the lake, beneath six fathoms of water. As I gazed down through the limpid medium, my head grew dizzy, and the canoe seemed suspended in air.

The voyageurs richly enjoyed this part of their voyage. Their lives were suddenly made easy, and they tasted pleasure for a sweet bit. They no longer had to carry the canoes and cargo on their shoulders, nor did they have to paddle upstream against a river current. At times they did not have to paddle at all, for when the wind was at their backs, they hoisted small sails from the canoes, and our tiny fleet coasted effortlessly across the broad bosom of an inland sea.

Yet danger remained our companion. Campion and the men were ever wary of running the canoes onto submerged rocks, especially when the wind blew from the south. We proceeded westward, following a string of islands, which aided our passage by sheltering our canoes from the strongest winds and the most violent waves. The greatest danger arose when we had to cross an open stretch of water, which the voyageurs called a *traverse*, for there the canoes might capsize or be broken to pieces if overtaken by a sudden wind. Before setting off on such a traverse, Campion watched the sky in an effort to anticipate the weather. At such times he spoke aloud to the wind, calling it *la vieille*, or "the old lady." He asked the old lady where she was hiding, and whether she was about to play a trick on him. When Campion finally issued an order to start out across a traverse, the men bent over their paddles with furious intensity, straining to cross the open water as quickly as possible.

Traveling ever westward, we passed islands that were barren or scantily covered with scrub pines. "The Upper Indians believe some of these islands are the homes of powerful spirits," Campion said. "They never set foot on them, except perhaps to escape a storm. They tell stories of fearful magic and enchantment suffered by the poor souls who tried to take shelter on these islands."

We passed a rocky peninsula known as *Point de Grondeur*, or "Point of Grumbling," aptly named for a mysterious sound the waves made in striking the rocks. On one rock I saw an Indian painting in the shape of a canoe with seven canoe men. Above the canoe towered a giant monster, raising two enormous hands above the canoe, as if in warning. I gazed upon the painting with apprehension, for I sensed that it held a special warning for me.

We arrived at an island called *La Cloche*, so named for a rock standing on a plain, which rang like a bell when struck. On the island lived a large band of Indians, who behaved quite civilly toward me at first. I bartered a few trade goods to them for dried fish and meat. But when they discovered that I was English, they declared that the Indians of Michilimackinac would surely kill me, and so they claimed the right to share in the plunder. Acting upon their dire predictions, they demanded a keg of rum from me, and they made it clear that if I did not give the rum to them, they would simply take it. I gave them the rum, and they let me depart without further insult.

By this time the repeated warnings of my sure death at Michilimackinac began to weigh heavily on my mind. The warnings seemed to concern Campion as well, for he suggested that we return to Montreal, or at least turn southward toward

Detroit, which lay in British hands. I urged him not to worry on my account, however, saying that I had recognized the danger of the voyage when I began it, and I would not turn back now. I added that we had no choice but to proceed, for our food was nearly exhausted. Campion agreed, but he went on to suggest another possible form of escape for me. Observing that the Indians we had met were hostile only to me, an Englishman, Campion suggested that I disguise myself as a French voyageur to avoid any further hostility. To this I readily agreed. I laid aside my English clothes and covered myself with a loose shirt, a sash, worsted leggings, and a red cap. I took the paddle of a voyageur, and Campion took my place as the bourgeois. The men were ordered to keep secret the fact that I was English.

The next day we met several canoes of Indians, and I used my paddle with as much skill as I could muster. None of the Indians suspected me of being English. But as we drew ever nearer to Michilimackinac, I became increasingly convinced that I was about to die. I felt quite alone, as we crossed the water toward my doom.

Late one afternoon a dark wall of clouds arose in the west. The voyageurs fell silent. Campion became pensive and alert. He pointed to a broad band of gray in the sky above the lake, which he said was falling rain. We paddled cautiously onward, as the sky darkened. When the storm was almost upon us, we paused for a few moments alongside a small island. Drops of rain dappled the swelling surface of the lake. Campion finally made a simple observation: "She spits, but she does not blow."

With this we stripped off our shirts and dug our paddles into the water. Sheets of rain engulfed our little fleet, and the men burst into a song about bathing in a clear fountain:

> *A la claire fontaine*
> *M'en allant promener,*
> *J'ai trouvé l'eau si belle*
> *Que je m'y suis baigné.*

I joined in the singing, and my spirits soared. I was infused with courage to face whatever dangers awaited me at Michilimackinac.

6

The Isle of Michilimackinac appeared on our horizon early the next morning, ascending out of the water like the shell of a great green turtle. The island rose so high above the lake that we could see it from twenty miles away. On this beautiful island, I thought, my fate would be decided.

Campion suggested that we visit a Chippewa village on the island before proceeding on to the fort. He warned that passing the village without stopping might arouse suspicion among the Indians. As we paddled our canoes toward a narrow beach on the island, I strained my eyes to catch a glimpse of the Indians about whom I had heard so much. In the trees overlooking the beach, I spotted a number of birchbark lodges, some with rounded roofs, others with pitched roofs. As we neared the shore, a welcoming committee of noisy, naked children and silent, wolflike dogs appeared on the beach. Not far behind the children stood the rest of the populace.

We pulled our canoes onto the beach, and I stole a closer look at the Chippewas. I was startled by the savage appearances of the men, some of whom had their faces painted in bizarre patterns, apparently to make themselves as unlike anything human as possible. They wore feathers in their hair, earrings in their ears, breech clouts about their waists, and little else. The women, on the other hand, wore modest dresses of deerskin. They wore their hair neatly parted over the forehead and braided behind. Their cheeks were painted with vermilion, to heighten the color.

Two chiefs stepped forward to greet Campion as the leader of our voyage. He spoke to them in the Chippewa tongue. The voyageurs took the opportunity to light their pipes, which they shared freely with the Chippewas. I was at a loss about just what to do. To avoid being approached by an Indian, I pretended that I was securing merchandise in the canoes. I clattered about the pebbled beach, passing from canoe to canoe, untying and tying knots. I tried to behave as inconspicuously as possible, but a young Chippewa man noticed me, stared at me for a moment, and for some reason pointed me out to another. Both men laughed at me. Fortunately, in spite of whatever they found amusing about me, they left me alone without suspecting that I was English.

Finally Campion bid adieu to the Chippewa chiefs and ordered us back into our canoes. We pushed off and steered a course across a broad strait toward Fort Michilimackinac, which was situated on the mainland, several miles to the southwest. As we proceeded, Campion informed me that the Chippewas of the island had asked him for news from Montreal —particularly whether any English were on their way to the Upper Country.

By early afternoon we arrived within hailing distance of the fort, at which point the voyageurs let out with their finest canoe songs, which were answered by gunshots and shouts of greeting from the fort. A number of residents came out on the beach to mark our arrival. When our canoes touched shore, the Canadians said hello to one another, and I quietly surveyed the fort. The stockade was a wall of cedar posts, some thirty feet tall, and sharpened to points at the tops. A corner of the fort stood at the very edge of the water, so that waves lapped against its base. Atop the stockade were six watchtowers—one above each of four corners, and one above each of two gates. In each tower that guarded a gate was mounted a brass cannon, which I later learned had been taken by Canadians who went on a plundering expedition against British forts on Hudson's Bay. Most notable to me was a French flag, which still flew over the fort.

Campion took charge of my property, and I continued to perform in my role as a voyageur. Pretending that I was ill, Campion found me a small house within the fort and had me retire there. But our ruse was to no avail. One of our men must have betrayed our secret to the residents, for several Frenchmen soon came calling on me. Rugged frontiersmen all, they behaved as gentlemen toward me. They welcomed me to their wilderness community, and each in turn shook my hand. Their chief spokesman, a man named Farli, was a portly, whiskered fellow with greasy black hair, who could speak a little English. In an urgent and conspiratorial voice, Farli warned me that I could not stay at Michilimackinac without risk of imminent death.

"The Chippewas have lost many young men fighting the English," Farli said. "They hate the English, and they consider themselves to be at war with the English. When they find you here, they will make a brutal ceremony of killing you. Your death will be a painful one, I can assure you. You must lose no time, monsieur. Make your escape to Detroit, where the English soldiers can protect you."

But Farli's dramatic warnings only served to make me stubborn. Something in his solicitous manner made me distrust him. I could not believe that he was as concerned for my safety as he pretended to be.

"Monsieur Farli," I replied calmly, "I intend to stay here with my canoes and my property."

Farli shook his head vehemently. "No, monsieur! The Chippewas will kill you. Only a few days ago another English trader arrived here, a man named Bostwick. He had many years of experience in the Indian trade in the Ohio Country, and he was wise enough to recognize the dangers here. When I told him of the hatred the Chippewas feel toward the English, he did not hesitate to flee to Detroit. Now you, my young friend, you must follow his example. Do not be so foolish as to tempt fate by staying here. It would be the last mistake that ever you make."

"Monsieur Farli," I replied, "thank you for your concern for my safety, but I intend to stay here. I expect to be here for some time to come."

With much shrugging of shoulders and shaking of heads, my French visitors finally left me alone. But before they left, Farli wagged a finger in my face. "We have warned you," he said.

I immediately went in search of Campion, whom I found at the lakeshore, supervising the unloading of the canoes. I related to him what had happened, and he praised me for the determination I had shown. "Matters may not be as bad as they seem, Alex. The French traders here, despite their great show of concern for your safety, may be every bit as hostile as they claim the Indians will be. The residents resent an Englishman coming here to compete with them for the Indian trade."

With Campion's tentative assurances I returned to my house, where I spent the night in fitful sleep and worried wakefulness.

I was aroused early the next morning, well before dawn, by loud knocks at my door and Campion's voice. "Monsieur Henry! Up now! You have callers!"

In an instant I was awake and standing at the door, in my nightshirt.

"The Chippewas are coming," Campion said. "They must know you are here. Their canoes are on the lake."

I stared at him blankly, hoping for some bit of useful advice.

"I will be at your side. We will see what happens."

I dressed quickly, this time in my English clothes, and Campion and I hastened to the lakeshore. Looking across the lake, I saw a distant flotilla of canoes, approaching with the dawn.

"What do I need to know?" I asked Campion.

"Two things are important. You must show your respect for the Chippewas, and you must show your determination."

I suggested that I show my courage by meeting the Chippewas at the lakeshore, but Campion disagreed. He advised me that it would show more courage (which was to say less fear) to await their arrival at my house.

A hundred thoughts raced through my mind. I thought of my French visitors of the day before. I asked Campion about the man named Farli.

"Farli holds great sway among the Chippewas," Campion said. "He has a Chippewa wife."

"Perhaps he will help us," I suggested.

"Perhaps he has already betrayed us."

"Yes. But even so, it may be wise to have Farli on hand when the Chippewas arrive. Let him show us his colors."

Campion considered the idea. "Very well. It may be better to have Farli at our sides than at our backs."

We called on Farli, and after a heated discussion, he agreed to accompany us, but he made one thing clear. "I will not risk my life to protect yours," he declared. "I warned you yesterday of the danger you are in. Today I will go with you to meet the Chippewas, but what they decide to do with you is out of my hands."

I asked Farli what he thought the Chippewas might do with me.

"It is their usual custom to welcome a stranger with a gift, and to expect a gift in return. But the Chippewas have far more in mind for you, my English friend. After all, you are much more than a stranger to them—you are their blood enemy." Farli smiled and shrugged. "More than this I cannot say."

I was standing at my window when sixty Chippewa warriors, all in battle dress, entered the open gates of the fort and walked toward my house in single file. Each carried a war hatchet in one hand and a scalping knife in the other. As they approached my house, I felt my heart rise in my chest.

Without knocking, the chief of the Chippewas opened my door and entered my house. His warriors followed. The chief made a sign, and he and his followers seated themselves on the floor. Campion, Farli, and I sat in chairs and looked down on the assembled warriors. We sat in silence and waited respectfully for the Chippewas to announce their purpose.

Without rising, the war chief began to speak. He ignored me entirely, as he calmly asked Campion how long it had been since we had left Montreal, and whether any other Englishmen were on their way to Michilimackinac. He remarked casually that the English must be brave men, not afraid of death, to venture alone among their enemies. The chief was a muscular man, perhaps forty years old. His entire face was painted white, but for a slash of red across his mouth and a band of black across his eyes. His eyes glittered menacingly from out of the blackness that surrounded them. A tuft of fur hung from a silver ring through his nose, and the fur moved with his every breath. His face held an indescribable mixture of good and evil.

The chief made a sign, and each warrior drew forth a pipe and gravely smoked from it. They smoked in silence, as I, with some trepidation, took the opportunity to survey the war party more closely. They were a fearsome lot. Their bodies were naked above the waists, and some were embellished with strange figures painted in charcoal, vermilion, or white ochre, worked up with grease. Their faces were covered with starkly painted patterns. The face of one was half white and half black, calling to mind a half moon in the night sky. The face of another was red, with a black circle at the chin and black lines radiating up from the circle, as though a black sun were rising into a red sky. Another had covered his face with diagonal bands of black and yellow. Feathers, animal skins, and silver ornaments hung from their heads and necks. Some had feathers through their noses or their ears. I could easily imagine any one of them rising to his feet, walking up to me, splitting my head open with a war hatchet, and tearing off my scalp.

When the warriors had emptied their pipes, a period of silence ensued.

Finally the chief took in his hand a string of wampum beads. He rose to his feet and stood directly before me. He stared fiercely into my eyes. I did my best to return his stare and to keep from glancing at the war hatchet and knife that hung at his belt.

"Englishman. It is to you that I speak, and I demand your attention! I am Minavavana, war chief of the Chippewas.

"Englishman. You know that the King of France is our father. You know that he promised to be such, and we, in turn, promised to be his children. This promise we have kept. But your nation has made war upon our father. You are his enemy. How can you be so bold as to venture among us, his children? Surely you know that our father's enemy is our enemy."

Minavavana punctuated each point in his speech by lifting a bead on his string of wampum. He spoke in his own language, and his speech was translated for me by Campion.

"Englishman. We are told that our father—the King of France—is old and sick. Fatigued with making war upon your nation, he has fallen asleep. During his sleep your nation has taken advantage of him. You have possessed yourself of Canada. But his nap is almost at an end. Listen! I hear him stirring and asking for his children—the Indians. When he awakes, what must become of you? He will destroy you utterly!

"Englishman. You think that you have conquered the French. But you have not conquered us! We are not your slaves! These lakes, these woods and hills were left to us by our ancestors. They are our inheritance. We will part with them to no one. Your nation supposes that we, like the white people, cannot live without bread and pork and beef. But know this. The Great Spirit has always provided food for us in these great lakes and on these wooded hills.

"Englishman. Our father has called upon our young men to make war upon your nation, and many of our young men have been killed in the war. It is our custom to retaliate for their deaths. Till such time as the spirits of our slain brothers are satisfied, we will strike against the English. The spirits of our slain brothers and sons can be satisfied in one of two ways—one is by spilling the blood of the nation by whose hand they fell; the other is by covering the bodies of the slain with gifts, to ease the pain of their families.

"Englishman. Your king has never sent us gifts, nor has he entered into a treaty of peace with us. Therefore we are at war with your king. We have no father among white men but the King of France.

"Englishman. As for you, we know that you have risked your life to come among us, expecting that we will not harm you. We see that you do not come here armed, with the intention of making war against us. You come here in peace, to trade with us and to supply our needs. Therefore we will regard you as a brother. You need not fear us. You may sleep peacefully in our country, without fear of the Chippewas. As a symbol of our friendship, we offer you this pipe of peace."

A warrior approached me and handed me a large pipe with a bowl of carved red stone and a long stem of wood. From the stem hung a braid of hair, a bunch of colored feathers, and a pair of white wings, spread as if the pipe were about to take flight. I lifted the pipe to my mouth and drew smoke from it, as the words "you may sleep peacefully" echoed through my mind. I was relieved to the point of elation, yet I smoked from the pipe with the solemn gravity for which the occasion called. When I had drawn smoke three times from the pipe, it was carried to Chief Minavavana for him to smoke, and then to all the warriors. When all had drawn smoke from the pipe, Minavavana grasped my hand in a show of friendship and gave me the string of wampum which he had used in his speech.

Campion motioned for me to reply to the speech of Minavavana. As I rose to my feet, I felt a certain weakness in my knees and a tightness in my chest. I recalled Campion's advice that I show respect and determination.

"Chippewas. Thank you for your kind welcome. I am not surprised by your kindness, for I was emboldened to come here by reports of your good character. I now see that these reports were true. You know that the King of France has surrendered all Canada to the King of England. Therefore, you must regard the King of England as your new father. I assure you that he will behave toward you as a kind and generous father. The King of England has sent me here to furnish you with the goods you need. My canoes are loaded with merchandise, and your kind treatment of me will encourage other English traders to come into your country, to bring you more merchandise."

The Chippewas seemed to be satisfied with what I told them. They all muttered "Eh!" when I was finished with my little speech. Following Campion's advice, I gave them gifts—a rope of tobacco, a box of rings, and a box of glass beads. Chief Minavavana accepted my gifts, but he had a further request of me. He asked that his young men be allowed to taste what he called English milk, meaning my rum. He said it had been a long time since his warriors had tasted liquor, and they were curious to know whether English milk was as good as French milk, meaning brandy.

I shuddered at the thought of giving rum to the Chippewas, for my past experience with drunken Indians had left a strong impression on my mind. I was about to refuse them the liquor, when Campion, speaking in English, suggested that I comply with their request. Accordingly, I told Minavavana that I would give his men a small cask of rum when they left the fort. He, in turn, said that some of his people would return in several days to trade with me.

Our meeting ended with what seemed to be the most cordial goodwill.

7

Michilimackinac is the Chippewa word for "Great Turtle." The Isle of Michilimackinac was so named for its shape, which resembles the shell of a giant turtle.

Five miles southwest of the island, on the southern mainland, stood Fort Michilimackinac, which guarded a broad strait of water that joins Lake Michigan with Lake Huron. Within the fort lived as many as thirty French families, who earned their livelihoods by servicing the fur trade. The old fort, I was told, was built by the French in 1712 and was garrisoned with a small number of French militia, some of whom married Indian women and raised children. The French soon became more like settlers than soldiers. They lived in tidy houses made of planks, daubed with plaster, and they grew vegetables and kept livestock in neatly plotted gardens outside the fort. Their little village within the fort included a commandant's house, a guardhouse, a powder magazine, five long barracks for soldiers and voyageurs, a small parade ground, and a wooden church in which a Jesuit priest celebrated the Mass.

Throughout the history of New France, Michilimackinac had served as the point of deposit and departure for a major part of the Canadian fur trade. Each summer trade goods from Montreal were assembled at Fort Michilimackinac into outfits and dispersed to all parts of the Upper Country—to the shores of Lake Superior and Lake Michigan, to the headwaters of the Great River Mississippi, to the Illinois Country, and to the Northwest. Each summer packets of furs—the riches of the Upper Country—were collected at Fort Michilimackinac and sent down to Montreal.

I was eager to resume the tried and true customs of the fur trade at Fort Michilimackinac. But before I had a chance to do so, Monsieur Farli came calling on me again, this time to warn me that he expected the Ottawas to be far more hostile toward me than the Chippewas had been. He again warned me to flee to Detroit, this time before the Ottawas learned of my presence at the fort. He told me of an Ottawa village known as L'Arbre Croche, located some fifteen miles west of the fort, that was far larger than either the French settlement at Fort Michilimackinac or the Chippewa village on the Isle of Michilimackinac. Farli said the Ottawas of L'Arbre Croche could raise all of two hundred fifty warriors.

By this time, however, I had grown tired of hearing Farli's urgent warnings. I presumed that the Ottawas would treat me as kindly as had the Chippewas, for I knew the two nations were closely allied with one another. I cheerfully advised Farli that I would take as great a pleasure in meeting the Ottawas as I had in meeting the Chippewas.

Relieved (as I imagined myself to be) of any reason for anxiety, I joined Campion in hiring a number of agents, or *engagés*, who were to carry my trade goods into remote parts of the wilderness. The engagés were expected to spend the winter trading with the Indians, then return to Michilimackinac in the spring with furs they had purchased on my account. Campion himself was planning to lead several canoes into the Northwest.

All was ready for the departure of the engagés, when I received word that an Ottawa war party was on its way to pay me a visit. I hastened to seek out Campion and Farli, to ask them to accompany me to the meeting. This time, however, Farli angrily refused, calling me "a damned fool of an English boy."

Late that afternoon two hundred Ottawa warriors marched into the fort, without so much as a word or a gesture of greeting for me. They took up lodging in several houses belonging to the French.

The next morning the Ottawas summoned me to a council in the commandant's house. Campion and I conferred briefly and agreed that we should attend the council. Upon entering the commandant's house, we were confronted by a group of men decorated more outlandishly and more frightfully than even the Chippewas. They sat on the floor, most of them naked but for breech clouts. Their heads were clean shaven but for short tufts of hair at the crowns. (This fashion, Campion later explained, made it difficult for their enemies to seize them by the hair.) But what the Ottawa warriors lacked in hair they made up for in gaudy headdresses of feathers or dyed animal hair that stood up like crests from their shaven heads. The Ottawas were variously adorned with pieces of silver through their noses, collars of wampum about their necks, and bands of brass or silver about their arms. Some wore a dozen or more earrings in each ear. Some had gaping holes stretched into their earlobes, from which were suspended pieces of shell or pounded copper. (For this custom the French called the Ottawas *les Courtes Oreilles*, or "the Cut Ears.") Some sported tattoos from head to foot. All wore red and black paint on their faces.

Campion and I took our seats on the floor facing the Ottawas. Their war chief, a man named Mackinac, rose to address us. Chief Mackinac was short and rather stout, but he seemed to tower above us. On each of his cheeks was painted a red hand print, and on his chest and shoulders were a half dozen more. The effect was as if a wounded and bloodied enemy had tried to push him away.

"Englishman," Mackinac said. "We are warriors of the Ottawa nation. Some time ago we were told of your arrival in our country and of your bringing merchandise which our people need. We were greatly pleased at hearing this, for we believed that, with your help, our wives and our children would be able to survive another winter. But how great was our surprise when, a few days ago, we learned that the goods we thought were intended for us were on the eve of departure for distant countries, some of which are inhabited by our enemies! Our wives and children heard this and came crying to us. They begged us to come to the fort, to learn the truth with our own ears. So we embarked, almost naked as you see us now. Upon our arrival here, we saw the truth with our own eyes. We saw your canoes ready to depart. We heard the truth with our own ears. We heard that your men were engaged for the River Mississippi and other distant countries.

"Englishman. We have considered this matter carefully. We have called you here that you might hear our determination. We demand that you give to each of our men, young and old alike, merchandise and ammunition to the value of fifty beaver skins. We demand that you provide us these goods on credit. Have no doubt that you will be repaid in the spring, when our men return from the hunt."

Chief Mackinac sat down without offering me so much as a pipe of peace, a string of wampum, or a hand shake.

I was speechless. I knew that the Ottawas' outrageous demand was impossible for me to meet, even if I wanted to, for it would strip me of all my merchandise. What was more, Campion had warned me that some of the Ottawas were bad paymasters, not to be trusted with goods on credit. I sat in silence for some minutes, collecting my thoughts.

Campion, speaking to me in English, offered just two words of advice: "Be resolute."

When finally I rose to speak, my reply was brief and to the point.

"Ottawas. I have come to your country intending to deal with your nation in good faith. But I tell you that I cannot provide you with the merchandise you request, for I have already promised much of it to other nations. I tell you that you must greatly reduce your request for merchandise, or I will not consider it."

I remained standing as Campion translated my speech.

Without hesitating, Chief Mackinac rose to his feet and announced that he had nothing more to say to me, except that his warriors would await the morning for me to reconsider my decision. He said he would not ask again. If I did not agree to his demand by morning, his young men would simply take my property from me. He said his people considered my property to be theirs, because I had brought it into their country while my nation was at war with theirs.

Campion and I returned to my house to discuss matters. We were not surprised when Farli soon came calling on us. This time Farli warned that the Ottawas intended to put me to death that very night, without so much as waiting for the morning. He said it was too late for me to flee, and my only safety lay in meeting the demands of the Ottawas. He urged me to hand over all my property to them.

Farli left, and Campion and I returned to our deliberations with renewed interest. Campion paced back and forth across the floor, deep in thought, as I volunteered ideas, asked questions, and formulated bits and pieces of desperate plans, all in random order. I was relieved when Campion finally interrupted my rambling thoughts with an opinion.

"Farli is trying to prey upon your fears," Campion said. "He wants to convince you to abandon your property and to give up the trade. He is conspiring with the Ottawas to frighten you off. Perhaps he has offered the Ottawas the hope that they might control the fur trade for themselves. Many years ago, in the early days of New France, the Ottawas acted as middlemen in the trade. They may be so foolish as to think they can do so again. But whatever the Ottawas are planning, we have no choice but to take Farli's warning seriously. We must stand ready to defend ourselves."

"How can we defend ourselves against two hundred Indians?" I asked.

"I will gather the men together."

The idea struck me as preposterous. "Why would Frenchmen risk their lives to protect the life or the property of an Englishman?"

"Make no mistake, Alex. The men hold no great love for you, or for any Englishman. But their loyalty runs deep. Their code of honor requires that they faithfully serve their bourgeois. They will not abandon you."

An hour later I was surprised to see Campion return to my house at the head of a ragtag brigade of more than thirty voyageurs. He apologized that more of the men had not joined him. We broke apart our packets of trade goods and armed ourselves with muskets, pistols, and hatchets. We trusted in my small house as a fort, and we posted sentries at the windows and the door. The rest of us sat on the floor and smoked our pipes.

As the night wore on, the talk among the men turned to fighting Indians. One of the men, an older fellow named Tibeau, said he once witnessed the raising of a war party among the Illinois. He told us of how the Illinois made ready for war.

"A war chief visited the young men of the village in early April and said to them, 'It is time to hunt for men. It is time to pay homage to our birds, so they will favor us in the hunt.' That evening each Illinois warrior drew forth from his lodge a case made of reeds. In each case was the skin of a bird—in one an owl, in another a hawk. With loving care, each man spread his bird skin on the ground before him, and all night long the men sang to their skins, beseeching the spirits of the birds to help them in the battle to come. One man prayed to the eagle for the strength of the eagle. Another asked the falcon for the falcon's speed in attacking its prey. Another man prayed to the crow for the crow's cunning. At the break of dawn, all the men who were willing to join the war party brought their bird skins to a feast with the war chief. The warriors ate the flesh of a freshly sacrificed dog, as the war chief harangued them. 'You all know that I have spent this year mourning for my brother, who was killed by the Kickapoos. If my strength were as great as my courage, I would go alone into the country of the Kickapoos to avenge the death of my brother. But alone I am not strong enough to overcome the Kickapoos, so I ask that you, my brothers, help me win the vengeance I seek. You see that our birds have promised us victory. With their protection, and with your courage, we will risk everything!' The war chief moved about among his comrades and placed his hands on the head and shoulder of each man in turn. Each man responded by saying that he was ready to join the war chief in hunting Kickapoos. Each promised that he would shout the cry of his spirit bird, when the time came to attack his human prey."

Tibeau's story was followed by silence. The thought of an Indian attack seemed to cast a pall over the spirits of the men, who stared at their pipes and smoked in silence. The air in my little house turned white with tobacco smoke.

Sensing the somber mood, Campion spoke up. "My friends, in the war I saw many an Indian shot, and I assure you, they are not spirits—they are men. The Indians bleed as freely as do the English." Campion winked at me, then clapped his hands sharply. "Porlier, you are the dancer here. Dance for us a fine war dance. Help us find our courage."

The crippled Porlier rose to his feet and, favoring his right leg, began dancing to the rhythmic claps of the others. His dancing was fashioned after an Indian war dance, and strange to say, it picked up our spirits nicely.

The night passed without incident.

Early the next morning the Ottawas again summoned me to council. But this time Campion warned me that any hope of resistance would be lost if I delivered myself into their hands. I quite agreed with him. We sent word to the Ottawas that we refused to attend their council, and we braced ourselves for the worst.

Another hour passed, with still no sign of an attack.

Campion now volunteered to leave the protection of my house and mingle with the French residents of the fort, in hopes of learning the plans of the Ottawas.

Two hours later he returned with most excellent news—a detachment of three hundred British soldiers was at that moment afloat on Lake Huron and approaching Fort Michilimackinac in bateaux. The troops were expected to arrive the next morning.

On hearing the news I fairly shouted for joy. My joy, however, was not shared by my French comrades at arms, who fell silent and grew sullen.

Despite the news, the danger did not end. Another long night had to be passed within my house, and our fates might well be decided before British troops arrived the next morning. For a second night we stayed on the alert, our weapons charged and by our sides. About midnight we received the ominous news that the Ottawas were meeting in council and that no white man but Farli was allowed to attend the council. We now knew beyond a doubt that Farli was our worst enemy.

A second night passed quietly.

The next morning, by the first dim light of the dawn, we looked out our windows and saw several Ottawas moving about outside. They seemed to be making up their bundles. At sunrise Campion ventured forth and soon returned to report that not a single Ottawa was to be seen anywhere within the fort. I ventured forth myself, and I found the situation altogether changed. The French residents, who had avoided my house while the Ottawas were about, now approached me and offered their congratulations. They said the Ottawas had urged them to join in a surprise attack on the soldiers who were approaching the fort. The French claimed that it was only their refusal to do so that convinced the Ottawas to leave peacefully.

8

Late on the afternoon of September 28, 1761, troops of His Majesty's Sixtieth Regiment of Royal Americans pulled their bateaux onto the beach at Fort Michilimackinac. I cannot express the relief I felt at seeing their familiar uniforms—scarlet coats, blue trousers, white leggings, and three-cornered hats. The soldiers were mustered into a tight formation by their lieutenant. All had bayonets drawn and muskets charged, and I was impressed with the fine figure they presented under arms. Their arrival at Michilimackinac dispelled all my fears. As things stood at the fort, the British soldiers had no real cause for concern. The gates of the fort stood wide open before them, and virtually all the French residents milled about outside the fort to witness their arrival.

The French populace now stood silently by as the British commander, Captain Henry Balfour, proclaimed that he was taking possession of Fort Michilimackinac in the name of His Majesty, King George. An advance party of ten British soldiers entered the fort to search for a possible ambush. Then, to the sounds of bagpipe and drum, the main body of troops paraded through the open gates and into the fort, where they were met by a single uniformed Frenchman, Lieutenant Charles Michel de Langlade, acting commandant. Langlade, I knew, was a legendary war hero among the border French and the Upper Indians. He was of mixed blood—French and Ottawa. His face was full and brown; his eyes were dark; his eyebrows were thickset and black; his body was square-built and solid; his movements were slow and purposeful. Yet he presented as fine a martial appearance as any man I ever beheld, standing erect in his white dress uniform with silver scabbard, gold belt, and tall military hat.

Lieutenant Langlade stepped forward, identified himself to Captain Balfour, and saluted smartly. Captain Balfour, a thin Scot with a ruddy complexion beneath a white powdered wig, returned Langlade's salute.

Two British soldiers stepped up to the flagpole and lowered the French colors—three gold fleurs-de-lis on a field of blue—and raised the British colors—the Cross of Saint George on a field of crimson. With great show of respect, Captain Balfour presented the French flag to Lieutenant Langlade. The French residents of Michilimackinac did not shrink from this painful business. They stood erect and proud, as they witnessed their country changing hands. A few of the French did not hide their tears.

My first impulse was to rush up to my fellow Englishmen and congratulate them on their conquest, but I thought better of it. I was mindful of the French voyageurs who had stayed by my side through two perilous nights. I now stood by their sides, as they watched my countrymen take possession of their homeland.

Captain Balfour and Lieutenant Langlade retired together to the commandant's house, as British sentries were posted atop the stockade, at the gates, and along the beach. Other soldiers were put to work unloading the bateaux.

Unable to contain myself any further, I strode up to a burly sergeant who was overseeing the men on the beach, and I greeted him. "Welcome, sir, to Michilimackinac. I am Alexander Henry, fur trader of these parts, formerly of . . ."

My announcement was cut short by a look of utter astonishment on the sergeant's face. "Whoa!" he cried out. "Who are you?" He reached instinctively for his musket. His exclamation drew the attention of his men, who laid down their loads and gathered about to inspect me. The sergeant ordered the men back to work, then looked up and down the beach, as if to see where I had come from. He eyed me from head to toe with a skeptical squint.

"So you're English, are you?"

"Yes, sir, I am."

He shook his head. "My boy! You should have led a regiment to this godforsaken place. You could have saved us the trouble." He let out a short burst of laughter, then returned to his inspection of me.

"How long have you been here, lad?"

"Six days, sir."

"Six days, is it? And what have you learned in all that time?"

"Sir. The Ottawas are most hostile to British rule. Last night they planned to attack your detachment."

The sergeant cocked his head and squinted all the harder. "I think the captain will want to speak with you. Come along. I'll make the introductions."

As I followed the sergeant across the parade ground, I spotted Campion. Without thinking, I approached Campion and suggested that he accompany me, to report what we had learned to the captain. Campion stepped to within a few inches of my face. He spoke vehemently, but in a low voice. "Monsieur Henry. We are partners. We are comrades. But I have never given you reason to think that I would offer aid to enemy soldiers who have seized my country."

Campion turned abruptly away and stalked off.

The sergeant and I waited for some minutes outside the commandant's house, till Lieutenant Langlade departed. Then we entered without knocking, and the sergeant announced my presence. "Captain, this lad made it here before us. He says he's English."

Captain Balfour rose to his feet, more out of surprise than courtesy, and looked me up and down. He shook my hand, then introduced me to his second-in-command, Lieutenant William Leslye, who sat to one side of the captain's desk. The captain motioned for me to be seated.

"So, laddie, did you care for the bagpipe?" Captain Balfour asked. "It was a bother hauling the thing about in the boat, but ah, there's nothing like the cry of the pipes to announce the arrival of His Majesty's troops."

The captain proceeded to take off his dress coat, loosen his collar, and remove his wig, revealing a bald pate fringed with gray hair. A purposeful, plain-spoken Scot, the captain posed his questions to me simply, and he paused after each of my answers to consider what I had said.

"Tell me, lad, what is your business in these parts?"

"Sir. I am engaged in the Indian trade here."

"Ah. And are other English about?"

"No, sir."

"Who are your assistants?"

"Canadians, sir. Voyageurs from Montreal."

"And do you trust them?"

"Most have served me well. Most have been loyal employees."

"Have you seen any French militia about the place?"

"No, sir. I was informed that the French garrison left some time ago, bound for a fort they call *de Chartres*, located on the River Mississippi several hundred miles south of here. From there they hoped to control the Illinois Country. I was told that Lieutenant Langlade, who was second-in-command here, refused to leave with the others. He stayed on here, without so much as a single soldier to command."

"And what do you know of this man Langlade?"

"He is a half-breed, sir, the son of an Ottawa mother and a French father. I was told that he led the border French and the Upper Indians into battle against the British. He is regarded as a great war hero by the French and the Indians hereabouts, who tell stories of his courage in battle. They say he led the war party that surprised General Braddock's army at Fort Duquesne. They say he defeated Rogers' Rangers in battle. He holds great sway among the Ottawas and the Chippewas, who believe that he has supernatural powers. They believe that he is invincible in battle."

"Do they now? And is Langlade stirring up the Indians against us? Is there any fight left in him?"

"Sir. I do not know."

"What of the French traders, lad? They must not take very kindly to an English trader in their country."

"Some have claimed to be friendly toward me. Others have tried to frighten me off."

"And how did they try to run you off?"

"They told me that the Indians were planning to kill me."

"And was there truth to it?"

I considered my answer carefully. "Sir. I cannot say for certain. The Chippewas made a show of welcoming me here, but they also made it clear that the British are their enemies. The Ottawas demanded that I hand over all my trade goods to them. When I refused, they threatened to seize my property. I was told by a Frenchman that the Ottawas planned to kill me and to attack your detachment before it arrived here."

At this the captain stiffened in his chair. "This'll not do," he said softly. He pursed his lips in thought for a minute or two, then turned to Lieutenant Leslye. "What do the devils intend to do with us? There's the nub of the matter, lieutenant."

Lieutenant Leslye shifted uneasily in his chair and said nothing.

Captain Balfour turned back to me. "You seem to have a head on your shoulders, Mister Henry. Tell me, do you trust anyone in this nest of heathens?"

"I trust my Canadian partner, a man named Campion, and I trust many of the voyageurs in my employ. They were ready to fight alongside me last night."

"Ah, come now, lad. If the fighting had started, do you think the Frenchmen would have risked their lives for yours?"

"Yes, sir, I do. I think I owe my life to them—to them and to the arrival of the three hundred soldiers under your command."

At this Captain Balfour raised an eyebrow, glanced at the lieutenant, and chuckled. "Mister Henry," he said in a secretive half-whisper, "if you'd been counting hats this morning, you'd know that we don't have but a hundred twenty men with us. And on the morrow, most of them will be gone."

The captain turned to the lieutenant. "You see there, lieutenant? In this godforsaken country you must strive at all times to know between fact and fancy. There will be rumors aplenty floating about. And yet you must take every rumor in deadly earnest till you know the better of it. For now, you had best take heed of the lad's warnings. Issue orders at once that no Indians are to be permitted within the fort. The gates are to be closed and strictly guarded, and the stockade is to be manned at all times by four sentries. As for the French, issue the order that they are not to bear arms while inside the fort. Mind you, lieutenant, you must be on the alert at all times. With only thirty men at your command, you'll have the devil to pay if you let your guard down."

The captain's words startled me. "Thirty men, sir? Did you say thirty men?"

Again the captain chuckled. "Take heart, lad. Thirty men are thirty more than were here yesterday."

Captain Balfour rose from his chair. "Mister Henry, you must excuse me now. Another long voyage awaits me on the morrow. I ask this of you, lad, that you report everything you hear to Lieutenant Leslye, no matter how foolish it may sound to you. What you hear may save his life, your life, and the lives of thirty British soldiers. The lieutenant will tell you what you need to know of our plans for this place. I expect you to keep secret everything he tells you. You're a brave and bonny lad, and I wish you good fortune."

Captain Balfour shook my hand and left the room. I turned to Lieutenant Leslye. "Thirty men?" I asked.

The lieutenant was young and seemed to be something of a dandy, in his neatly turned uniform and powdered wig. He answered me sharply, as if he had no time for me. "Tomorrow morning Captain Balfour will place Fort Michilimackinac with a garrison of twenty-eight men under my command. Captain Balfour and the others will then proceed on to Green Bay, and from there to Saint Joseph, where they will garrison those forts as well."

"Do you think you can hold this place with twenty-eight men?" I asked bluntly.

The lieutenant bristled. "Sir, I have no doubt of it. As for now, I have orders I must issue. If you will excuse me."

Lieutenant Leslye rose to leave, but paused at the door long enough to issue a new order, especially for me. "Mister Henry, by order of His Excellency, Sir Jeffrey Amherst, any English traders in this country are henceforth prohibited from selling guns and ammunition to the Indians. I trust that you will faithfully obey this order."

I went in search of Campion and found him standing at the edge of the parade ground. He was watching the British soldiers as they secured the fort. I approached Campion and apologized for having asked him to meet with the British commander. We stood side by side for a time without speaking. It seemed as though we were standing on opposite sides of a centuries-old conflict.

"Are the canoes ready to depart?" I finally asked.

"The canoes will be ready in the morning. As for the men, they are all too ready to leave this place. All of us will be happy to leave."

I was stung by Campion's angry response, and I was dismayed by the realization that he would be departing the next day for the Northwest. In a moment of weakness, I considered asking Campion to stay on at Michilimackinac, to help me deal with the Ottawas and the Chippewas. But out of pride, I said not a word.

Campion and I fell silent again. We watched as Lieutenant Leslye paced about the fort, issuing orders to his troops. We watched as two soldiers approach a pair of Indians who were sitting idly on the far side of the parade ground. Motioning with bayonets, the soldiers signaled that the Indians must leave. The Indians rose slowly to their feet, all the while glaring hatefully at the soldiers. Impatient with the Indians, the soldiers leveled their bayonets and prodded the Indians out of the fort, as if driving a pair of cattle before them.

Campion grimaced at the sight. He and I stood in awkward silence, till I again spoke. "General Amherst has forbidden British traders from selling guns or ammunition to the Indians. We will have to put up our guns and powder."

Campion turned to me slowly. "Do you understand what this will mean? Indians will starve! Alex! People will die!" He seized me by the front of my coat, and pinned me against a wall.

I shrugged innocently.

Campion's voice rose to an angry shout. "Do the English think they can conquer the Indians? Do they think they can starve the Indians into submission?" He held my coat with one hand and gestured wildly with his other hand. "This is madness! The English cannot hold this country with a few dozen troops!" His voice fell to a sudden whisper. "There will be another war!"

Campion released me, turned away, and stormed off.

But later that night the loyal Campion returned to my house. Working together, we removed muskets, lead, flints, and gunpowder from my trade goods. We hid the munitions within my bedroom, which was the safest place we could think of. We worked under cover of darkness, for Campion warned that I would be in great danger if the Indians knew I had munitions hidden within my house.

When we finished the job, Campion turned to me with a low laugh. "Monsieur Henry. The Chippewas promised you that you would sleep peacefully in their country. But tonight you will sleep atop twenty kegs of gunpowder. *Bon soir*, monsieur."

I arose early the next morning to find the beach at Fort Michilimackinac alive with activity. Captain Balfour's troops were readying their bateaux for the voyage to Green Bay. The voyageurs in my employ were loading their canoes for the return trip to Montreal. The voyageurs' task was an easy one, for their canoes were empty but for dried meat, corn, and a few skins which I had managed to collect. The engagés were busy dividing up my merchandise among their canoes. Campion supervised the distribution of the trade goods among the canoes, and recorded the details. I left it up to Campion to explain to the men the notable absence of guns or ammunition.

The day was exhilarating. The air was clear, and a brisk, cleansing wind blew from out of the north. The leaves of the trees were brilliant with hues of orange and gold. The sky was deep blue, and the lake a deeper blue. But the men were all business. All seemed eager to embark. They knew the season was growing late for a voyage into the Upper Country.

I still harbored some doubts about trusting my merchandise to the engagés, who seemed wild and undisciplined. I expressed my doubts to Campion, who assured me that the men were not only trustworthy but quite indispensable to our enterprise.

"Do not trouble yourself, Alex. The Indian trade has operated on the principle of credit for more years than any man can remember. Just as you purchased your goods on credit from the merchants at Albany, it is now time for those goods to pass into the hands of the engagés, again on credit. They will carry your merchandise into distant parts of the Upper Country, where they will sell it, again on credit, to the Indians. The Indians will put the merchandise to good use through the winter, and in the spring, when they return from the hunt, they will pay off their debts with animal skins. The engagés will deliver the skins here to you, and you will transport the skins to Montreal, to sell them and to settle accounts with the Albany merchants. So you see, Alex, the fur trade has always been based on the loyalty of men like these, and on the unswerving honesty of the Indians. I assure you, the engagés will go to great lengths to repay their debts, as will the Indians."

I had heard the story before. Yet it seemed incredible to me that the fur trade, involving thousands of people across thousands of miles of country, could be conducted on such a simple system of credit. I had my doubts about whether the system would work as well for me, an Englishman, as it had for the French.

At one point during the morning, Campion put his arm around my shoulders and led me off along the lakeshore. "Alex," he said, "do not hide yourself here, thinking that you will be safe among the English soldiers. You will not be safe. The English have come here thinking they can rule this country by force. I tell you, they cannot. Do not rely on the soldiers, Alex. Follow instead the example of the French traders who came here before you. From the earliest days of New France, we Frenchmen have lived with the Indians. We have become friends of the Indians, and brothers and husbands as well. If you wish to succeed in the trade, you must do the same. You must live with the Indians. You must learn their languages and customs. You must win their friendship and trust."

It soon was time for my canoes to depart. One large trade canoe was bound for the Grand Village of the Illinois, by way of the portage at Chekagou. Campion selected for this service men whom he positively knew to be loyal, and he instructed them to disguise the fact that they were working for an English trader. The Illinois Country, Campion said, was still controlled by French traders out of Louisiana. Another trade canoe was bound for the River Saint Joseph, which empties into Lake Michigan from the southeast. At Saint Joseph my engagés were to trade with Potawatomis, Miamis, and Weas. A third canoe was dispatched to Green Bay, there to trade with the Menominees, Winnebagos, Sauks, and Foxes. A fourth canoe was bound for the headwaters of the Great River Mississippi, where the engagés were to trade with the western Chippewas and the Issati Sioux. Theirs was considered a dangerous assignment, for the headwaters of the Mississippi were known as the Road of War, where the Chippewas and the Sioux were forever sending out war parties to attack one another.

Finally, Campion was to lead four canoes into the Northwest. He and his men were to follow the north coast of Lake Superior to Grand Portage, where they were to carry across into a vast maze of lakes and streams, the waters of which flow slowly northward toward Hudson's Bay. Campion had built for this voyage smaller canoes, known as *canots du nord*, or "canoes of the north." He said smaller canoes were easier to maneuver through the twisting streams and across the tangled portages of the Northwest.

My duty was to remain at Michilimackinac, where I was to establish trade with the Chippewas and the Ottawas, whose acquaintances I had already made.

By midday only Campion's four canoes remained on the beach in front of the fort. When all was ready for his departure, Campion and I embraced, and he waded into the water to take his place at the stern of one of the canoes. As the canoes set off, Campion abruptly stood up in his canoe, turned to me, and shouted. "Alex! In another year we will be rich men! Rich, I tell you! *Riche! Riche! Riche!*" He waved his arms and laughed boisterously. The men in the canoes joined in his laughter, and took up his chant: *"Riche! Riche! Riche!"*

I laughed too, but I did not know quite why.

9

Lieutenant Leslye kept his small garrison on full alert during their first few weeks at Fort Michilimackinac. From time to time he asked my advice regarding the Indians, and I gave him the best advice I could think of. But the practice worried me, for I realized that I was a blind man leading the blind.

With the help of a Jesuit priest, Lieutenant Leslye invited the Ottawas to a peace council at Fort Michilimackinac. I suggested that the lieutenant present a gift to the Ottawas, and I recommended generous amounts of tobacco and beads, and a small keg of rum. These goods I sold to him.

The Ottawas accepted the lieutenant's invitation, and an Ottawa delegation soon arrived at the fort, led by a chief named Okinochumaki. In council the chief professed a newfound friendship for the King of England, and he gave a collar of white wampum and a beaverskin robe to the lieutenant. He then asked the lieutenant for guns, lead, and powder, so the Ottawa hunters could provide for their families during the long winter that lay ahead. Lieutenant Leslye replied that he could spare neither guns nor powder for the Ottawas, but he added that English traders would arrive at Michilimackinac the next spring, and they would provide for all the Ottawas' needs. (As I listened to the fine speeches of the chief and the lieutenant, I suspected that neither Ottawa nor Englishman was telling the whole truth.)

One afternoon in mid-October I was informed that an Indian wished to see me outside the fort. On the beach I found an older Chippewa man with his wife. He introduced himself as Wawatam and his wife as Ocqua. I noticed that the man's eyes seemed to shine with inexplicable eagerness. We shook hands, and his face opened into a broad smile. His wife smiled as well. Their smiles startled me, for they were the first smiles I had ever evoked in Indians.

Wawatam's face was at once delicate and rugged: a high forehead, a long nose, and narrow, piercing eyes, surrounded by roughly weathered skin. His black hair was streaked with white, indicating an age of perhaps fifty—yet his lithe body seemed to belong to a man in his thirties. His hair was parted above the forehead, braided at each temple, and left to hang freely behind. On his forehead was painted a white V. He wore deerskin leggings and a red blanket draped over one shoulder.

Ocqua was short and powerfully built. Her face was as round and flat as Wawatam's was angular, and she possessed a lively, gap-toothed smile, which seemed to hold a special warmth for me. She had spots of red painted on each cheek and her chin. From holes in her ears hung white shells. She wore a neatly turned dress of deerskin and a white blanket over both shoulders.

I asked a Canadian to interpret for us.

"I have come to welcome you," Wawatam said. "More than that, I have come to tell you that I have seen you before. Four years ago, during the Moon of the Wild Rice, I was fasting in solitude, when the Great Spirit sent a vision to me. It was the vision of a young man with eyes the color of the sky and hair the color of dry grass. The Great Spirit made me understand that the young man was an Englishman, that he was a brave and good man, and that I would some day befriend him. When I learned several days ago of the arrival here of a young Englishman, I hastened here to see his face." Wawatam paused. "Now I see your face. Now I know that you are the young Englishman whom I saw in my vision."

As Wawatam's words were interpreted for me, he searched my face for understanding. I had no notion of how to respond to his peculiar story, so I only nodded.

Wawatam continued. "I have come to tell you that I wish to be your friend, as the Great Spirit has commanded. I have brought you this gift, which my wife has made for you."

Wawatam handed me a long, hooded robe of deerskin. Across the back of the shoulders were sewn porcupine quills, woven into patterns of squares and triangles. Across the front were simple paintings of people and animals. I put on the robe, and it hung comfortably to my knees. I thanked Wawatam for the gift of the robe and for the greater gift of his friendship. I complimented Ocqua on her fine quill work. I invited the couple to my house, but as we approached the gates of the fort, we were stopped by British sentries on the stockade, who refused to let my new friends enter. I went alone to my house and returned with a few of my finest trade goods. To Wawatam I gave a large hunting knife, with a handle of inlaid silver. To Ocqua I gave earrings of silver.

Following our exchange of gifts, Wawatam drew forth his pipe, and the three of us sat on the beach together and passed the pipe about, occasionally grinning at one another. At one point during our smoking, Wawatam motioned upward, toward the brilliant sun, and said, "The Great Spirit smiles upon us today."

When our smoking was finished, Wawatam and Ocqua took leave of me. Wawatam said they would visit me again, before his family left for its winter hunting ground.

By this time my life at the fort had settled into a comfortable routine. By day I traded with the Indians and learned a little of their languages. By night I socialized with Lieutenant Leslye and his sergeant. The three of us sat before a fire in the lieutenant's hearth, smoked from our clay pipes, drank glasses of high wine, and spoke earnestly of the future of Canada.

My newfound Chippewa friend soon proved good to his word. A week after his first visit, Wawatam again came calling on me. This time he brought with him his entire family—his wife, two sons, a daughter-in-law, and a young daughter. All were adorned in their finest ceremonial dress. Wawatam wore white feathers at the back of his head and a fillet of pearls suspended across his forehead. He wore bands of mink skin about his arms, a collar of white wampum about his neck, and a sash of red cloth about his waist, from which hung a medicine bag made from the skin of a silver fox.

Wawatam introduced me to his sons and his daughters, each of whom carried a bundle of goods, which made me think that the family had come to trade with me. We sat on the beach together, and Wawatam drew forth his pipe to smoke. But I noticed that his demeanor was much changed from his earlier visit. He now seemed serious and pensive, as if conducting some sort of important business. I noticed, too, that his pipe was filled not with tobacco but with the bark of the *kinnikinnick*, or "red willow," a sacred plant in the minds of the Chippewas. When we had emptied his pipe, Wawatam removed from his neck his collar of wampum, and held it toward me in both hands.

"My friend. Six days ago my wife and I came here to learn if you were the young Englishman whom I saw in my vision. I gazed upon your face, and I recognized you as the same young man. I offered you my friendship, and you, with your good heart, offered me your friendship in return. But when last we spoke I did not tell you all that needed to be said. Today I have returned to tell you all."

Wawatam drew a deep breath.

"In the vision in which I first saw you, the Great Spirit instructed me to take you into my family. I have come today to ask you to be my brother and my son."

I was speechless. The only sound to be heard was the washing of waves on the beach. I looked for a time into Wawatam's eyes. Then I looked into the eyes of his wife, his sons, and his daughters. All solemnly returned my gaze.

Wawatam continued. "I give you these gifts to soften your heart, so you will agree to join my family."

Ocqua and the others rose, opened their bundles, and set before me smoked meat, dried fish, Indian corn, maple sugar, and pelts of beaver and otter.

I stared at the pile of gifts before me. Questions filled my mind. What did Wawatam mean by asking me to join his family? Did he expect me to live with his family? How did the others feel about me? How could I be a son and a brother of the same man? I found myself thinking of my true family—my dead mother and father.

Some moments of silence elapsed before I realized that a reply was expected of me. I made my answer simple and direct. "Wawatam. I am honored that so good a man as you has asked me to be his brother and his son. I thank you for these fine gifts. I will gladly join your family." .

I started off to fetch gifts for Wawatam and the others, but he put his hand to my arm to stop me. "Your gift to me this day is your kinship," he said. "I am well satisfied."

Smiling broadly, Wawatam stepped forward to place his collar of wampum about my neck. "We are brother and brother, father and son," he said. He raised his hands and looked upward, as if speaking to the sky. "Nothing can break the cord that binds us together."

10

Wawatam's family soon left for their winter hunting ground, located more than a hundred miles to the south, on a river called *Aux Sables*.

I stayed on at the fort.

As winter began to show its icy teeth, men and beasts alike exerted themselves to leave Michilimackinac. The weather turned cold, and I saw long flights of swans, geese, and cranes flying southward. Ducks, all but a few, disappeared silently. The songbirds had departed weeks earlier. The people of Michilimackinac seemed to agree with the birds—all who could go did go. A number of French residents quit the fort and headed for remote trading posts in the wilderness. Fewer and fewer Indians visited the fort, as most of them separated into families, and each family returned to its traditional winter hunting ground. In this the Indians were following an ancient custom—as food became scarce in one place, the families spread out across the land, so that each family could find enough food to feed itself.

By the beginning of December only two Indian families still resided near the fort. One was the family of a minor Chippewa chief, who claimed to be warmly attached to the English. The chief had been taken prisoner by the British several years earlier, during the siege of Fort Niagara. Sir William Johnson, a shrewd officer who understood how to deal with the Indians, had surprised the chief by giving him not only his liberty, but a medallion and a British flag as well. Won over by these unexpected acts of kindness, the chief returned to Michilimackinac full of praises for the English. He hoisted the British flag over his lodge, but the act nearly cost him his life, for hostile Indians soon broke apart his lodge and tore his flag to pieces. The pieces of flag he gathered together and preserved with pious care, and whenever he came to the fort, he made a custom of showing the tattered rags to us. We, in turn, made a custom of giving the chief as much rum as he said he needed to make him weep over his lost flag.

I quickly learned that money was altogether out of the question at Fort Michilimackinac, where the sole medium of exchange was animal skins. When I visited the canteen, I took along a marten skin to pay my reckoning. A pound of marten skin was valued at a half dollar, a pound of otter at six livres, and a pound of beaver at a dollar. But while the prices for skins were low, the prices for food were high. I had to pay forty livres' worth of skins for a bushel of dried Indian corn, and a dollar's worth for a pound of tallow to mix with it. A Frenchman who killed an ox and sold beef by the quarter was able to demand as payment the full weight of the beef in beaver skins.

The high cost of food made me diligent in fishing, and fortunately I found the lake to be full of fish—trout, sturgeons, and whitefish. Trout were the principal winter food of the residents of the fort, and several Canadians kindly taught me how to fish. We took trout by cutting holes in the ice, through which we lowered baited lines, in some places to a depth of fifty fathoms. We left the lines in the water for days at a time. The trout we caught weighed from ten to sixty pounds each. We also took whitefish in nets, which we set beneath the ice. The whitefish were smaller than the trout, usually weighing just three to seven pounds apiece, but we caught them in astonishing numbers, and their taste was delicious. I could have eaten whitefish all winter long without losing my taste for them, which is more than I could say for trout. At the end of December the fishing suddenly failed, but by that time I had laid up a stock of dried fish sufficient to last me through the winter.

The Canadians helped me with fishing, but they held little interest for me socially. They talked mostly of fast canoes, beautiful women, and strong men who could fight a good fight.

But one day in mid-January I had the pleasure of meeting a truly remarkable Frenchman. He was Father Louis Jaunay, an old and venerable Jesuit priest, who had toiled for much of his life in the Mission of Saint Ignace at L'Arbre Croche. The hooded, black-robed priest came knocking on my door, in the midst of a howling blizzard, to ask if I had heard any news of the Indians. In particular he wanted to know how the Indians were faring with their winter hunt. He said he had heard reports that they were suffering greatly from want of food, for the winter had been a hard one. Heavy snow had fallen in early December, followed by bitter cold, followed by more snow.

I said I had not spoken with an Indian in more than two weeks, but I invited Father Jaunay to visit with me awhile, as he waited for the blizzard to subside. He accepted my invitation, and we sat before my fire and shared a kettle of tea. As we talked, the wind howled over my chimney and threw pellets of snow against my window.

Father Jaunay was thin and frail, and his hair was as white as his Roman collar. He informed me that he had been educated and ordained in Paris, and that he had first come to the Upper Country as a young priest, when he was assigned to the remote Mission of Saint Ignace. (I had seen this so-called mission. It amounted to nothing more than a log hut, decorated with a cross, standing amidst the birchbark lodges of the Ottawas.) From his tiny chapel Father Jaunay had devoted much of his life to converting the Indians to Christianity.

I complimented Father Jaunay on a fine cross I had seen standing in the Chippewa village on the Isle of Michilimackinac. The Chippewas had erected the cross in October, to ask for God's help with their winter hunt. They had adorned the cross with ropes of tobacco, arrows, and strings of wampum.

"My heart rejoices when I see a cross standing in the wilderness," Father Jaunay replied, but he shook his head. "I am filled with doubts, however, when I see sacrifices hanging from the cross. You must understand, my son, that many of the Indians of this country have accepted our Lord as their God—but not as their only god. They have welcomed our Holy Father into their prayers—but only as a sort of chief spirit among many spirits.

"My son, when first I arrived in this country, I was pleased to observe that the Indians possessed some of the principal virtues of true Christians. They were generous and deeply spiritual, and they trusted in their spirits to protect them and to provide for them. These qualities made me think the Indians would be fertile ground in which to plant the seeds of our faith. Yet over the years I have come to wonder if any of them have truly accepted Jesus Christ as their savior."

Father Jaunay seemed eager to confide in me, perhaps because I was a stranger.

"Ever since the Mission of Saint Ignace was established in this country, more than a century ago, we Jesuits have taught the Indians to pray to the Master of Life, which was the name we gave to God, to help the people better understand him. The Indians said they recognized our God as their Great Spirit, or *Gichi Manido* in their language. Many Indians obliged us by being baptized and praying to Gichi Manido, but few of them gave up their ancient idolatry to do so.

"My son, I will relate to you some of the evil superstitions I have witnessed in this country, which keep these poor people from their salvation. The Indians believe in a pantheon of spirits, as did the pagans of old. They believe that some spirits are good, such as the sun and the moon, the lakes, rivers, and forests; and that others are evil, such as the cold, storms, snakes, and toads. Whatever seems helpful or hurtful they call a *manido*, or 'spirit,' and they invoke their manidos whenever they go hunting, fishing, traveling, or to war.

"I once witnessed a pagan feast in honor of the sun, at which a man gave thanks to the sun for lighting his way. He prayed that the sun continue its kind care of his family. The guests at the feast were expected to eat their food to the last morsel, for the food was supposed to be a sacrifice to the sun. When the feasting was finished, the host broke a cake of tobacco and threw it into the fire. All in attendance cried aloud, as the tobacco burned and the smoke rose aloft. The tobacco was considered a sacrifice to the sun as well, and the people believed that the smoke would carry their prayers upward to the sun. When I challenged the host on his idolatrous practices, he claimed that he was only praying to Gichi Manido, who lives above us in heaven.

"In a storm on the open water, I have seen Indians sacrifice a dog by tying its feet together and throwing it into the lake. 'This is to calm you,' they said to the lake. 'Be quiet.'

"At dangerous rapids I have seen Indians try to appease the rushing waters by offering gifts. On River of the Foxes, above Green Bay, I once came upon a stone idol, silently watching over a fall in the river. The stone was in the shape of a man's head, and was painted in the most handsome colors the Indians could find. I was told that the Indians, when they ventured over the fall, never failed to offer a sacrifice of tobacco, beads, or some other gift to the idol, to gain its protection. When I discovered the stone idol, I ordered my companions to destroy it. They threw it into the depths of the river, never to be seen again.

"But an army of Christians could never destroy all the idols of the Indians, for their greatest idols are their pipes, and every family has one. The Indians honor their pipes as powerful spirits, as arbiters of life and death. They have pipes of peace and pipes of war, distinguished only by the colors of the decorations. They use a pipe of peace to seal alliances and welcome strangers. With such a pipe an Indian can venture alone among his enemies, who will lay down their weapons before it, even in the heat of battle, for fear of offending the pipe.

"I have seen Indians make a solemn dance to a pipe, treating it as though it were the most mysterious thing in the world. The host of the dance began the ceremony by presenting the stem of the pipe to the sun above, then to the earth below, then to the four points of the compass, then to the mouths of each of his guests. The bowl of the pipe was made from a red stone, polished to a luster, and its stem was decorated with brightly colored scalps of birds and the wings of a raven. The owner of the pipe spread its wings, as if to make it fly, and he danced about with it and sang to it. He then made a sign to another man, who took up arrows and a war hatchet and pretended to attack the bearer of the pipe, who in turn used only the pipe to protect himself. One man attacked; the other defended himself. One man struck blows; the other parried. One man took flight; the other pursued. Then he who was fleeing turned about and made his opponent flee. The spectacle was done to the slow and measured cadence of voices and drums, and it could have passed for the beginning of a fine ballet in Paris. But it grieved my soul deeply to see it."

Father Jaunay stared into the flames in my hearth. His voice was full of weariness.

"I have seen a wooden idol standing in the middle of a village. Many dogs were sacrificed to it, so that the idol would send away a sweeping sickness that was killing the people.

"The Indians believe that disease is caused by an evil spirit that enters a person's body. Their common cure is to send for a so-called medicine man or sorcerer. The sorcerer attends to the ill person by leaping and dancing about, to the accompaniment of a drum or a rattle, and devilish incantations. He then falls upon the diseased part of the patient, puts his mouth to it, and by sucking, pretends to draw from it an evil spirit. He displays a little stone or a shell, which he claims came from the patient's body and caused the illness.

"I once saw a sorcerer practice this false medicine on a young man who was seized by a rampant sickness. The sorcerer pretended to suck two dog's teeth out of the man's body, and he proudly passed the teeth about to the spectators, to prove that he had done his job. But I challenged the sorcerer, saying, 'These are not what caused the man's sickness. Rather, it is the tainted blood in his body.' I drew blood from the sick man and showed it to the sorcerer. 'This is what was killing him,' I said, 'not some alleged dog's teeth. You should have drawn from him every drop of this corrupt blood.' But the sorcerer refused to listen to me. Instead, he made the patient swallow some sort of potion. The man soon lay as if dead, and the sorcerer, much surprised by the turn of events, confessed that he had killed the patient. He begged me not to forsake the man. I baptized the sick man in the name of Saint Ignace, hoping that our blessed patron would confound the evil spirit of the sorcerer and save the life of the patient. Saint Ignace did not forsake the man, but gradually restored him to life.

"The Indians of this country believe that every sort of animal, fish, and bird has a special spirit that watches over the creature and protects it from harm. The Indians revere all creatures, as I once observed with a mouse I had killed and thrown from my lodge. A young girl snatched up the dead mouse and was about to eat it, when her father took it from her and bestowed a thousand caresses upon it. I asked him why he treated the mouse with such affection. 'Because,' he said, 'I wish to appease the spirit of the mice, so that the flesh of the mouse will not harm my daughter.'

"My son, I could relate a thousand stories of the paganism I have witnessed in this country. The Indians believe that the souls of dead fish pass into the bodies of newborn fish. They never throw fish bones into the fire, for fear of angering the souls of the fish, which would then refuse to enter their nets.

"There are certain animals whose spirits the Indians honor far more than others. One cannot believe the veneration they have for the bear. After killing a bear, they hold a solemn feast with special ceremonies. They save the bear's head and paint it with their finest colors. During the feast they put the bear's head in a place of honor, where it receives the praises that all bestow upon it, one after another, with their finest songs.

"And it is not only the animals they worship—they also pay homage to plants, lakes, rivers, and even to rocks. When I was a young man I visited the Jesuit mission at the Great Village of the Illinois. A band of Illinois escorted me to their country. As we followed the west coast of Lake Michigan, the Indians insisted on entering the mouth of each river we came to, so they might offer a sacrifice to that river. Despite my efforts to dissuade them, the Illinois left strips of meat hanging from stakes planted at the mouth of each river, to be disposed of as the river saw fit.

"The Indians are so convinced that they honor their false gods with such external worship that even those who are baptized continue to observe the same sort of worship toward our one true God.

"The Indians recognize no purely spiritual divinity, but believe that the sun is a man and the moon is his wife; that the snow and the ice are a man who comes in the winter and leaves in the spring; that the crow, the hawk, and the other birds are spirits that speak as we do; and even that some Indians understand the languages of the birds."

As Father Jaunay spoke, I could hear the blizzard blowing over the fort with a muffled roar. The priest glanced out the window at the storm.

"It has been a cruel winter, my son. I pray that my flock survives."

I thought of Wawatam and my adopted family.

"Instead of praying to our Heavenly Father for their sustenance," Father Jaunay continued, "the Indians seek visions of the animals they wish to kill. They weaken themselves by fasting for days on end, in hopes of seeing in a dream that which they seek—perhaps a bear or a herd of elk. They believe they cannot succeed in the hunt till they first see their prey in their dreams—not so difficult a task for empty minds, exhausted from hunger, thinking all day of nothing else.

"The Indians are held spellbound by their dreams. Their entire lives revolve around doubts and fears they learn from their dreams. I remember an Ottawa man, a father of many children, who visited my mission some years ago. He said he felt drawn to Christ. I was preparing the man for his baptism when he was attacked by a sudden illness and a high fever. He tossed about for days, half conscious, while I prayed over him. But when he recovered from his fever, he fiercely refused to listen to any more of my teachings. He said he had seen a vision during his fever, in which he was climbing a ladder to heaven. When he reached the top of the ladder, he saw a wide and beautiful plateau, full of flowers and birds. He looked about this supposed heaven, and he saw many trails and the tracks of countless men. But when he looked more closely, he noticed that all the tracks had been made by Frenchmen. Search as he might, he could not find the tracks of any Indians. In the midst of a beautiful paradise, he became terrified. He feared that he would never again see his countrymen, in this supposed heaven of Christians. He ran back to the ladder and descended back to the earth as quickly as he could. When he reached the earth in his dream, he awoke from his fever, and he proclaimed to me that he would never again listen to the teachings of what he called 'the French god.' Several months later I found the man giving a feast to a wolf skin. He and his family have remained obstinate pagans to this day."

Father Jaunay bowed his head, put one hand to his forehead, and shut his eyes.

"My son, I believe that Satan keeps his hold on these poor people through their dreams."

The priest remained bowed over, as if in forlorn prayer. We sat side by side, in silence. I looked out my window at the gray sky, filled with blowing snow. I felt pity for the old man, and a bit of scorn as well. To my way of thinking, he had wasted his life—his only life—on a false hope for eternal salvation. And yet I searched my recollections of Bible scripture for words that might comfort him. Finally I recalled a passage from the Book of Ecclesiastes.

"Father," I said, "remember the words of King Solomon:

> *He that observeth the wind shall not sow; and he that regardeth the clouds shall not reap. As thou knowest not the way of the spirit, nor how the bones do grow in the womb of her with child; even so thou knowest not the works of God who maketh all. In the morning sow thy seed, and in the evening withhold not thine hand; for thou knowest not which shall prosper, this or that, or whether they both alike shall be good."*

The words rang hollow in my mouth, for I did not believe in them. Having delivered my little sermon, I glanced sheepishly at the priest.

Father Jaunay raised his head and repeated the words: *"Sow thy seed . . . withhold not thine hand."* A smile creased his face, and he stared into my eyes for a time. "I am sorry, my son, for having burdened you with my doubts. It has been a true blessing to spend a few moments with a man of faith."

The old man rose to his feet, warmly shook my hand, blessed me, and walked to the door. He was smiling as he stepped into the blizzard.

11

I could have endured the tedium of an entire winter spent at Fort Michilimackinac—hunting and fishing by day, smoking and socializing with the British soldiers by night—but I did not forget Campion's advice that I should leave the fort, to educate myself in the ways of the Indians. In mid-March, as the weather began to ease, I traveled to the Sault de Sainte Marie, to visit the home of one Jean Baptiste de Cadotte, an elderly fur trader widely respected by the Indians of the Upper Country. Campion had advised me that I could learn much from Cadotte.

My route to the Sault lay overland to the northeast, through a thick forest, and I made the journey in two days. By the time I reached the Sault, I was troubled by a painful disorder in the backs of my legs, which the French called *le mal de raquette*, or "the snowshoe trouble," a malady caused by the weight of the snowshoes straining the tendons of the legs. The usual remedy was to lay a piece of smoldering touchwood on the sore tendon, to deaden the nerves. But although I had seen the treatment succeed with others, I could not be persuaded to perform it on myself.

The Sault de Sainte Marie was named for a tempestuous rapids, where the waters of Lake Superior fall into Lake Huron. In autumn the Sault is a source of vast numbers of whitefish, which the Chippewas scoop up in nets, while standing in their canoes in the midst of the rapids. When I arrived at the Sault, however, the place was almost deserted. I found only a modest fort, standing on the south bank of the rapids, and consisting of but four houses surrounded by a palisade of stakes. The only persons living within the fort were Cadotte and his family, which consisted of his Chippewa wife and their two sons.

Monsieur and Madame Cadotte welcomed me warmly to their lonely outpost, and seemed genuinely pleased to have the company of another person, even that of an Englishman. With their assistance I soon learned to speak the Chippewa language tolerably well, for in their household only the Chippewa tongue was spoken.

Cadotte informed me that the winter had been a hard one at the Sault. He said the snow, which had laid deep on the ground for much of the season, had spoiled the hunting, and the fishing had failed as well. Fortunately, Cadotte and his family had prepared for the winter by putting up large supplies of dried fish, Indian corn, wild rice, and maple sugar. Others were not so fortunate. Several families of Indians showed up at Cadotte's house seeking food. They were in appalling condition, being but skin and bones. Cadotte shared his family's food with them.

Cadotte blamed the plight of the Indians on the hard winter, but also on the recent war. "The Indians of this country have depended for their survival on guns, powder, and other goods which the French once sold to them. But with the war and the fall of Canada, the supply of these goods has been cut off. Now, Monsieur Henry, the Indians desperately need traders like yourself to bring them new merchandise."

I did not tell Cadotte that General Amherst had forbidden the sale of guns and ammunition to the Indians. Nor did I tell him of the guns and powder locked away in my house at Michilimackinac.

It was the beginning of May before the last of the ice melted from the bays and inlets near the Sault, allowing me to return to Michilimackinac by way of Lake Huron. I did so by riding in the canoe of a Chippewa family headed in that direction.

With the opening of the lakes, the pulse of life at Fort Michilimackinac began to quicken. Chippewas and Ottawas returned with furs for me, to pay off their debts from the previous autumn. Unfortunately, some who were in my debt returned empty-handed, claiming that the hard winter had prevented them from catching the beaver and other animals. They emphatically promised to repay me as soon as they could, and I did not doubt them, for I was well aware of the hardships they had suffered during the winter.

To my great relief, Wawatam and my adopted family returned to Michilimackinac in late May. The entire family came to my house to say hello, and I welcomed them with a meal of whitefish and grouse, seasoned with maple sugar. The entire family was in good health and good spirits, although Wawatam said they had gone hungry many times during the winter. When they had most needed food, he said, Gichi Manido had sent the animals to them. They had often lain in ambush for the animals near springs of open water, a hunting method which had served them well. Wawatam said his family was fortunate to have three hunters to feed six people.

In mid-June the voyageurs in my employ arrived from Montreal in seven canoes, loaded with merchandise. I greeted them as old and loyal friends.

Unfortunately, other canoes arrived as well, similarly loaded with merchandise but belonging to other Englishmen. Rival traders set up shop at Fort Michilimackinac—among them John Tracy, Stanley Goddard, and Ezekiel Solomons. All were eager to compete with me for the Indian trade. As I no longer held a monopoly in the trade, I was inspired to redouble my efforts to form friendships with the Indians.

Through the month of June my engagés returned from their winter camps in the hinterlands. Most of my outfits had done well for themselves. My canoes were filled to the gunwales with packets of fur—soft, lustrous, and foul-smelling. By the end of June all the engagés had returned, except for Campion and his men, who were inexplicably tardy.

Each day of June brought a new band of Indians to the fort, and soon all the nations of the Upper Country were represented—Ottawa, Chippewa, Potawatomi, Cree, Sauk, Fox, Kickapoo, Mascoutin, Winnebago, Illinois, Miami, Huron, Iowa, Menominee, Nipisingue, Amiquois, Mississaugi. As the nations gathered, Michilimackinac bustled with the activity of a summer fur fair. Beached canoes, piles of furs, and stacks of merchandise lay scattered about the beach. *Wigiwams* of birchbark, *tipis* of deer hide, tents of canvas, and lean-to's of logs stretched along the lakeshore for a half mile in both directions from the fort. A populous village took shape almost overnight. Festooned with feather flags and French laundry, the village was as colorful and ephemeral as a Bedouin encampment.

The arrival of each new canoe at Michilimackinac was boisterously announced to the village by its occupants. The Indians arrived with wild yelps and war whoops, and sometimes with flying arrows. At first I was alarmed by their warlike gestures, but I soon realized that all their belligerence was merely for show. The Indians were bedecked in their finest jewelry, feathers, and paint. The voyageurs, on the other hand, arrived to the cadence of gay canoe songs and flashing paddles. The men were freshly washed and shaved when they arrived, and they wore calico shirts, red sashes, and scarves. I commented on their unusual cleanliness, and was told that the voyageurs made a practice of stopping before they reached the fort, to attend to their toiletries. As they arrived, the voyageurs were particularly interested in the Indian women, some of whom traded sexual favors for European trinkets. (I confess that I too participated in this wicked commerce.)

Two distinct classes of voyageurs now resided at Michilimackinac. One class was the *Montrealers*—men who transported trade goods from Montreal to Michilimackinac each spring, and made the return trip in late summer with packets of furs. The Montrealers were the workhorses of the trade—strong men who loved the challenge of a long wilderness voyage but spent the winter safe and warm in Montreal. The other class of voyageurs was the *hivernants*, or "winterers"—men who carried merchandise into the wilderness each autumn, traded with the Indians through the course of the winter, and returned to Michilimackinac with furs in the spring. The hivernants were the true frontiersmen of the trade, as expert in hunting, trapping, tracking, and generally surviving as were the Indians themselves.

The hivernants were a strange and wild breed of men. All wore feathers in their hair as a special badge of their calling. Many sported other savage emblems—copper earrings, necklaces of wampum or animal teeth, stone amulets, or medicine pouches made of animal skins. Some wore tattoos. One referred to himself as *un Francais sauvage*—"a French savage." Some of the hivernants were *metis*, or "half-breeds," the sons of French fathers and Indian mothers. The half-breeds called themselves *bois brule*, or "burnt wood," in reference to their dark skins, but there was no lack of pride among them. One swaggered about boasting of his two noble bloodlines: that of a French lord, and that of Potawatomi chief. To draw attention to his esteemed pedigrees, he had tattooed the coat of arms of his French ancestors on one shoulder, and the figure of an otter, the symbol of his Potawatomi clan, on the other shoulder.

Each group of men—hivernants and Montrealers—seemed to despise the other group as an inferior class of commoners. Each group haughtily set up its tents and shacks in a separate camp, and those who enjoyed a good fight sometimes paid a visit to the enemy camp. One evening I saw a hivernant calmly stroll into the camp of the Montrealers, with his shoulders thrown back. Straightaway he picked out the biggest Montrealer he could find and insulted him. "You! You dumb pork eater! Do you call yourself a man? You could not catch a hare if your life depended on it."

To this the Montrealer had a ready reply. "I would not bother myself with chasing the small animals. But I do know how to treat a French lady. I will not have to marry a greasy squaw."

This was all that needed to be said. The two men threw themselves at each other. They wrestled, punched, kicked, bit, butted, and clawed, all to the wild cheers of the voyageurs who gathered about. Their savage fighting continued till one man lay silent on the ground. But all was soon forgiven, for later that night I saw the two men dancing merrily with one another.

The great pastime of the Indians at Michilimackinac was a game they called *baggatiway* and which the French called *le jeu à la crosse*. The game was played with an intricately carved wooden ball and sticks about four feet long with small nets or racquets at the ends. The game took place between two posts planted in an open field some distance apart. Each team defended its own post and tried to throw the ball to the post of its opponent. There were no boundaries to the field, so the game could range across a mile or more of country. At times more than two hundred Indians played at the game, with one nation competing against another, and with each Indian fiercely swinging his racquet. In such a game all that could be seen was the flourishes of racquets. The yells of the players and the cracks of jarring sticks produced a din that sounded like pitched battle. Games of la crosse often resulted in broken bones and cracked heads.

As the trade in furs flourished at Michilimackinac, I noticed that many of the Indians were conducting a secret trade all their own. It was a trade entirely beyond my understanding, a trade in mysterious objects reverently drawn from medicine bags—perhaps a bit of powder or a bone, a shell or a piece of birchbark with strange figures cut into it. Such paltry items commanded handsome prices among the Indians, and were traded for truly valuable goods such as peltries and silver. I saw one piece of birchbark traded for a whole packet of beaver skins, and I asked the Indian who sold the skins why he paid such a dear price for the bark. "The birchbark holds a magical song," the Indian said. "A packet of beaver skins has little value compared with a magical song to which all the beavers on the earth must listen."

One day in late June I noticed a group of Indians milling about, whispering and gesturing, as though they were uneasy about something. I asked them what was the matter. They pointed to a man who did things beyond their understanding—they said he possessed an evil spirit. I approached the man, who introduced himself as a Frenchman from River of the Missouris. I remarked that the Indians were nervous about his presence, and he confided in me that he was a master of the sleight of hand. With his magic, he said, he was able to hold great sway over the Indians of the Missouri Country, who called him *Minneto*, or "Spirit." As we spoke, a Cree passed us carrying a beautifully wrought pipe of polished black stone. Minneto stopped the Indian to admire the pipe and asked to see it. The Cree handed him the pipe, and Minneto examined it closely, remarking that the pipe must hold a powerful spirit. As Minneto held the pipe, he offered to buy it, but the Cree said he would not part with the pipe for anything. Suddenly the entire pipe seemed to leap into Minneto's mouth, and he seemed to swallow it whole. The Cree was speechless with astonishment, for the pipe was three times bigger than Minneto's mouth. Minneto calmly told the Cree not to trouble himself about the pipe, and assured the Cree that he could have the pipe back in two or three days. After three days had passed, Minneto called on the Cree to return the pipe, which Minneto said had just passed through his body. The poor Indian looked at the pipe as though he could not bear to part with it, yet he refused to lay his hands on it. Minneto kept the pipe for nothing.

That summer I witnessed a singular event at Fort Michilimackinac. A small delegation of Issati Sioux arrived in late June, having made the long voyage from their homelands, which lay far to the west, on the headwaters of the Great River Mississippi. Their appearance was a rarity, for the Sioux and the Chippewas were blood enemies, and the Sioux were greatly outnumbered at Michilimackinac. The Sioux came only because Lieutenant Leslye had called for a council of peace between the warring nations, and he had promised the Sioux that they would be safe at the fort. (I considered the lieutenant's promise to be a brash one, for if the Chippewas had taken it into their heads to attack the Sioux, there was little the lieutenant could have done to prevent a massacre.)

Yet the Sioux arrived with a great show of confidence. As they pulled their canoes onto the beach, they haughtily returned the hateful glares of the Chippewas. Some of the Sioux wore the tails of skunks tied to their heels, indicating that they, like the self-assured skunk, never ran from their enemies. The Sioux envoys seemed to calmly hold their lives in their hands. One warrior sat on the lakeshore and sang his death song, to show that he was not afraid to die.

The Sioux were all proper men, dressed in paint. They wore their hair short, worked up with grease, and sprinkled with feathers. From their shoulders hung small shields, covered with painted feathers in the shapes of animals, the sun, or the moon. From their ears hung ornaments of yellow copper. From their medicine bags hung bears' claws and carvings of buffalo horn. Their leggings were embroidered with pearls and porcupine quills. Their knives were a foot and a half long, and their wooden clubs were shaped like back swords, some with rounded heads. One had the skins of rattlesnakes hanging from his elbows.

A chief of the Sioux, a man named Ouasicoude, carried in one hand a tall war flag of eagle and vulture feathers, and in the other hand an elaborate pipe. The pipe had a stone bowl as big as a fist and a wooden stem four feet long, decorated with the tail feathers of eagles and the brilliantly colored scalps of woodpeckers and ducks. He wore a magnificent robe of buffalo hide, with porcupine quills and sweet grass sewn in a pattern across the back.

Lieutenant Leslye made a clumsy effort to greet the Sioux, but he found he could not make himself understood. The Sioux language, he quickly learned, was altogether different from the languages of the Upper Indians. At one point he said he had a mind to have a Highland Scot speak to the Sioux, for he said the two harsh tongues sounded much the same. At last he found a Winnebago who could converse with the Sioux, and the lieutenant proceeded with his welcoming ceremony.

The Chippewas, not to be outdone when it came to pageantry, returned to their lodges to prepare for a grand council. They passed the pipe of peace about, from lodge to lodge, and from mouth to mouth. The men took great pains to paint their faces in precisely the patterns they considered appropriate for the occasion, and no two patterns were alike. Then they dressed for the event and started a grand procession, in which they marched to the beat of drums and the flutter of feather flags. When they arrived at the council ground, they planted their feather flags in the sand. A band of musicians, made up of older men, sat on the ground under the flags and made rhythm with drums and rattles. A chorus of singers, made up of women wrapped in blankets, their eyes fixed on the ground, muttered a melancholy chant that sounded like a storm growling in the distance. Inspired by such sounds, the young warriors hopped about in a wide circle, shaking the tails of raccoons, skunks, and foxes, tied to their wrists, ankles, heads, and backsides.

Once in council, Lieutenant Leslye presented generous gifts to both nations. He informed them that the King of England wanted the Chippewas and the Sioux to put down their war hatchets and to live in peace.

The chiefs representing the two nations responded at first by airing old grievances and by leveling new accusations against the enemy. All were reluctant at first to show any desire for peace. But gradually and grudgingly, the chiefs of each nation finally admitted that peace would be a welcome change, if only the other side could be convinced to stop its vicious attacks. Both sides warmed to the idea of peace, and by the time the council ended, great promises were being made, the principal one being that the Chippewas would not venture west of the Mississippi River if the Sioux would not come east of the river. The chiefs of both sides now spoke eloquently of peace.

I thought the speech of Mongazid, a chief of the Fond du Lac Chippewas, was a particularly fine one. "When first I heard the voice of the Englishman coming from across the great water," he said, "it was no more than a murmur on the wind. Yet I rose from my mat and I hastened to answer the voice. I traveled across the great water to reach this place, and as I traveled, the sun shone brightly upon me, to light my way. Today I see that the sun shines brightly upon us all. I see the blue sky above our heads. Surely the Great Spirit desires for us to live in peace. Today I hear nothing but pleasant words from my enemies. Surely we can live in peace with one another. Today I hear no eagle cry, 'Come. The feast is ready. The Indian has killed his brother.'"

When all speeches were finished, the soldiers butchered a fatted ox, and the Chippewas and Sioux feasted together. Far into the night the two nations danced the peace pipe to one another and brightened the chain of friendship in a very decent way.

(The peace did not last long, however. Within a few months a Chippewa or a Sioux, depending on who told the story, had spilled the blood of the other nation. Ancient hatreds boiled over, and the two nations entered a new cycle of killing and being killed.)

But at least the peace council served my own purposes, for it presented me with an opportunity to introduce myself to the Sioux and to buy skins from them. The Sioux were exceedingly interested in trading with me, as they were with the other English traders. They honored me with a feast of dried buffalo meat, at which they offered me the choicest parts—the hump and the tongue—which were delicious. They blew on the hot meat before giving it to me, as a special gesture of friendship, and they placed the first three morsels in my mouth.

The Sioux were especially interested in buying muskets from me, which they called *mauza ouackange*, meaning "iron that has understanding." They appreciated the fact that a musket ball can break an enemy's bones, while their arrows could only pierce his flesh. I informed the Sioux that I had no guns to sell to them, but I assured them that I would send several canoes full of merchandise to their country the next winter, to furnish other needs they might have. I gave them a few trade goods, and I sold them a great deal more. As the Sioux departed from Michilimackinac, they professed their friendship for the King of England and for English traders.

I stayed busy that summer, securing furs, sorting them into packets, distributing trade goods among the engagés, and trading with the Indians. But in conducting all this business, I sorely missed my partner, Etienne Campion. The month of July came and went, and I grew increasingly worried for his safety. My greatest fear was that he and his men had starved to death. I frequently found myself scanning the horizon of the lake, hoping to spot Campion's canoes.

In trading with the Indians, I was continually beset by their pleas for guns and ammunition, which they said they needed in order to feed their families. Some of the Indians threatened me; others cajoled; others begged. I, in turn, lied to them all. I claimed that no guns or ammunition were available for the Indian trade. Finally the Indians grew so distressed by the supposed lack of guns that Minavavana, a chief of the Chippewas, demanded to speak to Lieutenant Leslye. A council was called, in which Minavavana was to speak to the lieutenant on behalf of the chiefs of several nations.

On the day of the council more than a dozen chiefs assembled in the commandant's house. Most wore black paint on their faces, as a symbol of mourning. In council Minavavana spoke of Indians who had starved to death during the preceding winter. He named and praised his dead brethren at some length, and he mentioned Indians of other nations who had died. In this he seemed to be speaking not so much to the lieutenant as to the ghosts of the dead. He said many Indians who died would have lived, if only they had guns and powder for the hunt. The assembled chiefs accompanied Minavavana's speech with moans and murmurs of grief.

Suddenly Minavavana turned to the lieutenant and spoke directly to him.

"My brother. We have heard reports that the English intend to destroy us. I cannot believe such a thing of our English brothers, but I tell you that many Indians do believe it. Many Indians ask why the English soldiers do not give us powder or lead, as the French once did. They ask why the English traders do not sell us guns. They ask why English gunsmiths do not come into our country, to repair our old guns.

"My brother. Can these reports be true? Do the English plan to make war on us? Do the English seek to destroy us?

"I call you my brother, for you have told us that the English will act as our brothers. You have told us that the King of England will act as our father. You have spoken of peace, and you have said that the English will be generous in supplying our needs. But I tell you, the French were far more generous in their day. When the French ruled Canada, we never wanted for guns or powder. You must help us to understand this, my brother. Has the King of England forgotten us? Does he seek to destroy us?"

Lieutenant Leslye rose to make his reply. He stood stiffly before the chiefs, who sat on the floor before him.

"I am surprised, my brothers, at your folly in listening to such idle and wicked reports. Have you no reason to doubt them? Do you not see proof every day of English kindness? Do you not see us showing mercy to our worst enemies, the French? Do you not see us showing mercy to the Indians? What other nation on earth would behave as mercifully toward its enemies as have the English? How then can you doubt our good hearts? You must drop your evil suspicions and behave as good brothers should. Do not give us reason to think your suspicions arise from your guilt. Do not give us reason to doubt your friendship."

To this Minavavana offered no reply. He and the other chiefs rose in a body and stalked out of the council room. It was clear that the lieutenant's haughty response had angered and insulted them, and I warned the lieutenant of their anger.

"Mister Henry," the lieutenant replied curtly, "do not expect me to try to placate the Indians, when they present me with such veiled threats. You know as well as I that the savages respect just one thing, and that is strength."

It soon became clear, however, that Lieutenant Leslye placed at least some credence in my warnings. He ordered his garrison to redouble its guard, and he again forbade any Indians from entering the fort. While a great concourse of peoples resided on the beach outside Fort Michilimackinac, the soldiers inside the fort did not show themselves. The British behaved as prisoners within their own fort.

12

On the afternoon of August 5, 1762, I looked up from a pile of skins to see Etienne Campion striding across the beach toward me. Before I could speak, he pulled me into his arms and clutched me with a rough passion. I was filled with joy, but my joy was supplanted by concern when I saw deep lines etched into Campion's face and a hollowness about his eyes. He seemed to be a different man—an older man.

"What has happened?" I asked.

"It was a cruel winter, Alex. Four of my men died. The rest of us are fortunate to be alive."

I led Campion directly to my house, where I set before him a meal of duck meat, corn meal, and tea. I was full of questions for him, but Campion refused to answer any questions before learning the fate of the other engagés and the condition of our enterprise. Only after he was satisfied with the general state of our affairs did he began to tell me of the hard winter through which he and his men had suffered.

"We followed the north coast of Lake Superior and reached Grand Portage by the end of October. We made haste to carry across, for the season was growing late. A thin skin of ice covered the small bays. Snow began to fall, warning us.

"I separated our four canoes and sent each to a different part of the Northwest, so as to spread our trade among as many peoples as possible. Four of us paddled a single canoe westward, toward the country of the Issati Sioux. In places we paddled across open water, but in other places we had to break the ice with a paddle or an axe, to make a channel before us. Finally we were forced to build a sled and pull our canoe across the ice. As we traveled, we ate our stock of Indian corn."

Campion stared at the plate of food I had set before him.

"We stopped at Lac à la Pluie, where we set up camp, and we began to trade with the Sioux and the Crees, who were happy to see us in their country.

"But powdery snow—snow the Chippewas call *peewun*—fell from the sky as if sifted. It lay soft and deep on the ground and would not bear us up, even when we made snowshoes six feet long and a foot and a half wide. We could not turn on our long snowshoes without falling, and when we fell, we had trouble rising again. We made such a noise, thrashing about in the snow, that the animals heard us from a long way off. We could kill nothing.

"A band of Issati Sioux came to us in great want, being but skin and bones. They begged us for food and ammunition. They said their hunting and fishing had failed them, and a band of renegade Indians, known as *Pilleurs*, or 'Pillagers,' had stolen their stores of wild rice. The Issati promised that they would return to us in the spring with a canoe full of pelts, if only I would sell them powder, lead, and two or three muskets. But how could I help them without risking the lives of my men? I made excuses, telling the Issati that I had no spare guns or ammunition, and precious little food. I offered to sell them knives, traps, and blankets on credit. But on hearing this, they raised their spears against us and demanded our food, our guns, and our powder. They said they were deeply ashamed to be stealing our property from us. They admitted that they were acting like hungry dogs, which steal a piece of meat from the dish and run. They beseeched us to understand that they must save the lives of their children, which were the dearest things in the world to them. They acted out their shame by weeping over us and letting their tears fall on our heads. They chanted countless prayers over us. They gave us so-called magical songs, which they said would help us with our hunting, but which amounted to nothing more than drawings on birchbark. They left us with just enough Indian corn to last us a week. They promised they would return to us with food as soon as they succeeded with their hunt. Their actions distressed me deeply, but I could not blame them for preferring their children's lives to our own.

"Heavy snows were followed by bitter cold. Cold was followed by snow. Our bellies ached for want of food."

Campion spoke with a flat, expressionless voice, as if in a trance.

"To add to our misery, we learned that more than a hundred Crees were on their way to our camp, hoping we could help them survive. When the Crees arrived, they asked us for food, and when I told them we had no food, they ran their spears into the snow to find where we had hidden our supplies of Indian corn. But try as they might, they found nothing but our knives and kettles, and these were of no use to them, for they had no food to cut or to cook. When they realized that we were as destitute as they, they cried aloud to their gods of heaven and earth.

"Each day brought a new family—half-dead, flying from famine.

"In their first days with us, the Crees killed and ate their dogs. We soon found ourselves going back over their tracks, to search for the bones of the animals they had killed. Happy was he who found what another had thrown away. We boiled the bones three and four times, to draw the substance out of them. We ground the bones into a powder, and from it we made a tasteless sort of bone soup, which nourished our imaginations rather than our bellies.

"In early January there appeared two strangers, Issati hunters, with a dog. The men were well fed, but the dog was as lean and hungry as we were. I offered to buy the dog, but the Issati refused to sell it, saying they loved their animal. Their refusal angered me, and I made up my mind to eat dog flesh. That night I approached their lodge, and the dog came out to greet me, wagging its tail for friendliness. I led the dog a little distance away and cut its throat. While the Issati slept, I carried the dog's carcass back to our lodge. Then I returned to gather up the bloody snow, which I used to season the kettle. I broiled the dog's carcass like a pig, and I caught the fat in a kettle for broth. I gave the pieces, guts and all, to my men and to a few Cree children.

"But there was no end to the cold, which was extreme. Soon we lacked the strength to gather wood for a fire, or to haul our snowshoes after us. We tried to dig for roots, but the earth was frozen two or three feet deep, and the snow lay in drifts five or six feet above it. Our sustenance was the bark of the bittersweet vine, which we ground into a powder and mixed into a broth.

It amused our appetites, but we became dryer and thirstier than the wood we ate.

"Next we ate the skins we used for shoes and clothes—even the beaver skins in which the children had beshat a hundred times. We burned off the hair. The rest went down our throats. We ate heartily of things we should have abhorred. We chewed so eagerly that our gums bled like fresh wounds.

"All cried out for hunger. The women became barren and dry like wood. The men ate the cords of their bows, for they lacked the strength to pull them. The children . . . the children died. With each dawn the mothers and fathers opened their eyes to look upon their little ones, to see which of them still had life. They mourned their dead children with cries that made our hearts stop."

Campion paused and shut his eyes.

"And we—we Frenchmen—we who called ourselves masters of the earth—we too tasted of this bitterness, and we prayed to escape it. We became the very image of death. The Crees, who could not see my face beneath my beard, thought I was well fed and suspected that some devil was bringing me food secretly. But if they could have seen my body, they would have known the truth.

"Wolves circled our camp. Crows and eagles flew above it. The creatures sought to eat the flesh of dead humans. We humans gazed back at the creatures, and desired devoutly to eat their flesh, but we lacked the powder with which to shoot them.

"My friend, they say that calm follows the storm. But we dreaded the calm, and we prayed for a storm. At last, in mid-February, our prayers were answered. A night of wind and freezing rain cleared the forest about us. We awoke in the morning to find the snow crusted over with a shell of ice, on which we could walk. We discovered that the deer and the elk, already weak from hunger, broke through the ice with every step, and were pinned as if by stakes. It suddenly became an easy matter for us to approach the animals and slit their throats with our knives.

"It was God." Campion reached across the table to grasp my arm. "It was God, in his infinite mercy, who rescued us from famine. At a time when we were too weak to walk, God sent us animals we did not have to chase.

"At first we could eat but little of our new food, for our guts had been straitened by long fasting. But we grew stronger daily.

"A band of Issati Sioux came to us in early March, bringing us venison and beaver. They were the same people who had taken our food and guns from us in November. I accepted the food from them in silence. A month earlier I would have wept with joy to receive it.

"In May we returned to Grand Portage, where we expected to rendezvous with the other three canoes. We waited there a week, but one canoe failed to return. I took three of my healthiest men with me, to search for the missing canoe. We pushed northward as rapidly as possible, crossing countless lakes and portages.

"At Lac des Isles we heard an alarming story from a band of Crees. They said four French traders had frozen to death that winter. A Cree offered to show us the graves of the Frenchmen. He led us northward to a spot on the shore of Lac Nipigon, where we found four fresh graves, each marked with a cross of sticks. From each cross hung tatters of worsted cloth, and from one cross hung a string of rosary beads. We recognized the scraps as having once belonged to our comrades. Our Cree guide said the four Frenchmen had been caught on the ice by a storm of sleet, that was followed by a cruel north wind. The Frenchmen froze to death before they could find their way to shore. All the Crees found of them was their bones, torn apart and gnawed by wolves, and a few pieces of cloth, scattered across the ice. Ah, *misère*!

"The Crees gathered together the bones and buried them in four separate graves, each marked with a cross, just as they knew the French would have wished. They attached the tatters of cloth and the string of rosary beads to the crosses, so the dead who were buried there might be identified by their countrymen.

"We prayed over the graves of our dead comrades and offered them their last rites as best we could."

Campion looked into my eyes. "Alex. I pray that I never see such a winter again."

We sat in silence for some minutes.

Finally Campion asked me about the guns and ammunition that he and I had hidden in my house the previous autumn. I opened the door to my bedroom to let Campion see for himself. There were the guns and kegs of powder, just as we had left them nine months earlier. Campion stared blankly at the munitions.

"The governor forbade us from selling guns to the Indians," I said.

For the rest of the day Campion busied himself in discussing business affairs with the voyageurs in our employ. His many questions covered such matters as the quality and abundance of furs, prices of merchandise, and political intrigues among the Indians. At day's end Campion complimented me on the way I had run our business in his absence, saying that he agreed with most of the decisions I had made. He then surprised me by saying that he planned to travel to L'Arbre Croche the next morning, to visit Father Jaunay.

Late the next day Campion returned from L'Arbre Croche and immediately set about visiting the lodges of the Indians camped near Fort Michilimackinac. I noticed that he carried pen and paper with him as he made his rounds. When he was finished, he showed me a list of the names of more than a hundred and fifty Indians who had starved to death the previous winter.

Campion then made a startling proposal to me. He proposed that he return with the trade canoes to Montreal, where he would sell my pelts, purchase trade goods, and proceed on to Albany, where he would pay off my debts. Then he intended to travel to New York, where he would seek an audience with General Amherst. He intended to persuade the general to permit the sale of guns and ammunition to the Indians of the Upper Country.

I rejected Campion's proposal outright, for I planned to return with the trade canoes myself. I had my heart set on spending the winter in civilization. I assured Campion that I would do my best to communicate his arguments to the general. Surely, I pointed out, I could be more persuasive with the general than could a Frenchman.

But Campion was adamant. He paced about me in circles, at times clasping his hands before my face, at times pounding his fists on the table, at times shaking me by my shoulders, and all the while bombarding me with his arguments. After a few minutes of such rigorous treatment, I felt compelled to admit that Campion was far more determined than I to argue his cause before the general. I further admitted that he would be more effective than I in selling our furs and bartering for new merchandise. Finally I threw up my hands and agreed that Campion should be the one to travel to Montreal. With a sinking heart I resigned myself to another long winter in the wilderness.

But my partner had still one more surprise for me. "Cheer up, Alex," he said. "I have good news. I have spoken with an English trader here who has agreed to pay you handsomely for the guns and ammunition hidden beneath your bed."

"And what does he propose to do with them?" I asked, knowing the answer.

"He did not say," Campion replied innocently.

"You know full well that he intends to sell the guns to the Indians," I charged.

Campion shrugged. "I only know that he will pay you for merchandise you cannot use. I know, too, that there is no law against selling guns to an Englishman." Campion winked. "And I know that you will again be able to smoke in your bed."

I stiffened at Campion's jest.

"Alex," Campion said in a low voice, "more good people will die if they do not have guns and powder. You must do this for them."

Again I had to agree.

That evening Campion and I transferred our guns and ammunition from my house to the storehouse of a rival English trader.

Late that night I sat up alone, thinking of Campion and marveling at the sense of urgency he felt to save the lives of the Indians. I admired his fervent compassion, and I wondered at it, for I felt nothing like it within myself. I confessed that I cared but little about the lives or deaths of one hundred fifty Indians.

13

As Campion and his voyageurs left for Montreal, the Indians and the engagés all left for the hinterlands, and I resigned myself to another tedious winter at Fort Michilimackinac. I tried to convince myself that I was lucky to have the company of the British soldiers, to help me while away the long winter months. We amused ourselves in hunting grouse and a species of large hare that turns white in the winter. Yet I soon grew weary of chasing the little animals about the forest. I longed for the more refined distractions of civilization.

The tedium I experienced at the fort was interrupted briefly in mid-November by the arrival of a fresh detachment of troops from Detroit. The detachment was led by Major George Etherington, a young and darkly handsome officer who was supremely confident of his own abilities. The major took command of the garrison at Fort Michilimackinac, and Lieutenant Leslye stayed on as second in command.

Several days after his arrival, Major Etherington entertained the English traders at the fort with a splendid dinner of roast beef. Through the course of the meal, the major immodestly recounted his brilliant acts of heroism, while fighting under the command of General Amherst, in British victories at Louisburg, Ticonderoga, and Crown Point. He claimed to be a trusted confidant of the general's, and as if to prove the point, he shared with us the strategic thinking employed by General Amherst in ruling Canada.

"There are those among His Majesty's forces who would seek only to appease the Indians with expensive gifts and lofty speeches of friendship," the major asserted. "But Sir Jeffrey realizes that the savage mind understands but one thing, and that is unflinching strength. Sir Jeffrey has advised that I offer no gifts whatsoever to the Indians, for he considers such gifts to be nothing more than bribes, which will buy the good behavior of the Indians only till such time as they demand more bribes. Sir Jeffrey prefers quite a different policy—he prefers to punish the Indians if ever they misbehave."

As the evening wore on, too many glasses of high wine loosened the major's tongue still further, and he decided to tell us a humorous story regarding the British commandant at Detroit, a Major Henry Gladwin.

"Mind you, Major Gladwin is a fine officer," Major Etherington avowed. "But he spends much of his time cultivating supposed spies among the Indians, whom he pays handsomely for their alleged secrets. Of course, the scoundrels are all too happy to take his money from him, and for their part of the bargain, they fill his head with dark stories of conspiracy and intrigue."

Major Etherington leaned back in his chair and chuckled.

"Why just last spring, fully two years after the end of the war, Major Gladwin wrote to General Amherst to warn of a far-flung French conspiracy against us. The conspirators, he claimed, were urging the Indians to rise up and attack the British. Gladwin reported that certain Frenchmen in Montreal, including a number of Jesuit priests, mind you, were sending war belts of wampum to Indian nations throughout the Upper Country. The conspirators, he claimed, were trying to excite the Indians with stories that the British planned to build new forts in the Indian countries, and intended to take lands away from the Indians. The alleged war belts urged the Indians to attack all the British forts in the Upper Country, then proceed on to Niagara, where they would be joined by the Six Nations, the Wolves, the Shawnees, and the Illinois. Then all together, this grand alliance of savages would seize British munitions at Oswegatchi, and would mount an attack on Albany."

The major rapped the table with his mug and laughed so deeply he could hardly speak.

"Then, mind you, these savages . . . these victorious savages . . . would be joined by a war fleet sent to America by the French. And as if the French were not enough for us to handle, the Spaniards would come along as well . . . just for the chance to fight us. And we . . . we poor British . . . we would be swept off the continent and into the sea." Major Etherington swept his arm across the table top. "And so . . . all last spring . . . poor Major Gladwin spent his time nervously expecting the onslaught . . . the onslaught of an army of savages . . . and the arrival of the French Armada."

We laughed heartily at the major's story. Yet somehow the thought of war belts being circulated through the Upper Country made me uneasy.

14

In late December I again traveled to the Sault de Sainte Marie, where I spent the remainder of the winter enjoying the hospitality of Monsieur and Madame Cadotte. I found I now preferred their company to that of the British officers at Fort Michilimackinac.

Late in May I returned to the fort, where I found that a number of French traders had arrived from different parts of the country. These men were of the general opinion that the Indians had grown hostile to the British. A few even predicted an Indian attack. One trader, a man named Laurent Ducharme, positively warned Major Etherington that the Indians had conceived a plan to destroy the garrison at Fort Michilimackinac, as well as other British forts in the Upper Country. The major, however, only scoffed at the warning and dismissed Ducharme as an ill-disposed idler. The major threatened to send the next man circulating such a story to Detroit, as a prisoner.

At the time the British garrison at Fort Michilimackinac consisted of ninety privates, two subalterns, the major, and four English traders. As strong as we were, none of us worried much about the Indians, who had no weapons but small arms.

Meanwhile Indians from every quarter, and in unusual numbers, were arriving daily at the fort. They had every appearance of being friendly. They frequented the fort and sold their pelts in such a civilized manner as to dispel most everyone's fears. But when a Frenchman informed me that no fewer than four hundred Indians—most of them warriors—were encamped within a few miles of the fort, I took the liberty to observe to Major Etherington that little trust should be placed in the Indians. I repeated the Frenchman's warnings, but in response the major only rallied me on my timidity.

"Mister Henry, I grow exceedingly weary of hearing the frightful stories, which you and your Canadian friends are so intent on telling me," the major said. "Such stories are the foolish twaddle of old women."

Yet I must confess that if Major Etherington ignored the growing signs of danger, so did I.

On the second day of June my adopted father, Wawatam, appeared unexpectedly at my door. He told me that his family had just returned from its wintering ground. I greeted him warmly, but I was surprised when he did not observe the usual ceremony of smoking his pipe with me. Wawatam seemed sad and thoughtful. I asked after everyone's health, but without answering, he said he was sorry to find that I had returned so soon from the Sault. He said that he and his family intended to leave for the Sault the next morning, and he urged me to go with them. To this he added a strange question—he asked whether the major had heard any bad tidings during the winter. Wawatam said that he himself had been disturbed often by "the noise of evil birds."

I paid but scant attention to my father's remarks. I told him that I could not think of leaving for the Sault, because my business required me to be at Michilimackinac for the return of my engagés. My refusal to accompany him seemed to distress Wawatam, and he left my house without further discussion.

The next morning, however, Wawatam again appeared at my door, this time accompanied by Ocqua. She kissed me on the cheek and presented me with a gift of dried venison. Wawatam again expressed a vague sort of concern for my welfare. He remarked that many Indians were encamped within a few miles of the fort, many of whom had not yet shown themselves at the fort. He warned me that the Indians were planning to come in a body the next day, to demand rum from the major. He advised that I should leave the fort with him, before the Indians began drinking and became dangerous. He made several vague observations about dark clouds and an evil wind—none of which made much sense to me. (By this time I had learned the Chippewa language well enough to converse in it, but I did not understand the extravagantly figurative manner of Chippewa speech well enough to comprehend the full import of Wawatam's comments. If only I had known the language better, I might have pieced together enough information to save myself, and my countrymen as well. As it was, I turned a deaf ear to everything Wawatam said.)

At last Wawatam drew forth his pipe to say good-bye. As we smoked, Ocqua sighed and moaned in a sing-song voice.

Later that day a large number of Indians entered the fort, to visit the English traders. They bought from me a number of "tomahawks," which were small hatchets of one pound weight. Several Indians asked to see the silver armbands and other jewelry I had for sale, but none of them bought any silver from me. After turning the jewelry over in their hands, they put it down again, saying they would call on me again the next day. (Their motive in this, I soon learned, was to see where I stored my silver, so they could lay their hands on it in a moment of pillage.)

That night I turned over in my mind the visits of Wawatam and Ocqua. I was puzzled and strangely uneasy, yet nothing could make me think that serious trouble was at hand.

15

The next day was the fourth of June—the King's birthday. The morning was still and sultry.

A Chippewa came to tell me that his nation planned to play at la crosse against the Sauks for a high wager. He invited me to watch the match, and he added that Major Etherington would be on hand and would bet on the side of the Chippewas. I decided not to attend, however, for a canoe was ready to depart for Montreal, and I busied myself writing letters.

The la crosse match was played just outside the gates of the fort, and from my desk I could hear the tumultuous cries of the Indians as they struggled for the ball. An English trader by the name of John Tracy called on me, to report that a canoe had just arrived from Detroit. He suggested that we go meet the canoe, to learn of any news. Again I declined, saying that I would join him as soon as I finished with my letters. Mister Tracy turned to leave, and he shut the door behind him.

In the next instant an Indian war cry pierced the air, followed by a harsh bedlam of screams and yells. I sprang to my window, and from it I saw a crowd of Indians within the fort. More Indians were pouring in through the gates. All had tomahawks in their hands, and they were furiously cutting down every British soldier they could find.

I seized my fowling piece, which was loaded with swan shot, and I stood by my window, waiting to hear the drumbeat to arms. During the dreadful interval that followed, I saw several of my countrymen fall, and more than one struggle between the knees of an Indian, who was scalping him. In particular, I witnessed the horrible deaths of Mister Tracy and Lieutenant Johnson. At length, disappointed in my hope of seeing any resistance made, and realizing that no effort of my own could avail against four hundred Indians, I thought only of seeking shelter.

Amidst the slaughter that was raging, I noticed that the French residents of the fort were calmly looking on, neither opposing the Indians nor suffering any harm. From this fact I seized upon the idea of finding shelter in one of the houses of the French. I fled out my rear door and leapt over a low fence that separated my yard from the yard of my neighbor, Charles Michel de Langlade. I burst into Langlade's house without knocking, and found Langlade and his children at the window, calmly gazing at the bloody scene before them. Madame Langlade, a French woman, stood trembling in one corner, her hands covering her face. I immediately addressed myself to Langlade and implored him to save me from the attack. I begged him to put me in a place of safety till the heat of the battle was past. Langlade only turned, glanced at me for a moment, shrugged his shoulders, and turned back to the window.

"What can I do?" he asked, with his back to me.

This was a moment of great despair for me. But as I stood there, dumb with fear and uncertainty, I saw that a servant of Langlade's, a Pawnee woman, was beckoning to me with her hand. For want of a better idea, I went to her, and she silently led me to a door that opened to a stairway. She whispered that I should hide in the garret of the house, and I gladly took her advice. I climbed the stairs to the garret, and the kind-hearted woman followed me, locked the garret door behind me, and had the good sense to take the key away with her.

Having gained this shelter, if shelter it was, I was anxious to see what was occurring outside. Putting my eye to a crack in the wall, I beheld in forms most terrible and grotesque the ferocious triumphs of barbarian conquerors. Dead soldiers were being scalped and mangled. The dying were writhing and shrieking under the knife and the tomahawk. The bodies of some soldiers were ripped open, and the butchers were drinking blood scooped up in the hollow of joined hands, quaffed amidst shouts of rage and victory. I was shaken with horror and fear. I believed that I was about to experience the same suffering.

Soon I heard an Indian cry, "All is finished!" Then I heard Madame Langlade shriek, "They are coming! They are coming!" An instant later I heard Indians enter the house below me.

The garret I occupied was separated from the room beneath it by just a layer of thin boards, so I was able to hear everything that was said below me. I heard the Indians ask Langlade if there was an Englishman in the house.

"I do not know of any," Langlade replied calmly. (In this he did not lie, for the Pawnee woman had hidden me by stealth, and had kept my hiding place a secret. Langlade was as far from any wish to destroy me as he was careless about saving me.)

"You can look for yourselves," Langlade volunteered.

My heart jumped to my throat.

I heard the footsteps of Langlade and the Indians, as they climbed the stairs to the garret door. Arriving at the door, Langlade was delayed by the absence of the key, which allowed me a few moments to seek a hiding place. In a corner of the garret I saw a heap of birchbark vessels, of the sort used in making maple sugar. I scurried beneath an opening in one end of the heap, just as the door was being unlocked and opened. An instant later the Indians entered the garret.

From my hiding place I could see four Indians, all armed with tomahawks, all besmeared with blood, who walked to every corner of the garret. One of them approached so close to me that, if he had put out his hand, he would have touched my face. I could hardly breathe, yet the throbbing of my heart was so loud that I thought it would surely give me away. Somehow I remained undiscovered, perhaps because of the dark color of my clothing and the darkness of my hiding place. The Indians took several turns about the garret, all the while boasting to Langlade of how many English soldiers they had killed and how many English scalps they had taken. Finally they returned down the stairs, and I, with emotions not to be expressed, heard Langlade lock the garret door behind him.

As I regained my wits, I noticed an old feather bed on the floor. I threw myself on the bed and, after several hours, I fell asleep, exhausted as I was by fear and anguish. My sleep lasted till dusk, when I was awakened by a second opening of the door. The person who now entered was Langlade's wife, who was startled and alarmed at finding me in her home. Overcoming her surprise, she informed me that the Indians had killed most of the British soldiers in the fort. To this she added the sentiment that she hoped I might survive. In a timid voice she told me not to worry, but she offered no reason why I should not. As she left, I asked her to send me a little water, and she did so.

As night came on, a shower of rain drummed steadily on the roof over my head. I lay on the feather bed and turned over in my mind my desperate plight. Try as I might, I could think of no way to save my life. I realized that a flight to Detroit had no real chance of success, for the distance was four hundred miles; I was without food; and the route lay through Indian countries where the first man I met would surely kill me. Yet to stay where I was promised the same result.

I considered whether Langlade might be convinced to help me. I tried to recall everything I had heard about the man, hoping to hit upon some insight into his character. I knew that he was a half-breed—half French and half Ottawa—and that he was a great war hero among the Indians, who told stories of his courage. It was said that he had accompanied his first war party at the age of ten; that he had recruited the Upper Indians to fight in the war against the British; and that he had inspired some of the Indians to go to war by dancing the dance of the dog's heart to them. In this dance he had tied the hearts of freshly sacrificed dogs to the tops of stakes, and as he danced about the stakes, he had bitten off and swallowed pieces of raw heart. The dance was an ancient ceremony, and Langlade had used it to challenge the Indians to follow him to war and so to prove that they had brave hearts like his. It was said that the Indians could not resist in joining the dance, and soon they were in a warlike frenzy, eager to follow Langlade off to war. Yet it was also said of Langlade that he was so calm in the heat of battle that sometimes he smoked his pipe while waiting for his gun to cool. The Indians called him *Akewaugeketauso*, which means "He Who Is Fierce for the Land." The more I considered the man, the more fully I realized that I could not rely on his help.

After some hours of desperate thought, fatigue of mind again suspended my cares by casting me into sleep.

I awoke before dawn the next morning and was again placed on the rack of apprehension. At sunrise I heard Langlade's family stirring about below me. A short time later I heard Indian voices within the house, telling Langlade that they had not found my hapless self among the dead. The Indians said I must be hiding somewhere.

It now became obvious to me that Madame Langlade had told her husband of my hiding place, for the woman declared to her husband in French that he could no longer keep me in the house, but must hand me over to the Indians. Langlade at first resisted the idea, but Madame Langlade argued that if the Indians were to find me hidden in her house they might take revenge on her family. She said it was better that I die than her children, and with this Langlade quite agreed. He announced to the Indians that he had just learned I was hiding in his house. He said he would lead them to me and place me in their hands. I heard Langlade's steps on the stairs, with the Indians at his heels.

There was nothing for me to do but resign myself to my fate. As the Indians entered the garret door, I rose to my feet and presented myself in full view. One of the Indians, a warrior named Wenniway, walked up to me and stood within a few inches of my face. His face and body were covered with black paint, but for white circles around his eyes. The young warrior, tall and powerful, seized me by my collar with one hand, and in the other hand he held a large carving knife, as if to plunge it into by breast. He fixed his eyes steadfastly on mine.

I awaited the blow of the knife.

But after pausing for what seemed an eternity, Wenniway dropped the arm that held the knife and said, "I will not kill you." To this he added, "I have fought many battles against the English, and I have taken many English scalps. Three years ago my brother Musinigon was killed in battle by the English. For this reason, I now claim you as my slave. I will adopt you into my family, and you will take the place of my brother. You will be called 'Musinigon,' to honor the memory of my slain brother."

This was welcome news indeed. A reprieve upon any terms placed me among the living and gave me back the sustaining voice of hope.

Wenniway ordered me down the stairs and to his lodge. But as we descended the stairs, it occurred to me that the Indians in the camp would be mad with liquor, and that death would again threaten me. I expressed my fears to Langlade and asked him to speak on my behalf with my new master. Langlade did so, and Wenniway agreed that I could remain in Langlade's house till he returned for me. Wenniway then left the house, and I climbed the stairs to the garret, to be as far from the reach of drunken Indians as possible.

Less than an hour had passed, however, before I again was called to the room below. There stood a lone Chippewa warrior, a huge man of portly girth, whom I knew as Otamigan. He swayed back and forth with drunkenness, and I noticed a fierce glint in his eyes. He ordered me to leave with him, saying that Wenniway had sent him to fetch me. But my knowledge of the man gave me pause. The previous autumn I had provided Otamigan with goods on credit, for which he had never repaid me. Just the week before I had upbraided him for his lack of honesty, and he had fiercely replied, "Englishman, I will pay you back before long." His reply now came fresh to my mind, and it made me suspect his intentions. I voiced my suspicions to Langlade and asked for his protection from the Indian. At this

Langlade glanced at his wife, who touched his arm in silent warning. Langlade shrugged and said, "You are not your own master. You must do as you are told."

Before leaving Langlade's house, Otamigan ordered me to undress, saying that my trousers and shirt would suit him far better than they suited me. I removed my clothing, and as I did so, the drunken brute howled with laughter at the whiteness of my skin. Rather than leave the house naked, I put on Otamigan's breech clout and deerskin leggings, even though they were besmeared with human blood.

When we finished changing outfits, Otamigan marched me out of the house and across the parade ground. As we passed through the gates of the fort, I turned toward the spot on the beach where the Chippewas were encamped. This, however, did not suit the purpose of my captor, who seized me by my neck and pushed me violently in the opposite direction. We walked for some distance above the fort, till I saw that we were approaching bushes and low hills of sand. At this point I decided that I would go no further. I turned to my captor and told him that I believed he meant to kill me, and if it were true, he might as well strike me where I stood. To this he coolly replied that I was quite correct. He said he was about to repay his debt to me by giving me his knife. Grinning devilishly, he pulled out a large hunting knife and showed it to me, holding it an inch from my face. He said he had taken my clothes from me to keep from staining them with my own blood. He suddenly seized me by my hair, jerked my head backward and downward, and held me in a position to receive his intended blow. He raised the knife.

I cannot say what happened next, for it was an affair of the moment. By some effort too sudden to be explained or remembered, I blocked Otamigan's descending arm and gave him a sharp push, turning him away from me. In an instant I was free from his grasp and running with all my speed toward the fort. My attacker was close at my heels, and I expected at any moment to feel his knife rip into my back.

I managed to reach the gates of the fort, where I spotted Wenniway and ran to him for protection. But Otamigan, mad for my blood, did not give up his hunt. He chased me in circles about Wenniway, all the while swinging his knife wildly at me and shouting with rage at his repeated failures to strike me. Wenniway ordered Otamigan to stop the attack, and he tried to keep the brute from harming me. The three of us—prey, predator, and guardian—scurried furiously about one another. The commotion we made drew a crowd of Frenchmen and Indians, who gathered around to cheer and to laugh. Finally we neared the door to Langlade's house, which stood open, and I took the opportunity to scurry inside. Otamigan gave up his chase at Langlade's front door.

With Langlade's permission, I climbed back up to my garret, with my heart racing. I threw myself on the feather bed and gasped for air. And yet I felt growing within me a sense of confidence in my own ability to survive.

The remainder of the day passed uneventfully, and Madame Langlade kindly provided me with food and water.

In the middle of the night, however, I was again aroused from my sleep, to resume my adventures. I was ordered downstairs, where, to my astonishment, I found Major Etherington and Lieutenant Leslye, both half naked, bruised, bloody, but very much alive. In grim and sullen voices, they informed me that they, together with a number of other soldiers, had been taken as prisoners by the Chippewas. They said the Chippewas had sent the British prisoners into the fort for the night, to be guarded by the French, because the Chippewas wanted to drink the rest of their liquor, and the chiefs worried that the soldiers might be killed if they stayed in the Indian camp.

I invited the major and the lieutenant to join me in my garret, where they informed me of the sad state of affairs. But in listening to them, I gathered that twenty captive British soldiers and perhaps three hundred Frenchmen were now within the fort, and that the Chippewas were getting drunk on the beach outside the fort. I suggested to the major that he seize the opportunity to recapture the fort. I urged him to ask the French to close the gates and help us fight off the Indians, if they mounted a fresh attack. Major Etherington considered the idea carefully and decided to seek the counsel of Father Jaunay. We summoned the priest to the garret and explained my idea to him.

Father Jaunay discouraged us, however, arguing that we could expect no mercy from the Chippewas if they regained the upper hand, and further pointing out that we had no reason to place much trust in the French. Major Etherington agreed with everything the priest said, and he rejected my plan for retaking the fort, despite the fact that we were to spend the night within the fort, while the Chippewas were to spend the night without.

The major and the lieutenant described for me the attack which the Indians had mounted on Fort Michilimackinac. The major credited the Chippewas with devising a brilliant plan of battle. The game of la crosse, it seemed, had been staged by the Indians to serve as a sort of Trojan horse—a ploy to provide an excuse for a large number of warriors to gather just outside the open gates of the fort. The game further served to draw Major Etherington, Lieutenant Leslye, and a number of other soldiers outside the fort. In the heated struggle of the game, an Indian threw the ball, seemingly by accident, over the stockade of the fort. At this signal the players rushed in through the open gates, all struggling with one another, all in apparent pursuit of the ball. Once inside the fort, however, the players suddenly became warriors and pulled tomahawks from under the blankets of their women. They fell upon the startled British garrison with such speed that the soldiers could offer but little resistance.

I did not press the major for too many details of the attack, for I understood that he was deeply ashamed of having lost the fort.

Thus the major, the lieutenant, and I spent the entire night in the garret, silently listening to the distant screams, yelps, drumbeats, and war chants of the Chippewas, who were celebrating their victory.

16

Master Wenniway called for me the next morning and ordered me to follow him. He led me to a small house, in which I found an English soldier, an English trader, and a third Englishman who had recently arrived from Detroit. Wenniway ordered that I join them, and the four of us, prisoners all, waited for we knew not what. About midmorning another Chippewa warrior ordered us to march to the lakeshore, where a canoe appeared to be ready for our departure. But instead of departing, we were ordered to sit on the shore, in the teeth of a cold north wind. The lake before us tossed angrily, and the wind tore ragged shreds of mist off the water. I was dressed in only a light shirt, which soon was drenched from the mist blowing off the lake. I suffered keenly from the cold, till a kind Frenchman named Cuchoise saw my plight and draped a blanket over my shoulders.

At noon our small company embarked. We were four English prisoners guarded by seven Chippewa warriors. The lone English soldier among us was ordered to lie on his back, and was tied by his neck to a bar of the canoe. The other three of us were left untied, given paddles, and ordered to use them. We were told to steer for Isle du Castor, a large island some fifteen miles off the coast of Lake Michigan.

By the time we departed, the wind had died, and our canoe was enveloped by fog. We paddled over the swelling surface of a gray sea, through an endless cloud of gray vapors. It seemed that we had lost every connection with the earth, but for the sound of waves breaking on an invisible shoreline, that lay somewhere off our port side. The warriors in our lone canoe pierced the dismal emptiness every so often with four yelps, shouted in unison. I gathered that they were boasting of the four "slaves" whom they guarded—for such is what they called us. Their cries seemed to be a waste of breath, however, lost altogether in the void that surrounded us.

A warrior had just announced that we were nearing Wagoshense, a point of land that extends westward into Lake Michigan, when we were startled to hear a lone voice call to us from out of the fog. The voice beckoned to us in the Chippewa tongue and invited us to come ashore. My Chippewa captors readily accepted the invitation, eager as they were to brag of their exploits in battle. As our canoe approached the shore, the disembodied voice made polite conversation with the Chippewas, and asked for news from Michilimackinac. Suddenly there arose a bedlam of yells. A crowd of Indians, brandishing spears, rushed upon us from out of the fog. The warriors seized us—Englishmen and Chippewas alike—and pulled us from out of the canoe. I recognized our attackers as Ottawa warriors, more than a hundred strong. I saw that they were wearing war paint, and I concluded that the last of my sufferings were at hand.

But no sooner were we dragged ashore than an Ottawa approached me and extended his hand to me, in an apparent act of friendship. I recognized him as Okinochumaki, an important chief of the Ottawas and a man with whom I thought I was on good terms. Okinochumaki greeted me by name and assured me that the Ottawas remained fast friends of the English. He said his people had stopped the canoe of the Chippewas to save the lives of the English slaves within it. He claimed that the Chippewas had intended to kill us and "devour" us as soon as we reached Isle du Castor. (When Okinochumaki said "devour," he meant just that, for it was the custom of the Upper Indians to eat a small part of the flesh of a slain enemy. In so doing, they believed they could acquire the courage of that enemy.)

Okinochumaki turned to our Chippewa captors, who were every bit as surprised as we were. He chided the Chippewas for not consulting with the Ottawas before attacking the English. The Chippewas tried to reason with him, but the matter was not open for discussion. Okinochumaki turned his back on the Chippewas and cordially invited my English comrades and myself into the canoes of the Ottawas. Before long we were again afloat on the great lake, but this time the shoreline lay off our starboard side. We were bound on a return trip to Michilimackinac.

By evening we were back at Fort Michilimackinac. There our Ottawa saviors (if saviors they were) made a show of marching us through the open gates of the fort in full view of the Chippewas, who were confounded by the actions of their Ottawa brethren. The Chippewas could do little about the turn of events, however, for the ranks of the Ottawas had swelled to more than two hundred strong, and the Ottawas far outnumbered the Chippewas. The Chippewas lost no time in asking the Ottawas for a council.

My three comrades and I were led to the commandant's house by several Ottawa warriors, who professed friendship for us but kept us under strict guard.

A council was held that night, around an enormous fire within the fort. Chief Okinochumaki invited me to attend the council. I sat off to one side, in the shadows, and behaved as inconspicuously as possible. I was a keen observer, however, for I realized that my life would likely depend upon the outcome of the council.

Minavavana, war chief of the Chippewas, rose to address the Ottawas.

"Ottawas. My brothers. Help me to understand what I have seen this day, for my heart is filled with disbelief and confusion. Can it be true that you have taken it into your hearts to oppose us? Can it be true that you have taken the side of our enemies against us? Can this be true, my brothers? Are not our nations— Ottawas, Chippewas, Potawatomis—still bound together as Nations of the Three Council Fires? Has this not always been so? Never before has one of our nations sided with an enemy against the others. Yet now you seem to take the side of the English in opposing us.

"Brothers. Surely you can see that the English have evil intentions against us. Surely you can see that the English are our enemies. The English do not supply our needs, as the French once did. When we visit the English soldiers, they do not offer us gifts of friendship. The English soldiers only insult us and laugh at us. When we visit the English traders, they refuse to sell us the guns and powder we need to support our families. The English seek only to destroy us, by starving our children.

"Brothers. Surely your prophets have heard the sound of war drums, carried here by the south wind. Surely you know that all Indian nations are rising up in a body, to fight the English. Surely you know that the King of France is calling upon his children, the Indians, to drive out the English dogs. The English are meeting their destruction here and on every other part of the earth. It is good, my brothers, that we wipe from our lands this nation that seeks only to destroy us.

"Ottawas, it is your duty to return our English slaves to us. As brave Ottawas, it is time for you to win honor by joining us in this war."

Minavavana placed a fresh scalp and a war belt of wampum atop a pile of gifts set before the Ottawas. The scalp was stretched across a wooden ring and was adorned with feathers and ribbons. The gifts consisted of plunder stolen from the fort. I recognized the scalp as that of Private Dunn, and much of the plunder as having once belonged to me.

A number of Ottawas grunted their approval at Minavavana's speech, but Chief Okinochumaki withheld a final response. He said the Ottawas would consider Minavavana's speech through the course of the night and would return with their reply the next morning.

Later that night, just outside the commandant's house, I listened as the Ottawas heatedly discussed the matter. Some wanted to hand their English captives over to the Chippewas, and to take up the war hatchet. Others argued they should not be so eager to join in a war that had been started without their approval, or even their knowledge. The Ottawas seemed to be deeply offended by the independent actions of the Chippewas.

I was beginning to think that the Ottawas might restore the peace, as well as my freedom, when three strangers appeared at the edge of the light cast by the council fire. All eyes turned toward the strangers, as they boldly entered the circle of light. Their arrival in the middle of the night seemed to surprise everyone. Two of the three strangers were decorated in war paint, in the Ottawa fashion, and carried muskets, tomahawks, and scalping knives. The third stranger seemed to be a foreigner, for he wore his hair greased and tied up in a scalp lock, in the fashion of the Iroquois nations. He was modestly attired, with just a few daubs of green paint on his body and a belt of black wampum hanging about his neck. Yet the appearance of the third man seemed to surprise the Ottawas more than anything else.

The Ottawas fell silent and made way for the three men, who seated themselves on the ground beside the fire. Okinochumaki welcomed the newcomers and asked for news from Detroit. One of the strangers announced that they brought an important message from Pontiac, a war chief of the southern Ottawas.

The modestly painted warrior was first to speak, and as he spoke, I noticed scowls on the faces of many in the audience.

"Brave Ottawas," the stranger said. "It must surprise you that I have journeyed here, into the heart of your country. I know that you think of me as your enemy. For longer than anyone can remember, your nation and my nation have made war against one another and have spilled one another's blood. Your ancestors fought on the side of the French. My ancestors fought on the side of the English. But I come to tell you that much has changed."

The stranger spoke in the Iroquois tongue, and I recognized him as a Seneca, one of the Six Nations of the Iroquois Confederacy residing near Lake Ontario.

"Ottawas," the Seneca warrior said. "I have come to speak to you of the English, for we Senecas know what sort of men the English truly are. When the Six Nations fought alongside the English in the recent war, the English promised they would keep their forts in our countries for only so long as it took them to defeat the French. The English told us they would tear down their forts when the war ended, and their soldiers would depart from our countries forever. But these promises the English did not keep. When the war ended, the English only strengthened their forts. They brought more soldiers and farmers and trappers into our countries, who sought to take our lands from us, and to steal our animals.

"When the English first arrived in our countries many years ago, we received them kindly. If they were hungry, we hunted for them and fed them. At first the English asked us only for furs and skins. They never asked us for anything else. Furs and skins we gladly gave them, and they in turn gave us iron, guns, and powder. But in recent times the English have asked us for land, and more land, and ever more land. We, proud warriors of the Six Nations, have told the English we are not willing to give away any of the lands in which the graves of our fathers lie. Yet now, since the war with the French has ended, the English believe they can take our lands from us. They believe they are the masters of our countries.

"Ottawas. The English believe they are the masters of your country as well. They believe they own all the countries of the Indians.

"Ottawas. We warriors of the Six Nations have at last come to our senses. We see the English for what they truly are—greedy men who seek to take our lands from us—cruel men who seek to destroy our people.

"Ottawas. The time has come for the Six Nations to join with all other Indian nations. Together we can rid our countries of the English. Take this war belt I offer you. It was made by a wise sachem of our nation. It symbolizes a new and powerful alliance that will bind your nation with the Six Nations of the Iroquois. We have sent war belts to other Indian nations as well. Soon all will join us to make war on the English.

"Ottawas. Take up this war belt I offer you. Join us in this war. The King of England is a giant in his cradle. We must destroy him while we are able."

The Seneca warrior placed his belt of wampum on the ground beside the fire. The Ottawas stared at the war belt as if it were a mysterious and powerful animal.

An Ottawa envoy now spoke. He was altogether naked, but for a headdress of feathers that radiated in all directions from his head, forming an unholy halo. His face was hidden behind black and red war paint.

"My brothers. I bring you news from your kinsmen at Detroit. A short time ago Pontiac, our great war chief, summoned Ottawas, Hurons, and Potawatomis to a war council at Detroit. Four hundred and fifty warriors attended the council. Pontiac declared to them that none but Indians should live on this part of the earth. He showed them war belts sent to him by the King of France, urging the Indians to attack the English. Pontiac spoke to the warriors of a mighty vision that has appeared to a prophet of the Wolf nation, in which the Great Spirit called upon the Indians to destroy the English.

"My brothers. Pontiac sent me here to tell you of the great vision that appeared to the Wolf prophet. Listen closely to what I tell you, for the vision of the Wolf prophet is a vision for all Indians.

"Wishing to see the Great Spirit with his own eyes, the Wolf prophet decided to make a journey to Heaven. Not knowing anyone who had been to Heaven, who could show him the way, the prophet began to conjure and to dream. In his dream he saw that he had only to start his journey, and his travels would lead him to Heaven."

The Ottawa envoy spoke in a hushed and reverent voice, so his audience had to strain to hear his words.

"Early the next morning, equipped as a hunter, the Wolf prophet set off. For eight days he marched toward the west, never doubting that he would reach his destination. As the sun set on the eighth day, he stopped to camp beside a stream that flowed past a small prairie. While preparing a bed of grass, he saw at the far end of the prairie three paths, all starting from the same place. The three paths seemed to shine with the light of the setting sun. While cooking his food, the prophet noticed that, as the sky darkened, the three paths shone all the more brightly. Frightened by this, he thought of moving his camp to a safer place. But he remembered his vision, and he understood that one of the three paths must be the road that would lead him to Heaven.

"The next morning the prophet started out on the broadest of the three paths, and he marched on it for half a day. When he stopped to rest at midday, a great flame suddenly rose up from the path before him. He bravely walked toward the flame, but it burned all the hotter. He recognized the flame as an ill omen, telling him to turn back.

"The prophet returned to the small prairie, and the next morning he started out on a narrower path. Again at midday he was stopped by a flame rising out of the path before him, and again he returned to the small prairie.

"The third morning the prophet started out on the narrowest of the three paths, and he marched on it for three days.

"At the end of the third day the prophet saw before him a mountain of splendid whiteness—whiter than snow that shines in the sunlight. He walked toward the shining mountain, but he found that the path he was following ended at the foot of the mountain. As he was wondering what to do, he looked up and saw a woman sitting atop the mountain. Her beauty dazzled him. Her dress was marvelously white, and her hair shone like the wing of a raven.

"The woman spoke to the prophet in his own tongue. 'You seem surprised that the path you have followed ends here. I know how long you have desired to see the Great Spirit. I know that you have undertaken your journey to see him. I tell you, the road to the Great Spirit's lodge leads over this mountain.'

"The prophet looked at the face of the mountain. It rose straight up before him and was smooth as glass. The beautiful woman understood the prophet's doubts, and she spoke to him. 'To climb this mountain you must leave behind all that you own. You must leave your gun, your powder, and your blanket at the foot of the mountain. You must bathe in a river which I will show you. Then, naked, you must climb this mountain, using only your left hand and your left foot.'

"This seemed impossible to the prophet, but the woman, understanding his doubt, said to him, 'Trust in your faith, and you will succeed.'

"The prophet followed the woman's instructions. He removed his clothing, and he left his possessions behind. He began to climb the mountain, using only his left hand and his left foot.

"After much hard work the prophet reached the top of the mountain, where he saw three beautiful villages, each filled with sunlight. He knew that he must be in Heaven. He marveled at the beauty he saw all about him. He walked toward a village that seemed to him most beautiful, but he suddenly remembered that he was naked, and he was too ashamed to go on. But he heard a voice speak to him, telling him to proceed and not feel ashamed, so he walked toward a gate to the village. Through the gate he saw the figure of a handsome man, clothed in white, coming toward him. The man took the prophet by the hand, and led him to a lodge of unspeakable beauty. The floor of the lodge was the green earth; the roof of the lodge was the blue sky; and the lodge fire was the sun. The man in white pointed to a golden circle and motioned for the prophet to sit on the circle.

"Suddenly all Heaven was filled with the voice of the Great Spirit.

"'I am Gichi Manido—the spirit whom you seek to know. Listen well to what I say to you, for I say it to all Indians. I am the maker of heaven and earth; of trees, lakes, and rivers; of all that you see on the earth. I am the maker of all the animals and all the people who live on the earth.

"'Because I love you, you must do that which I love. Because I love you, you must not do that which I hate. I hate that you drink till you lose your reason. I hate that you take two wives or run after the wives of others. You must have only one wife, and love her till death. I hate that you fight one another. When you go off to war against your brothers, you conjure and you join in the medicine dance, believing that you are speaking to me. But you are greatly mistaken, for it is Machi Manido—the Evil Spirit—to whom you speak. He whispers nothing but evil in your ears, and you listen to him, because you know me not.

"'I have made your country for you—not for others. Why do you suffer the white men to live in your country? Can you not do without them? I know that the white men have supplied your needs with their merchandise. But if you were not evil, you could live without the whites. You could live whole lives, as you did before you knew them. Before they came to your country, you lived by the arrow and the spear. You had no need of guns, or powder, or any of the white men's objects. Your brothers, the animals, fed you and clothed you. But when I saw you doing evil, I called the animals into the depths of the forests, so that you needed the white men to supply your needs and to cover you.

"'But hear this. You have only to become good, and do that which I love, and I will send the animals back to you.

"'You may allow the French to live among you, for I love the French. They know me, and they pray to me. As for the English—I love them not. They know me not. They do nothing but evil. The English are dogs clothed in red, who have come to trouble your lands. They are your enemies. Drive them away! Make war on them! Send them back to the country I made for them! There they shall remain!'"

Here the Ottawa messenger paused. Profound silence filled the night. The messenger drew forth from his bundle a primitive war hatchet, with a head of polished black stone. He passed the war hatchet about to all the Ottawas. All seemed mesmerized by the great vision of the Wolf prophet.

I grew increasingly nervous.

"Brother Ottawas. I bring you word from Detroit. The great vision of the Wolf prophet was spread from village to village, till it reached the ears of Pontiac, who recognized in the vision the words of Gichi Manido. Pontiac instilled the vision in the hearts of our brothers at Detroit, who picked up their war hatchets and chased the English soldiers behind the walls of the fort. Every day our brothers at Detroit renew their attack on the English fort, and every day the English grow weaker."

The Ottawa messenger drew forth a war belt, with beads of purple and black wampum. He proceeded to harangue his kinsmen, at the top of his lungs, with a call to arms. At the end of each of his proclamations, he raised a string of wampum above his head, and his Ottawa brothers shouted "Ho!" to voice their agreement. With each proclamation, their shouts grew louder.

"Brothers! The King of France tells us to strike a blow against the English. Shall we not listen to his words?

"Brothers! We will defeat the English! We will cut them off, so they cannot return to our country!

"Brothers! Other Indian nations have already joined in this war: Potawatomis and Hurons, Wolves and Shawnees, Miamis and Illinois. All are striking a blow against the English! Even our former enemies, the Senecas, are killing the English!

"Brothers! Shall not we Ottawas join them? Are we not brave men, like they?

"Brothers! Everywhere the English are being destroyed!

"Brothers! It is time!"

By the end of the short but fervid speech, the shouts of the Ottawas had risen to a crescendo of martial fury. A pipe of war in the shape of a war hatchet with a red blade was passed from mouth to mouth. All the Ottawas drew deep breaths from it.

An Ottawa sitting near me suddenly remembered that I was present. He turned on me, raised his tomahawk over my head, and ordered me to leave. I quickly obliged him.

The Ottawas did not wait till morning to make their decision. On the spot they made up their minds to deliver their four English slaves back into the hands of the Chippewas. They rousted us and marched us back to the camp of the Chippewas, where they invited the Chippewas to "make broth" of us.

The Chippewas placed me within a lodge that held fourteen captive British soldiers, all bound in pairs and seated back-to-back, with ropes about their necks fastened to poles at the center of the lodge. I was left untied, but I spent a sleepless night, for my bed was the bare ground, and I wore nothing but a shirt.

Late that night Father Jaunay, the French priest, appeared at the door of our prison lodge. He asked our Chippewa guards to untie the British soldiers, but the Chippewas refused to do so. The good father then knelt among us and offered to lead us in prayer. The soldiers all bowed their heads in the darkness, as best they could, but I politely declined to bow my head. I respectfully informed the father that I no longer had any faith in God, and so it was better that I did not pretend to pray.

At this a young private snarled at me. "Infidel! Is this how you thank Our Lord for saving your life?"

"Do you see the hand of God in this?" I replied scornfully. "Do you imagine that God saved my life, while he let your fellow soldiers die?"

The private glared hatefully at me and strained at the rope about his neck.

Father Jaunay interceded by gently placing his hand on the head of the young soldier. "My son, put away all wrath. Forgive others, as God in Christ forgives you. My son, I ask that you pray for Mister Henry."

While the others prayed, I sat alone, off to one side, and listened to their prayers. I was sorry that I had disturbed their simple service.

With prayers finished, Father Jaunay handed me a King James translation of the Bible, which he had retrieved from the barracks. As I was the only Englishman in the place with free hands, he requested that I read aloud from the Bible whenever the soldiers asked. This I promised to do.

Before Father Jaunay left our prison lodge, he inquired after our health. We said we were in great want of food, having eaten nothing for two days. He asked our Chippewa guards to feed us, and they agreed to do so. After the good father left the prison lodge, the Chippewas brought us bread, just as they had promised—but bread seasoned with a most gruesome sauce. They cut the bread with knives used in the attack—knives still covered with human blood. They moistened the blood with spittle, rubbed the blood on the bread, and put the bread to our mouths. They invited us to partake in the blood of our countrymen.

We had become the sport—or rather the victims—of events that seemed more like dreams than reality.

17

Such was my situation on the morning of June 7, 1763, when an event took place that again changed the color of my life. I was summoned to a council lodge, where I was seated opposite the war chief Minavavana and his son Wenniway. Suddenly my adopted father appeared at the door. In passing me, Wawatam gave me his hand, but said nothing. He went straight to Chief Minavavana and sat on the ground between Minavavana and Wenniway. Silence ensued, as the three men smoked from the same pipe. When their smoking was concluded, Wawatam rose and left the lodge, saying to me as he passed, "Take courage."

An hour elapsed, during which time several chiefs entered the lodge. Preparations seemed to be in the making for a council. At length Wawatam again entered the lodge, followed by Ocqua. Both were loaded with pelts, dried meat, and maple sugar, which they laid in a heap before the chiefs. After a few minutes of silence, Wawatam began a speech, every word of which was of extraordinary interest to me.

"Friends. Brothers. What shall I say? You must know how I feel, for you have brothers and sons whom you love as you do yourselves. How would you feel if you saw your brother held as a slave? How would you feel if you saw your son exposed every moment to insults and threats of death? But such is my plight. There you see my son—held among slaves—a slave himself!"

Wawatam pointed to me.

"You all know that I have adopted this young Englishman as my son and my brother. At the moment I did so, he became one with my family, and I promised him that nothing would break the cord that bound us together. This Englishman is my son. He is my brother. And just as I am your relation, he is your relation as well. How then can he be your slave?

"In the days before this war began, you worried that I might warn my son of your planned attack, and so reveal your plans to the English. You asked that I leave the fort and cross the lake, and this I agreed to do. But I did so with great reluctance, and before I left, I asked that you, Minavavana—you who planned the attack—promise to protect my son and keep him from all harm. You, Minavavana, best know whether you have kept your promise.

"You, Minavavana, promised me that you would hand my son over to me when the attack was finished. And so I come today to ask that you keep your promise. I come not with empty hands. I come with gifts, to buy off every claim that any man may have on my son as a slave."

Pipes were filled and lit, and a period of silent smoking ensued. Minavavana then offered his reply.

"Wawatam, my brother, what you have spoken is true. I knew of the friendship between you and the young Englishman. It is true that I asked you to leave the fort in the days before the attack, for I recognized the risk of having our plans discovered by the English. I asked you to leave the fort out of concern for you and your family, for if the English had learned of our plans, you would have been blamed for it. Whether guilty or not, you would have been caught up in troubles from which you could not have escaped. I am glad, my brother, that your English friend has escaped from harm. We accept your gifts. You may take the Englishman with you."

Wawatam thanked the chiefs and rose to his feet. Taking me by the hand, he led me to his family's lodge, where the entire family welcomed me and expressed the greatest joy at my rescue. Ocqua set boiled liver and maple sugar before me, and I ate my first meal since the attack took place. Ocqua's youngest son pressed me with questions about the attack, but Ocqua told him to keep quiet while I ate my food and rested. After four days of hardship and threats of death, I suddenly found myself in the bosom of a loving family.

18

On the evening of the day I was rescued, the Chippewas spotted a trade canoe out on the lake, advancing toward the fort. A cry went up, and a hundred warriors rushed into service. I watched from the door of my family's lodge as the canoe came on without hesitating. When the canoe touched land, its two passengers, both English traders, were seized by the Chippewas, dragged through the water, beaten, reviled, stripped of their clothing, and marched off to the Chippewa prison lodge. Meanwhile the French voyageurs in the canoe were not molested in the least.

Two days later a general council was held among the Chippewas, who decided to move their village to the Isle of Michilimackinac. There, they thought, they would command a more defensible position, in the event of an English attack. They prepared quickly for the trip, and by noon the women had broken apart the lodges and packed all their belongings. Late that afternoon a flotilla of Chippewa canoes crossed the water toward the island. I accompanied my family, which had managed to fit all its earthly possessions, including four dogs, into two small canoes.

We approached the Isle of Michilimackinac in the evening, just as the sun was setting off our port side and lighting the clouds above us with radiant hues of amber and rose. The lovely sunset seemed to bode well for me, and I was reflecting on its peaceful beauty, when I was startled by sudden, unearthly noises at my ear. I turned to see Ocqua, her mouth opened round, moaning in a resonant voice, and her daughters producing high, trilling sounds, like the cries of loons. The eerie chorus was unlike anything I had ever heard before. Precarious as my situation was, I feared that their cries heralded some new threat against my life. Wawatam, however, assured me that the women were only mourning dead relatives, as we neared a family burial ground on the island.

Twilight was upon us by the time we landed on the island, where we found the lodges of many Chippewas, who had gathered from other parts of the country. As we were beaching our canoes, a host of Chippewas clustered about us, and a number of them muttered about my presence among Wawatam's family. Suddenly a young woman brandishing a stick came running at me. Before I knew what to do, she rapped me sharply over my head, breaking the stick in two and knocking me to the ground. She commenced to pummel me with her fists and bombard me with oaths, till Wawatam managed to pull her off from me. Wawatam then made a point of telling the assembled Chippewas that I was his adopted son and that henceforth I was under his protection. (Wawatam later excused the actions of the young woman, saying that several of her relatives had been killed by the English in the war.)

I retired to my family's lodge that night with a knot on my head, and with the grim realization that my life among the Chippewas was likely to be a hazardous one.

I awoke the next morning drenched in sweat, with my head throbbing, and when I tried to stand, I had trouble keeping my balance. Ocqua, noticing my weakness, put a hand to my face and announced that I was ill. Wawatam lost no time in having built for me a sweat lodge—a small structure of bent poles, with moose skins thrown over the top. In the center of the sweat lodge were placed a number of boulders, heated till they were red-hot. Wawatam then removed all his clothing and instructed me to do the same, and we entered the sweat lodge, together with three other men, who were just as naked as we were. I tried to conceal my nakedness with a small animal skin, as Wawatam recited a number of prayers, then poured water mixed with tobacco over the boulders, filling the tiny lodge with hot steam. Wawatam and the others expelled their breaths violently, and Wawatam instructed me to do the same. He then began to sing in a thundering voice, and the others accompanied him, as they rubbed their hands over my entire body. Perspiration poured from me, and I felt as though I could not breathe. Finally I began to faint, and I had to be carried from the lodge. But after three or four such visits to the sweat lodge, I recovered nicely from my illness.

By this time I was completely confused as to what to expect from the Chippewas, among whom I had been attacked and vilified one day, then nurtured and healed the next.

A few days after my arrival on the Isle of Michilimackinac, the Chippewas counted their fighting men, who numbered all of three hundred and fifty. They seemed to expect an attack from the English, and so they had gathered together for the common defense. They thought the English would spare no effort in raising a grand army to recapture the Upper Country. They worried that the northern Ottawas soon would join Chief Pontiac at Detroit, leaving them alone to fight the English at Michilimackinac. They were uncertain as to whether the Potawatomis or the Menominees of Green Bay would join them, and they even worried that the Issati Sioux would join the war on the side of the English. Caution became the prevailing passion among the Chippewas. They kept a strict watch, day and night, and frequent alarms were sounded. The warriors stayed close to their families.

I enjoyed some freedom of movement on the island, and my situation was much improved over that of the captive soldiers, but I was by no means safe. Some in the village, including Chief Minavavana, welcomed me as an adopted member of a Chippewa family, but others refused to accept me as anything but an enemy, a slave, and an "English dog." Otamigan, my recent assailant, made it clear that he would like nothing better than to add my fair scalp to his other sundry trophies. My adopted father warned me to be on my guard at all times and to stay by his side whenever possible. During this period of nervous freedom, I returned frequently to the prison lodge, to read to the British captives from the Bible, just as I had promised Father Jaunay. Wawatam insisted on accompanying me on these visits.

One evening I noticed that the Chippewas were gathering in an open field near the village. In the middle of the field stood a post. As I watched from a distance, a warrior in full battle panoply, his hair and feathers flying in the wind, danced up to the post and struck it a sharp blow with his tomahawk. He then proceeded to boast of his heroic acts in killing two English soldiers during the attack on the fort. He acted out his struggles with the soldiers and described his valiant acts in gruesome detail. He punctuated his story from time to time with yet another blow of his tomahawk to the post. (In this he acted much like an English orator pounding his fist on a lectern.) When the warrior finished his story, his audience applauded him with war yells, trumpeted through cupped hands. Each warrior then in turn danced up to the post, tomahawk in hand, struck the post with the weapon, and proceeded to boast of his heroism. Those who had not killed any English soldiers boasted of past valor in fighting the Sioux. Some warriors had painted old battle scars with red vermilion. (I stayed far away from this ceremony, for I did not wish to take the place of the stalwart post as an object of some warrior's ferocity.)

Several days passed without event, till one morning a cry went up from a sentinel, announcing the approach of two trade canoes. While the canoes were still far out on the lake, a band of warriors crossed over to a point of land, where they lay in ambush. As the two large canoes turned the point, they suddenly were surrounded by a host of smaller Chippewa canoes, filled with howling warriors. The merchandise in the trade canoes would have been safe from the Chippewas, I think, if the voyageurs had only claimed that the merchandise belonged to a Frenchman. But the voyageurs concealed nothing. They said the merchandise belonged to an Englishman named Levy. Upon hearing the news, the Chippewas were all too happy to seize the property, which included eight kegs of rum.

Wawatam recognized the acquisition of rum as a threat to my safety. That evening he no sooner heard the sounds of drinking, than he warned me of impending danger. He admitted that he could not resist the temptation of joining his comrades in drinking the rum. But first he told me to follow him to a lofty hill at the center of the island. Using the last light from the setting sun, the two of us climbed the hill, which was thickly wooded and rocky at the top. We walked for almost a mile, till we came to a large rock, at the base of which was a dark opening that appeared to be the entrance to a cave. Here Wawatam said I should take up my lodging till he returned for me. He then left me alone.

I entered the cave, the mouth of which was almost ten feet wide. The darkness inside was complete. Feeling my way over the uneven floor, I came to the far end of the cave, which I found to be rounded in shape, like the inside of an oven. In the far wall I found a further passage, which was too small to be explored. I collected a few pine branches and, laying them on the floor of the cave for a bed, I wrapped myself in a blanket and retired for the night. I slept soundly till some time in the middle of the night, when I felt discomforted by an object beneath me. Pulling the object from under me, I found it to be a bone—I supposed the bone of a deer or some other animal that had died in the cave. Again I fell asleep.

When daylight visited my chamber the next morning, I opened my eyes to stare into the hollow eye sockets of a human skull. I fairly shouted with surprise. Looking about, I was horrified to discover that I was lying amidst a heap of human bones, which covered the entire floor of the cave. I scurried backward, toward the mouth of the cave, stumbling over bones as I went and leaving my blanket behind. I fled into the daylight with a gasp of relief, and I sat myself down in a sunny spot, a safe distance from the black maw of the cave.

The day passed without the return of Wawatam and without food. As night approached for a second time, I found myself unable to face the darkness within the charnel house of the cave, so I chose the shelter of a bush for the night's lodging.

The next morning I awoke wet, hungry, dispirited, and almost envying the dry bones within the cave. At length I heard the sound of footsteps, and I saw Wawatam climbing the hill toward me. He apologized for his long absence, the reason for which, he said, was his excessive enjoyment of rum. I told Wawatam of the bones within the cave, and he expressed great surprise to learn of them. We explored the cave together, with some trepidation. Wawatam gazed upon the bones with awe, and even dread. "These are not the bones of Chippewas," he said. "We Chippewas have always buried our dead." He concluded that the cave must have been filled with bodies in ancient times.

Wawatam and I returned to the village, where we told the others of the bones. All expressed surprise, and a large party immediately set off to visit the cave. Before anyone dared enter the cave, a prophet offered up prayers and incantations. Once inside the cave, the Chippewas treated the bones as things altogether sacred. Several theories were advanced regarding the origin of the bones. Some thought ancient residents of the island must have retreated to this cave when the great flood covered the land, only to be drowned as the waters continued to rise around them. Others theorized that the residents were discovered in the cave by a large war party of Hurons, and were slaughtered there. My own theory was that the cave served as an ancient receptacle for the bodies of slain prisoners. (I had already observed that the Indians paid particular attention to the bodies of their slain enemies.) The Chippewas debated the origin and significance of the bones throughout the day, and well into the night.

A few days later Chief Minavavana called on my family, to warn me that Indians were arriving daily from Detroit. Some, he said, had lost relatives or friends in the war and would not hesitate to retaliate with violence against any Englishman on whom they could lay their hands. Minavavana advised that I dress like an Indian, to try to escape harm. To this I readily agreed.

That very day my family transformed me into an Indian. They shaved my head, but for a spot of hair on the crown, which they dyed black. They painted my face in a fanciful pattern of red and white. My body was smeared with bear oil, and I was given a shirt painted with vermilion. A large collar of wampum was placed about my neck, and another was hung across my chest. Both my arms were adorned with large bands of silver above the elbows and smaller bands at the wrists. My legs were covered with *mitasses*, a kind of legging made of scarlet cloth. Over all I wore a scarlet blanket and a bunch of feathers on my head.

I regretted parting with my long blond hair, which I thought was quite becoming. But the ladies of the village now considered my appearance much improved. They condescended to call me handsome, even among Indians.

Protected in some measure by my new disguise, I felt more at liberty to venture forth from the village. I asked Wawatam to accompany me on a trip to Fort Michilimackinac, for the season was at hand when my engagés were to return from the interior, bringing with them my wealth in animal skins. We paddled across the strait to the fort, where I succeeded in finding some of my engagés—but none of my property. Either because of the turmoil caused by the war (as the engagés claimed), or because of their own misconduct (as I suspected), they brought me nothing.

Nothing, I began to think, was all that I would need for the rest of my life. To fish, to hunt, to collect a few skins for trade—this, it seemed, was my destiny.

19

Food soon grew scarce on the Isle of Michilimackinac, as the hunting and the fishing failed us. The Chippewas now had plenty of muskets and powder, plundered from the British fort, but the hunting was so bad that we often went whole days with nothing to eat. And yet the Chippewas never seemed to lose courage or hope. When they awoke in the morning and had no food, they blackened their faces with charcoal and grease and acted as cheerily as though they were in the midst of plenty. The hungrier they grew, it seemed, the happier they became, as if they positively enjoyed the hardship. (We English growl and curse when we fall into a state of want, but the Chippewas merely laugh and jest.)

During this time of hunger I was impressed by the generosity of the Chippewas. One day a hunter from another family brought in a large sturgeon, and I expected that he and his family would fall upon the fish like hungry wolves. Instead, the hunter asked his wife how the food should be shared. Following her suggestions, he gave portions of the fish to other families in the village, and I noticed that the portions he gave away were larger than those he kept for his family. As he gave part of the fish to Wawatam, I overheard him ask Wawatam for something in return. "I give you the last food I have," the hunter said. "In return, I ask that you pray to Gichi Manido on behalf of my family. I ask you to pray that the Great Spirit send the animals to us. Stand by me in your dreams, Wawatam. Remember me in your fasts."

Wawatam promised to do this for the hunter, and the hunter considered himself well paid, for he believed that Wawatam's prayers and visions would help him succeed in the hunts to come.

Wawatam later told me that all Indians were once as generous to those in need, but he added that many Ottawas and a few Chippewas who lived in close contact with the French had learned to live as the whites do, and to give only to those who could pay for the gift.

Hunger soon forced my family to leave the island in search of food. We departed for Bay of Boutchitaouy, some twelve miles distant, where we found waterfowl and fish in abundance. This was in July, which the Chippewas call the Moon of the Raspberry.

During this time I came to know my family well. Wawatam was in high spirits, although he worried for my safety. He seemed pleased with my presence in his family, and he remarked that my arrival made his family complete. He predicted that the days we spent together would be the happiest days of his life.

As soon as Wawatam and I grew familiar with one another, he asked me to take a second name for myself, a Chippewa name, and he suggested Mekawees, which in the Chippewa tongue means "Comes to Mind." He said the name described how I first appeared to him in a dream. I agreed to the new name, and soon even I thought of myself as Mekawees.

The others in my family seemed happy to have me as well. Ocqua asked that I call her "Old Mother." I, of course, politely declined, saying that I did not want to show her any disrespect. She puzzled over my refusal for a time, then asked me a second time. "Mekawees," she said, "the words 'old' and 'mother' are words of great respect. Why do you refuse to use them?" At this I recognized the error in my thinking, and I told Ocqua that I would be happy to call her "Old Mother."

What surprised me most about my new family, and the other Chippewa families as well, was that the women did most of the hard work. They cut and hauled firewood; they built lodges and broke them apart; they carried the heaviest burdens; they dug for roots and gathered food; and they often hauled meat back to camp after the men made a killing. The men, on the other hand, had only to hunt and make weapons. This unusual division of labor made the women very strong—stronger, I suspected, than the men. The hands of the women were tough and calloused, while the hands of the men were soft and aristocratic.

I once remarked to Old Mother that the men did most of the hard work among the English. I asked why Chippewa women had to work so hard.

"Mekawees," she said, "we Chippewa women have always performed the hard work, ever since the time we were placed on the earth. This is a good way for us to live, for it saves our men for the hunt, and it makes our women strong enough to protect our families when the men are away.

"Mekawees, I will tell you the story of a Chippewa woman who once used her strength to save her family. Her name was Miskogijik. She was of the Moose Clan, and she lived near Fond du Lac. When Miskogijik was a young girl, her mother fed her the beating heart of a turtle, and this made her grow strong and tireless. When Miskogijik was a woman with little children of her own, a Sioux war party attacked her family's camp, killed all the men, and took the women and children as slaves. They forced Miskogijik and the other slaves to march westward, toward the country of the Sioux. At one place in their march they came to a stream. The lone Sioux warrior who guarded the slaves was so foolish as to turn his back on Miskogijik, as he stooped to drink. Miskogijik approached him from behind, seized his genitals in one hand, squeezed them with all her strength, and with her other hand she plunged the warrior's head into the water. She climbed atop the warrior's back like a mountain cat climbs atop a deer. There she held him fast, with his head under the water, so he could not cry out for help. She quickly drowned the warrior, and without stopping to lift his scalp, she led her family and friends back to their own country.

From that time to this, the Chippewas of Fond du Lac have honored Miskogijik as a heroine and a chieftess."

Old Mother laughed as she described how Miskogijik drowned the Sioux warrior. She demonstrated with her own body how the heroine seized the warrior and grappled with him. As I watched her strong body act out the struggle, I had no doubt that Old Mother could accomplish the same feat to protect her own children.

The elder son of Old Mother was a slender fellow named Kisaiasch. I noticed that Kisaiasch differed from the other men of the village in that he seemed quite happy to help with the women's work, or to be more precise, with the work of one particular woman. He had just married a lovely young woman named Ozhawis and he was smitten with love for his new bride. He often returned from the hunt in the afternoon, to help her with her chores. He seemed to prefer spending time with her above all else, and she seemed pleased to have his attention. I once overheard Ozhawis tease Kisaiasch, saying that if he insisted on doing a woman's work, she would paint her face and go off to fight the Sioux. I noticed, however, that she never teased him in front of the others. A favorite chore for the young couple was to gather firewood in the evening, when they would stroll off into the woods together, axes in hand. Old Mother never failed to call out after them, "We will listen for the sounds of your axes." This made us laugh, for we were more likely to hear nothing at all.

Kisaiasch was just two or three years older than I, yet he already was considered one of the best hunters in the village. He was graceful like a deer, and he was renowned for his speed afoot. It was said that he could run down an elk and exhaust the animal before killing it. It was said that he once pursued an elk over such a long distance that he decided to chase the animal back to his family's camp, so he would not have to carry the carcass far. I never saw Kisaiasch run down an elk, and when I asked him about the story, he only passed the flat of his hand across his mouth, signifying that he had nothing to say on the matter. I can readily vouch for his hunting abilities, for I once saw him catch a moose in a snare. I saw him take ducks and fish together in the same net, and I saw him catch hares using nothing but his bare hands. He often returned to camp with ample meat for our entire family.

I once asked Kisaiasch to share with me his secrets of success in hunting. "Mekawees," he said, "you must listen to the spirits. Each animal, each place, each weapon has its own spirit. To kill the sturgeon, you must know the spirits of the sturgeon, the lake, the spear. To kill the moose, you must know the spirits of the moose, the swamp, the musket."

The younger brother of Kisaiasch was Sassaba, a youth of fifteen. He was a good hunter, like Kisaiasch, but this was their only similarity. In all else they differed. While Kisaiasch was tall and thin, Sassaba had the round face and squat physique of their mother. While Kisaiasch was quiet and reserved, Sassaba was boastful and full of talk. While Kisaiasch wore the simple trappings of a hunter, Sassaba dressed as a dandy. Sassaba's usual outfit included a three-cornered hat with feathers hanging from the hind corners and a piece of looking glass in the shape of a crescent moon attached to the front. A bronze medallion of unknown origin hung from a ribbon about his neck, and hawk bells hung from his leggings and jingled as he walked. He wore a brass ring through his nose, and he painted his face in stark and colorful patterns, which he never repeated from one day to the next. When Sassaba strode through the village in his outlandish costume, the old men often laughed at him. Sassaba seemed not to mind their laughter, however. He seemed to enjoy attention of any kind.

Sassaba's intemperate personality often placed him at odds with his family. During the evenings we spent together within the lodge, he often asked me about life among the English. His loud exclamations at some of my answers disturbed the others, and Old Mother had to tell him to keep quiet. Sassaba's frequent boasts annoyed the family as well, for boasting of the hunt was frowned upon by most Chippewas. When Kisaiasch returned from the hunt, he entered the lodge quietly, set his weapons in a corner, greeted his wife properly, and sat down by the fire. After some minutes of silence, the wife casually asked the husband if he had killed any animals, and only then did the husband describe the hunt, using the same calm tone of voice regardless of whether he had made a killing or not. For Sassaba, on the other hand, boasting of the hunt came naturally. When he returned from the hunt, the entire camp quickly learned of his exploits.

Late one evening Sassaba returned to camp with the forequarters and head of a huge buck elk. He proudly dragged the carcass up to the door of the lodge to show the family the rack of antlers on the animal. Kisaiasch, however, only frowned and turned away, remarking that good hunters do not boast of killing the animals.

Kisaiasch's rebuke angered Sassaba.

"Kisaiasch, I will soon be a better hunter than you," Sassaba declared. "And I will have three wives, each of whom will be more beautiful than yours."

At this Wawatam swiftly rose to his feet. "Sassaba!" he commanded. "Stand before me!" As the entire family watched, the father slowly ran his hands over the son's body, first down the right side, then up the left. When Wawatam's hands came to Sassaba's breast they stopped. "Ah! Be still. I feel it beating! So you do have a heart! I am glad to know it, my son, for I thought that you might not have a heart, judging by the way you treated your brother and his wife. I am glad to see that I was mistaken. So then, you have no excuse. You should feel your shame, Sassaba. In the future think of the heart that beats within you, and do not treat your family as you did today."

The youngest member of our family was Pukanabik, a girl of thirteen. She and Sassaba were fast friends and spent much of their free time together, with Sassaba demonstrating his hunting skills to his sister. Pukanabik was a serious child, with a perpetual frown of concentration on her face. Like Sassaba, she seemed to possess a certain desire for independence. She was a fine runner, and when there was not much work to be done, she sometimes went hunting with one of the men. Pukanabik once confided in me that she disliked her name, which in the Chippewa language means "Sitting Elsewhere." This name was given to her at birth by a relative, whose job it was to dream of the correct name for the baby. Pukanabik told me that some day, when she went in quest of her vision of life, she hoped to dream of a new name for herself. I asked her what she thought her new name might be, but she deferred, saying that a new name could be given to her only by her guardian spirit. She added, however, that she very much liked the name "Kiwita Asikek," which means "Sunshine All About."

While at Bay of Boutchitaouy, Ozhawis was taken in labor with her first child. When her labor pains started, Old Mother led Ozhawis away from the family lodge to a smaller lodge, which the women had built in less than half an hour.

The next morning we were told that Ozhawis was having great trouble with her labor. The news alarmed the family, all the more so because cases of difficult labor were rare among Chippewa women. Kisaiasch was beside himself with worry. In our general distress, Wawatam asked that I go with him into the woods. As we walked swiftly away from camp, Wawatam explained to me that if we could only find a snake, he would soon secure relief for his daughter-in-law. On reaching a patch of wet ground, we found a small snake, of the type called a garter snake. Wawatam seized the snake by the neck, and holding it fast as it coiled about his arm, he cut off its head and caught its blood in a cup. This done, he threw away the snake's body and carried the blood home with him. He mixed the snake's blood with water and gave the mixture to Ozhawis to drink, first a large spoonful, then a second.

Within an hour Ozhawis was safely delivered of a healthy baby boy.

The next day I found the new mother in high spirits, barefoot and knee-deep in water, laughing and joking as she helped load the canoes. Wawatam, the proud grandfather, smiled broadly at seeing his daughter-in-law in such good health. He declared that the remedy of the snake's blood was one that never failed.

With the birth of her first grandson, Old Mother set about making a *tikinagan*, or carrying board, for the baby. She cut a flat board of poplar wood, and on the board she sewed a thin shell of wood, bent in the shape of the baby, which stood up from the board like the sides of a violin. She filled the cavity with a mixture of dried moss, rotted cedar wood, and a cottony substance taken from the seed pods of a species of reed. This mixture, she said, could absorb moisture so well that the baby's dressing would seldom need to be changed. Old Mother fastened a stiff ring of cedar at the top of the carrying board, to protect the baby's head in case the board should happen to fall. To the ring, and within the baby's reach, she attached a number of playthings: a pair of tiny moccasins, a toy bow and arrow, a wooden ring, pieces of deer horn sewn to a strip of caribou hide, and a small sack that held the baby's umbilical cord. Ozhawis lovingly placed her son within the new carrying board and bound him up to his arms with coverings. Over the carrying board was laid an embroidered coverlet of sky-blue cloth, decorated with pearls. No European cradle, I thought, could be better crafted than this Chippewa tikinagan.

Once the baby was safely swaddled in his new carrying board, Kisaiasch and Ozhawis carried him about from lodge to lodge. The women of the village inspected the little one closely and lavished praise on the trinkets hanging from the carrying board, while the men blew smoke from their sacred pipes over the baby and spoke words of welcome to him. Through all this attention the baby remained remarkably quiet and stared about with bright eyes.

Ozhawis and Kisaiasch were enthralled with their new son. The baby went everywhere with the mother, as she pursued her daily chores. The mother was forever singing or talking to her baby, or sitting for a moment in the grass with him, lost in admiration of her little one. And when Kisaiasch returned from the hunt in the evening, he never failed to hold his son and speak to him.

Several weeks after the birth of my nephew, I was alarmed one evening by the sight of a canoe full of men, approaching our isolated camp with rapid strokes of their paddles. The men were wearing black war paint and were yelling frightful war cries. I turned to Wawatam for guidance.

"They are Chippewas of the Crane Clan," Wawatam said. "They are coming to steal my grandson."

Without further ado I ran to the lodge, where I seized a musket, balls, and powder. When I returned to the shore, however, Wawatam put his hand to my arm. "They mean us no harm," he said calmly. "Put away your gun, Mekawees. Use this as a weapon."

Wawatam handed me a bark dish, and he armed himself in the same fashion. Kisaiasch and Sassaba picked up dishes as well, as did two nephews of Wawatam's, who were visiting us.

The warriors came on with hideous yells. Following the example of Kisaiasch, we answered them in kind, and made the air ring with our war cries. Our enemies shot arrows over our heads, till Kisaiasch, acting as our war chief, led us in a sudden mad charge into the lake. We rushed upon our assailants and drenched them with water from our dishes. We pulled them from their canoe and thrashed about in the water with them. (I would have considered the wrestling match to be great fun, but for the fierce war cries howled in my ears, which kept me from quite believing that all was meant to be a game.) We fiercely defended our baby boy.

When finally we succeeded in chasing our enemies away, we waded back to shore like returning heroes. I asked Sassaba what I should make of the strange battle we had just won, and he explained that it was a custom among his people to fight off kidnappers who try to steal a newborn son. The sound of fighting in the baby's ears was believed to instill courage in the child. We returned, exhausted, victorious, and dripping wet, to our lodge, where we found our baby nursing at his mother's breast.

20

During my first few months as an Indian, I was probably the worst hunter the Chippewas had ever known. My blundering efforts to kill the animals were a continual source of amusement among the Chippewas, who told stories of me—"the clumsy Englishman." I was fast becoming a character of legendary proportions.

For some unknown reason, I also gained a reputation as an expert in English medicine. I was asked frequently to bleed the Chippewas, particularly the women, who seemed to enjoy the treatment. I sometimes had ten or more patients sit on a log, and I went from one to the next, first opening their veins, then dressing their wounds.

One evening as Kisaiasch and I returned from the hunt, Wawatam met us and asked that I visit a young girl in the village who was ill. Wawatam was worried about the girl, a distant relative of his, and he thought my knowledge of English medicine might be of some help to her. We found the girl, a child of seven, lying in her father's arms. She was suffering from a high fever and having great trouble breathing.

While we were visiting the girl, an old man entered the lodge. His face was painted red and green, and he carried under one arm a medicine bag, made from the skin of an owl. The old man was a *miday*, or "medicine man," a man who claimed to know the art of healing through sorcery. He was accompanied by several other elders, who served as his advisors. The girl's father was so eager to have the miday treat his daughter that he gave the miday all his silver as payment for services to be rendered.

The miday reached into his medicine bag and drew forth three hollow bones, from the wing of a swan. He placed the bones in a basin of water and commenced to sing his medicine song, while marking time with his *shishiquoi*, a rattle made from a gourd filled with corn. After singing for a time, the medicine man began to crawl back and forth beside the patient, fixing his stare on various parts of her body and acting much like a cat hunting a mouse, except that the mouse he hunted was the girl's illness. The miday finally took from the basin a polished bone and blew on the child's body through it. He put one end of the bone to the girl's breast and the other end to his mouth, and acted as though he were trying to suck something from the girl's body. Suddenly the bone appeared to leap into his mouth, and he seemed to swallow it whole. He doubled over in pain and fell to the ground, writhing and thrashing about. After a time, however, he must have found some relief, for he came to his senses, stood up, delivered a speech, and returned to his singing. As he sang, he struck his head, chest, sides, and back with the shishiquoi, all the while straining, as if trying to vomit forth the bone. Finally he gave up the effort and applied himself to suction with a second bone. Soon he appeared to swallow the second bone as well, and again he distorted himself in the most frightful manner, using every gesture imaginable to convey the idea of pain.

At length the miday succeeded, or pretended to succeed, in throwing up one of the bones. He passed the bone about to his advisors, who examined it carefully, but apparently saw nothing remarkable about it. The miday returned dutifully to his song and his shishiquoi, and in a short time he threw up the second bone. This he passed about as well, and in a groove of the second bone was found a small white object, like a piece of a quill. The miday gravely identified this tiny object as an evil spirit that was causing the girl's illness.

By the end of his bizarre treatment of the girl, the miday was perspiring profusely, and I must admit that, whatever his faults as an imposter, he certainly earned his pay by dint of strenuous labor. I now understood why the French called the midays *jongleurs*, or "jugglers."

Unfortunately the miday's efforts did the sick girl but little good. Her breathing came harder than ever.

The next morning I returned to the girl's lodge, where I found the poor child wrapped in a blanket, lying in her father's arms, gasping weakly. She seemed to be at her last breath. The father, his face askew with anguish, was gazing down at his daughter. The mother lay on the ground, her face buried under skins. All were perfectly still. No one looked up at me as I entered or took any notice of me as I left.

That evening as I returned from the hunt, I felt compelled to again visit the girl's family. I went to their lodge (or rather to the spot where I expected the lodge to be) but I saw no sign of it. I returned to my own family's lodge, where I found Old Mother drying fish and singing a low song of mourning. She said the girl had died that afternoon. According to Chippewa custom, the girl's parents had extinguished their lodge fire, destroyed their lodge, and gone off to live with relatives.

The miday's grotesque and futile efforts to save the sick girl left me with little confidence in Chippewa medicine. Yet several weeks later I watched a miday treat a deep chest wound, which then healed with astonishing speed. Much occurred in the treatment that seemed fantastic, but the success of the operation indicated something of substance.

A man had suffered the blow of an axe to his side during a quarrel. The axe was driven so deeply into his side that the man who swung the axe could not pull it out. The wretch left the weapon in the victim's side, and fled. The wounded man was found shortly after the wound was inflicted, and was carried to the village, but by this time his eyes were fixed, and his teeth were clenched. I thought his plight was hopeless. But the miday who examined the man sent for a medicine bag. From the bag, which was in the shape of an otter skin, he took a small amount of a pure-white substance, and he scraped it into a little water. He forced open the jaws of the patient with a stick and poured the mixture down the patient's throat. In a short time the wounded man moved his eyes and began to vomit, throwing up a clump of clotted blood. The miday then, and not before, examined the wound itself. From the wound hung a membrane, through which I could see bloody bubbles of the man's breath escaping. The miday did not try to push the membrane back into place, but instead, he cut it entirely away, minced it into small pieces, and made the patient swallow it. He then made a new cut above the patient's wound and poured warm water mixed with herbs into the wound. He forcefully moved the patient's body, causing the water, together with a bit of clotted blood, to the surface of the wound. This he sucked from the wound through a hollow bone. Finally the miday dressed the wound loosely with herbs and had the wounded man carried to a lodge.

The next day, much to my surprise, I found the victim still alive. By the sixth day the lucky fellow was able to walk, and within a month he was quite healthy, although suffering from a cough.

In mid-August, which the Chippewas call the Moon of the Whortleberry, I had the opportunity to witness a formal ceremony of the sacred order of the midays, known as the *Midaywiwin*, or Grand Medicine Society. Kisaiasch announced to us that he had seen a vision, in which his guardian spirit had advised him to induct his baby son into the Midaywiwin. I, being the baby's adopted uncle, was invited to attend the induction ceremony.

The next day several women gathered on a hill overlooking the lake, to build a temple lodge for the ceremony. The temple was constructed of poles, arched and joined at the middle of the roof, and covered with birchbark. The structure was forty feet long, with its entrance facing the east. Flanking the entrance were two posts, from which Kisaiasch hung sheets of brightly colored calico. The calico, which fluttered gaily in the breeze, was a special gift for the midays.

The next morning, with the ceremony about to begin, I entered the temple lodge. Within the temple were seven or eight midays, seated along one wall. Their faces were painted in various patterns of red and green, symbolizing the degree of authority each held within the Midaywiwin. Across from the midays sat Kisaiasch, the father, with his baby son lying in the grass before him. On either side of Kisaiasch sat a row of relatives, god-parents, and witnesses. All were in their Sunday best, which is to say, all had their faces painted fiery red, like fresh-boiled lobsters. A large drum stood in the middle of the temple. Next to the drum lay a large stone.

(I must confess that I understood but little of what I observed that day. I can only describe what I saw and heard.)

The eldest miday first delivered a speech to welcome us, then addressed a prayer to Gichi Manido. He blessed us, one and all, gesturing with his hands over our heads, much as priests do in Anglican churches. He assured us that righteousness leads to a long life, and that evil turns back upon the evildoer. He instructed Kisaiasch and Ozhawis to instill in their son the virtues of a miday. He said the boy should be taught to respect women and old people, to act thoughtfully, to speak softly, and to devote himself to learning the healing secrets of the Miday-wiwin. He said the boy should never lie, or steal, or drink liquor.

The midays then rose to their feet and formed a procession, as the guests made way by standing along the walls of the temple lodge. The midays paraded about, one after the other, each brandishing a medicine bag under his right arm. The medicine bags, or *pindjigossan*, were made from the skins of animals—a wildcat, an otter, a bear cub, a snake—and each bag retained more or less the shape of the original beast, as heads, tails, and feet remained intact. The bags contained sacred objects—stones, amulets, herbs, potions, and magical chants recorded on pieces of birchbark. The Chippewas imagined that the guardian spirit of each animal still lived within its skin, and that the breath of that spirit, when exhaled from the medicine bag, had the power to blow down and kill a person, as well as to restore that person back to life. The procession of the midays was based on these peculiar beliefs. As the drum was beaten with a powerful rhythm, the medicine men stalked about the temple, each eying the spectators with a fearsome stare, as if to identify his prey. When a miday spotted his intended victim, he held his medicine bag at charge, like a Cossack holds a lance, and started his attack with short, mincing steps, accompanied by a low war cry. As he increased the speed of his attack, his cry grew in intensity, and upon reaching his victim, the miday made a stab through the air with his medicine bag, thus allowing the breath of the animal's spirit to work its magic. The victim invariably collapsed at the feet of the miday and lay motionless as if dead. As soon as a miday blew down a guest, he slackened his speed, slowed his cries, and trotted back to his starting place, where he paused for a few moments to allow his medicine bag time to regain its strength. This done, he looked about for another victim.

Victim after victim was executed by medicine bag, all to the incessant beat of the drum and the rattle of shishiquois. A confusion of cries filled the temple: "Ho! ho! ho! Hohohoho! o!o!o!o!o!"

I found the ceremony to be bizarre and comical. I could not take my eyes off one strangely bedizened old miday, who invariably rushed upon his prey with a wild yell, took a prodigious bound, and puffed out his cheeks, as if to aid the deadly breath of his medicine bag. He then leapt atop his prey like a lion and made a critical examination of the person he had just killed, as if to convince himself that all had been performed properly. I was doing my best to keep from laughing at the spectacle, when I noticed that one of the medicine men had fixed his gaze upon me. I realized that he was about to draw me into the play. Before I had time to consider my response, the miday was bounding across the temple toward me and fiercely stabbing at me with his medicine bag. I was face to face with a sacred animal skin, in the shape of a snarling wildcat. Caught up in the spirit of the moment, I reeled backward, collapsed, and lay limply on the ground—a victim of death by medicine bag.

From my vantage point in the grass, I could see several girls lying in a heap, nudging each other and giggling. They kept their tittering and smiling to themselves, however, and the ceremony proceeded in a respectable fashion. With seven or eight medicine men continually bounding about the temple lodge, all the innocent bystanders soon lay on the ground, like so many playing cards scattered by the wind.

Fortunately, as soon as the midays had finished proving the destructive power of their medicine bags, they set about demonstrating the reviving strength of the bags. Resurrections were performed in the same fashion as executions, which is to say, through the breath of an animal spirit. The medicine men again charged about the temple, this time breathing life back into the assembled dead. None of the dead, not even the giggling girls, ventured to stir hand or foot till breathed upon by an enchanted animal skin. When the revival was concluded, I saw that one girl had been overlooked by the midays. She lay on the ground for some time after the rest of us had been restored to life. I could see she was indulging a quiet grin, but she dared not rise to her feet of her own volition. Finally one of the girl's companions timidly recalled a miday and pointed out his oversight. He held his medicine bag over the still body of the girl, and up she jumped.

Our trial by medicine bag was to be repeated several times during the course of the day, as a sort of interlude between other ceremonies.

I noticed one girl who seemed particularly attentive in the performance of her religious duties. When blown upon by an animal skin, she fell over in a heap and did not stir. When restored to life by the same skin, she sprang up like a champagne cork, and was all life and fun. When the sacred dancing started, she went through her various figures with the precision of a puppet. When there was anything to be sung or chanted, she was the first to join in the singing. In short, she knew her catechism by heart, and she performed her sacred duties with a pious countenance.

At the end of the first execution and resurrection, Kisaiasch solemnly lifted up his son and walked toward the midays. The young father was dressed grandly in full war panoply. His head was covered with feathers of the eagle, the hawk, and the raven, which served as symbols of his bravery. The skin of the fearless skunk was wrapped about his head like a turban, with the tail hanging behind, like a braid. Skins of skunks were tied to his feet as well, with the tails trailing behind, like long spurs. His face was painted fiery red, the color of joy, and it shone forth from among his skins, tails, and feathers like the sun shining forth from among the clouds.

Kisaiasch stood before the midays, holding his son in his hands, at times gazing lovingly at the child. Kisaiasch was most attentive in performing his duties. He seemed intent that his son should enjoy all the benefits of a proper initiation. He made a short speech, then presented the child to the midays, just as godfathers do in English christenings. (This made me think the ceremony was an imitation of a christening, probably introduced to the Chippewas by the Jesuits, and embellished with certain pagan customs. Wawatam later assured me, however, that the ceremony was an ancient ritual of the Chippewas.)

Each miday responded to the short presentation speech by Kisaiasch with a longer speech of acceptance.

Five women stood in a row behind Kisaiasch, as if to act as witnesses. They celebrated the baby's rite of passage with a dance, consisting of two quick leaps to the right, then two leaps to the left, all performed to the beat of the drum. They moved in unison, with such precision that they appeared to be five puppets pulled by a single string. At times Kisaiasch danced about with them, carrying his son in his arms, his tails and feathers shaking as though the animals themselves had been restored to life.

Following the induction of the child into the Midaywiwin, another trial by medicine bag was performed. This time everyone carried his or her own sacred bag, and everyone marched in the procession. Among the medicine bags I saw were the skins of owls, weasels, red and silver foxes, wolves, otters, wildcats, snakes, and bears' paws full of claws. The scene was most picturesque, and did not lack for noise, for many of the skins had hawk bells and pieces of metal attached to the feet and the tails. Half the occupants of Noah's ark were carried about the temple lodge before me, and I rather regretted that I did not have my own animal skin with which to join in the parade.

The procession ended the morning's performance.

When we returned to our places in the afternoon, I noticed that a pile of sticks had been placed near a large stone in the middle of the temple, and had been covered with a cloth. Wawatam warned me that the stone represented Machi Manido—the Evil Spirit.

The afternoon's ceremony began with everyone, medicine men and guests alike, dancing up to the cloth and looking within its folds. They apparently saw nothing there and danced on. But with a second approach, each performer scrutinized the cloth more closely, as if expecting to see something. With a third approach, each dancer was seized by minor spasms. With a fourth approach, each worshiper was completely convulsed, as if trying to expel something from his or her throat. Their violent convulsions lasted for some time, and pandemonium filled the temple lodge. I took the opportunity to peer into the cloth myself, and I was surprised to see two yellow shells lying within the folds of the cloth, like eggs within a nest. I was staring at the shells when a third shell fell into the cloth, and I looked up to see that it had come from the mouth of a woman. I watched more closely and saw that each dancer in turn was vomiting a shell into the cloth. The old midays took extraordinary pains to expel their shells, while the young people did not have so much difficulty, dropping shells from their mouths as easily as a smoker blows a puff of smoke. Soon everyone had managed to throw up a shell, and all recovered nicely.

The midays approached the cloth and inspected the shells carefully, while the young people paid no further attention to them.

A miday then spoke on the subject of evil. He said the shells represented the wickedness that exists in each of us. He cautioned that evil can be expelled only through zealous exertion and attention to religious duties. In his speech the miday never once mentioned the name of Machi Manido—the Evil Spirit—while he frequently called upon the name of Gichi Manido—the Great Spirit.

Each person then took a turn beating upon the drum and reciting a song. Each song seemed to be that person's prayer.

Kisaiasch gave gifts of calico and tobacco to the midays, who in turn gave him potions, powders, and dried roots, together with whispered instructions for putting these sundry items to use. Kisaiasch seemed half-pleased and half-embarrassed by the wealth of mysterious objects he received.

Finally an old miday offered up a concluding prayer, in which he thanked Gichi Manido for that spirit's bountiful mercy. In the silence that followed, a steaming kettle of broth, made from Indian corn, was served to one and all. I noticed that the parents fed their children before taking any food for themselves. Everyone seemed to enjoy the simple banquet, amply earned by good people through an entire day of religious exertion.

21

Late in August my family moved its camp to the Isle of Saint Martin, off Cape Saint Ignace, so named for the Jesuit mission of Saint Ignace that was once established there. Our object was to spear the sturgeon, and we did so with great success. We fished by night, when we hung torches made of sticks from the bows of our canoes. Guided by light from the torches, we were able to spear sturgeons that lay beneath as much as fifteen feet of water.

At the end of August, with autumn at hand, Wawatam announced that the time was approaching for us to leave for our winter hunting ground. It soon would be time for our family to fend for itself, apart from the other families. I welcomed the announcement, for I happily would have gone anywhere to escape the threats and insults from my enemies among the Chippewas.

Wawatam, however, was not especially confident about our prospects for the coming winter. He worried that we might be discovered by Indians who were at war against the English. He said our small family would be hard pressed to defend itself against such a war party.

We returned to Fort Michilimackinac, where we procured powder and lead, two bushels of Indian corn, and a few trifling articles, all bought on credit from a French trader.

My family and I then steered our two small canoes westward toward Lake Michigan, stopping on the way to visit the Ottawas at L'Arbre Croche. Chief Okinochumaki greeted me warmly and presented me with a loaf of bread made from ground Indian corn, baked beneath a fire. I never in my life tasted such delicious bread. Near the village grew fields of Indian corn, which the Ottawas harvested and sold for provisions to the voyageurs at Michilimackinac.

We paddled our canoes southward, along the east coast of Lake Michigan, and soon we came to a broad bay known as *Le Grande Traverse*, where we stopped to camp for the night. I was searching for driftwood on a sandy stretch of the lakeshore, when I heard a peculiar sound that seemed to come from above. Looking up, I saw nothing, but looking down, I was startled by a rattlesnake, no more than two feet from my ankles. The serpent was coiled. Its head was raised and ready to strike. If I had taken another step, I would have trodden upon it.

I hastened back to the canoes to get my gun, but Wawatam, noticing my haste, asked me what I had seen. I told him I was about to kill a rattlesnake. He warned me against it, however, and cautioned that the rattlesnake must be a powerful spirit, for such a creature had never before been seen in that part of the country. Wawatam and the rest of the family followed me, to pay the snake a visit. We found the creature in the same spot where I had left it. The entire family surrounded the snake, and each spoke to it in turn. Wawatam lit his pipe, and each member of the family cautiously blew tobacco smoke over the serpent, which it seemed to receive with real pleasure. The snake remained coiled and enjoyed the incense for some ten or fifteen minutes. Then, in a visibly good humor, it stretched its body more than four feet along the ground. After lying outstretched for a time, the snake crawled slowly away.

The next morning we continued our voyage, passing massive hills of sand, which my family knew as the Sleeping Bears. We passed several bays and rivers, where the banks of the lake consisted of pure sand, drifting from one hill to another, like snow. The sand seemed to have been deposited by the water, especially in places where the current of a river was met and driven back by the force of waves on the lake. Each river had managed to cut a passage through the sand and into the lake, but the passage was only as wide as the river was able to force. Behind the sand each river had hollowed out a basin of one, two, or even three miles in width. In the shallows of these broad basins we found wild rice growing on stalks of grass that rose six feet above the water. We stopped to gather the wild rice, which we did by pushing our canoes through the dense stalks, bending the stalks over our canoes, and knocking the grain loose with sticks. In the beds of rice we saw vast numbers of ducks, which made a noise like thunder when they rose into the air.

This was in the month of September, which the Chippewas call the Moon of Wild Rice.

Within a few days we arrived at River Aux Sables, so named for hills of sand at the river's mouth. Our family's principal winter camp was to be located on this river, fifteen miles above its mouth. As we entered the river, Wawatam offered a sacrifice to Gichi Manido by taking a favorite dog, tying its feet together, and throwing it into the water. As the dog drowned, Wawatam uttered a prayer in which he asked the Great Spirit to support his family through the perils of the long winter to come. "Gichi

Manido, you have made this land," Wawatam said. "You have made the animals that live on this land. You have made us, your children. It is within your power to make the animals come to us, so we will have food for the winter."

We reached the family's campsite the same day. With an Englishman on hand, however, Wawatam decided to set up camp a short distance away from the traditional site. Our new camp was situated atop a hill, bordered by the river on two sides, and by boggy ground on the other two sides. Wawatam said our new campsite could be more readily defended, if we were attacked.

Upon arriving at our winter camp, the women quickly built a *wigiwam*, or domed lodge covered with birchbark, so named for the *wigiwass*, or birch tree. They erected a frame of bent poles, freshly cut from ash saplings, then unrolled sheets of sewn birchbark, called *apakwas*, which they had brought with them in the canoes. The apakwas were spread over the frame, leaving only a hole in the top for smoke to escape and a hole in the side for people to enter. The apakwas were secured with cords of cedar bast, anchored at the sides with rocks. On the floor of the lodge were laid mats of bullrush reeds, called *pukkwi*, woven in bold patterns. I found our winter wigiwam to be most comfortable, with gay matting spread across the floor and a fire crackling in the center.

A few days after we set up camp, I returned one evening to find the lodge fire put out and the hole in the top of the lodge covered with skins, apparently to keep out the light. I noticed that ashes from the old fire had been removed from the lodge, and fresh sand had been spread over the hearth. A new fire was burning just outside the lodge, in the open air, and a kettle of water was hung over it to boil. By these signs I supposed that a feast was in the making, but I did not ask about it, for it would have been bad manners to inquire into the meaning of such preparations. (Good manners among the Chippewas required that I remain silent and await the results.)

At twilight Wawatam invited us into the lodge. As we entered, Old Mother cautioned me not to speak within the lodge, for she said a feast was about to be given to the dead, whose spirits delight in uninterrupted silence. We entered the lodge and seated ourselves on the floor, as the door flap was closed behind us. We found ourselves in total darkness. Each of us was handed a wooden spoon and a dish, into which were placed two ears of boiled Indian corn.

Wawatam then addressed us, or rather, he addressed the spirits of his departed ancestors. His deep voice rose from out of the darkness and enveloped us. He called upon the spirits of the dead to be present at the feast, and to share in the Indian corn he had prepared for them. We among the living then proceeded to eat the corn. The darkness was complete, and the silence was perfect, but for the sound of our grinding teeth. The corn was not half boiled, so it took me most of an hour to eat my share. Old Mother whispered that I should be careful not to break the spikes of the corn, as this would upset the spirits of the dead.

When all was eaten, the spikes were carefully buried in the ground beneath the lodge, as some sort of offering to the dead, and Wawatam made a second speech to the spirits of the dead. A fresh fire then was kindled inside the lodge, with sparks from flint and steel. This done, Wawatam began to sing and to beat his drum, and the rest of the family began to dance about the fire, I along with the others. Our dancing lasted the greater part of the night, to the great enjoyment of everyone.

The Feast to the Dead marked the new moon of November—a month the Chippewas call the Moon of Freezing.

By degrees I was growing familiar with my life as an Indian, and becoming as expert in Indian pursuits as the Indians themselves. Each day brought a new hunt, and I enjoyed a personal freedom unlike any I had ever known. Were it not for the idea that I was leading the life of a savage, or for the whispers of a lingering hope that some day I might escape from it, I could have been as happy in that life as in any other.

22

I was beginning to feel secure in my new life on River Aux Sables, surrounded as I was by the kind affections of my family, when my sense of security was rudely shaken. Late one evening Kisaiasch came loping into camp to warn us that four men, dressed as warriors, were approaching on a trail that passed through the family's hunting ground. The trail soon would lead them to within a half mile of our camp.

Wawatam ordered me to leave camp immediately. He handed me several blankets and instructed me to go to a certain spring of water, where I was to remain quietly till he sent for me. He said I was not to build a fire or to move about. I agreed to follow his instructions to the letter.

I waited at my lonely outpost till morning, when Sassaba appeared and invited me back to camp. He said the four warriors were Potawatomis from Detroit and were followers of Pontiac, the Ottawa war chief. They were on their way from Detroit to Michilimackinac, by way of Saint Joseph. They carried war belts, which they planned to use in urging the northern nations to join in the war against the English. The four warriors had spent the entire night with my family.

I returned to camp, where Wawatam told me of astonishing news he had learned from the four visitors. An Indian revolt had spread halfway across the continent, and Indians of various nations had attacked every British fort between central Pennsylvania and the Mississippi River. In the process, the Indians had seized large stores of British munitions.

One by one, Wawatam recounted for me the ruinous results of a wave of Indian attacks. Fort Saint Joseph, located near the southeast coast of Lake Michigan, had been overrun by Potawatomis, who had killed all but four British soldiers. Fort Ouiatenon, situated on a prairie south of Lake Michigan, had been captured by Weas and Illinois, who had sent the entire garrison, as prisoners of war, to a French settlement in the Illinois Country. Fort Sandusky, on the south coast of Lake Erie, had been burned to the ground by Ottawas and Hurons, who had taken the scalps of fifteen soldiers and twelve English traders. The only scalp the Indians had left in place was that of the commandant, whom they had let live as a sort of trophy, to be displayed to other Indian nations. The Miamis, acting in league with a number of Frenchmen, had captured Fort Miamis in the Ohio Country. The Miamis had surprised the garrison with the help of an Indian woman, who had been bedding with the commandant of the fort. Fort Edward Augustus, situated at the bottom of Green Bay, had been abandoned by its garrison even before the Indians had attacked the place. Meanwhile, in western Pennsylvania, the Shawnees, Senecas, and Wolves had been joined by Ottawas, Chippewas, and Hurons to attack Fort Presque Isle, Fort Venango, and Fort Le Boeuf. At Fort Venango the entire garrison had been killed. At Fort Le Boeuf the British soldiers had managed to escape into the forest, as the fort burned down around them.

Across a vast expanse of wilderness, Wawatam reported, the only fort still held by the English was Fort Pontchartrain at Detroit, and it had been saved only because an Indian spy had warned the commandant that an attack was imminent. I took no comfort even in this, however, for the fort at Detroit was cut off from any assistance, and it lay under heavy siege. Pontiac's warriors expected the fort to fall any day.

I was dumbstruck by the widespread catastrophe that had befallen His Majesty's forces, and I was dismayed by the utter hopelessness of my own situation. I now found myself many hundreds of miles from the nearest British outpost and surrounded by more than a dozen Indian nations, all of which were on the war path and eager for English blood. I saw no chance whatsoever of escaping my predicament, and countless chances of losing my life.

And yet, despite all the turmoil in the world about us, the month of December brought only peace and happiness to my family, isolated as we were on the remote banks of River Aux Sables. Hunger was not a problem for us, for our hunting went well. By the time of the winter solstice, we had collected a hundred beaver skins and as many raccoon, and had put up a large store of dried venison. We kept our wealth of skins and food away from the wolves by storing it on high scaffolds.

Late in December, which the Chippewas call the Moon of Little Spirits, my family decided to embark on a hunting trip into the interior of the country. The women made up our bundles, and early one morning we set off. I could not help noticing that the bundle handed to me was the lightest, and the bundles carried by the women were the heaviest.

On the first day of our march we advanced about twenty miles, then encamped. Wawatam killed a large deer, and the next morning we moved our camp to the carcass. There we stayed, while the women dried the venison by cutting the meat into slices the thickness of a steak and hanging it over a fire to be smoked.

Two days later we again broke camp and marched till midafternoon. While the women were busy erecting our lodge, I picked up my musket and strolled off, telling Wawatam that I intended to look for fresh meat for supper. He said he would do the same, and we headed in opposite directions.

The sun was shining brightly when I left camp, so I had no fear of losing my way. But in following several animal tracks, expecting at any moment to fall in with the prey, I must have walked for a considerable distance. It was almost dusk when I thought of returning to camp, but by then the sky had grown overcast, and I was left without the sun for a guide. I realized that I was not quite certain in what direction to proceed. No snow lay on the ground, so I could not retrace my steps. I began to walk more and more swiftly, making great strides through the forest, always thinking that I was approaching my family's camp. Soon it became so dark that I was walking into trees. Finally I resigned myself to the simple fact that I was lost—lost in a country entirely strange to me, where any Indian whom I came across would likely kill me. With the flint of my gun I made a fire, and I laid down to sleep.

Late that night I was awakened by the sensation of cold rain falling on my face. The rain fell harder and harder, and soon I was drenched and miserable.

By the first light of an overcast dawn, I arose and resumed my journey. All day I proceeded onward, under an overcast sky, sometimes walking, sometimes running like a madman, always without a clue as to where I was going. At some point in the afternoon I came to the shore of a broad lake, the opposite side of which I could barely see. I had not heard of such a large lake in that part of the country, so I concluded that I must be farther than ever from my family's camp. Relying on a sort of anxious logic that bordered on desperation, I reasoned that by turning myself about, I might save myself. I turned my face directly away from the lake, and I tried resolutely, as the day darkened, to hold my course to that direction.

As night settled over the land, snow began to fall, and I stopped to build a fire. Stripping a sheet of birchbark from a tree, I laid beneath it, so that it might shelter me from the snow. I lay awake for some time under my piece of bark and listened to the wolves howling all about me. The wolves were unusually bold in approaching my fire. They seemed to understand my misfortune. Amidst thoughts most distracted, it took me some time to fall asleep.

In the middle of the night I awoke. The snow was falling. The wolves were howling. Yet I felt strangely calm and self-possessed. I found myself wondering at the terror to which I had yielded myself the day before. I must have lost my senses, I thought, for it now seemed incredible to me that I could have failed to find my way back to camp. I recalled the simple lessons I had been taught by Wawatam. He had shown me that the tops of pine trees lean toward the rising sun; that moss grows on the north sides of tree trunks; and that the largest limbs of trees grow toward the south.

At daybreak I started my journey anew, this time determined to use my knowledge to direct my feet. As I trudged through a half-foot of new-fallen snow, I trained my eyes on the trees, and where the tree tops leaned in different directions, I looked to the moss or to the branches. By connecting one sign with another, I was able to make my way with some confidence. I reasoned that by traveling westward I would sooner or later reach the shore of Lake Michigan, and from there I could easily find the mouth of River Aux Sables.

About noon, to my great joy, the sun broke forth from behind the clouds, and I had no further need to examine the trees.

Late that afternoon, as I was walking down the side of a hill, I spotted a herd of elk approaching. Hungry and eager to kill food, I hid myself behind a low bush and waited in ambush. As a large elk passed near me, I raised my musket and pulled the trigger. The gun missed fire, and the elk walked calmly past, without taking the least notice of me. I reloaded, followed the elk, and again took aim. But now a new disaster befell me. On attempting to fire, I discovered that I had lost the cock to my musket.

Of all my misfortunes, this was the worst. The weather was growing rapidly colder; I had gone three days without food; and I now lacked the means of procuring either food or fire. Despair almost overwhelmed me. I fell to my knees in the snow, and buried my head in my hands for some minutes. In wondering what to do, I finally reached the conclusion that I could do no more than resign myself into the hands of divine Providence. I reasoned that God—whether real or imagined—could do no worse for me than I had already done for myself.

Cold and hungry, I resumed my march westward.

The sun was setting fast as I descended a lofty hill, at the foot of which lay a small, frozen lake. In the middle of the lake I saw a beaver lodge, which offered me some faint hope of food. On reaching the lodge, however, I found that it had been broken apart by hunters. As I stood there, staring down at the beaver lodge, it suddenly occurred to me that I had seen the lodge before. Turning my gaze around the edge of the lake, I spotted a fallen tree that was distinctly familiar to me. I recalled having cut down the very same tree with my axe a month or so earlier, and I realized that Sassaba and I had broken apart this very beaver lodge. Suddenly I was no longer lost. I knew both the route and the distance to my family's camp. I had only to follow a small stream which flowed into the lake, to eventually reach my family's camp. An hour earlier I had considered myself the most miserable of men. Now I shouted for joy and called myself the happiest.

Through the whole of that night and the next day, I followed the stream. At sunset I reached my family's camp, where I was greeted warmly by everyone. Old Mother cried to see me, for she thought I had died in the forest.

23

While hunting one day, in the coldest part of January, I happened to pass an enormous pine tree, the bark of which had been torn by the claws of a bear. Looking up, I saw a hole high in the trunk of the tree, around which small branches had been broken. Looking down, I saw no tracks in the snow, which had covered the ground for several weeks. The signs made me think that a bear was sleeping within the trunk of the tree.

I returned to camp and told my family of my discovery. Everyone followed me to the tree, where we concluded that a bear did indeed reside within the tree. We debated for a time as to whether we should come back the next morning to cut down the tree and kill the bear. At first the women opposed the idea, arguing that our small axes, of only a pound and a half weight, were not suited for the job. But our hopes of killing a bear, and of gaining a supply of bear oil, finally prevailed.

The next morning we surrounded the tree, men and women alike, as many at a time as could chop at it. There we toiled like beavers till the sun went down. The day's work carried us just halfway through the enormous trunk, which had a girth of more than three fathoms.

The following morning we renewed our attack. We stayed at it till midafternoon, when the tree finally came crashing to the ground. For a few minutes all was still within the tree, and I feared that all our work had been in vain. But as I cautiously approached the tree, a bear of extraordinary size suddenly reared up from out of the tree trunk. I shot the bear through the heart, before it had a chance to attack. When we were certain that the bear was quite dead, we drew near to it, and we determined that it was a pregnant female, just as Wawatam had predicted. He said the bear had spent the winter lodged within the tree, where she was to give birth to her young. High up in the tree, he said, her cubs would have been safe from the wolves. There was little the bear could do, however, to defend herself against humans with axes and guns.

Wawatam, Old Mother, and my brothers and sisters now dropped to their knees beside the bear's carcass, and each in turn, but especially Old Mother, lifted up the bear's head, stroked it, kissed it, and begged a thousand pardons for taking the bear's life. They called the bear their grandmother, and asked that she not blame them for her death, since it was truly an Englishman who had killed her. Their pleas for forgiveness did not last long, however, and if it was I who had killed their grandmother, they were not far behind in the work that remained. My accomplices and I skinned and butchered the bear, and we found her fat to be six inches deep in places. The fat alone was as much as two of us could carry, and the meat was a burden for four. All told, the bear's carcass must have weighed more than five hundred pounds.

Returning to the lodge with our booty, Wawatam reverently set the bear's head atop a shelf—a place of honor within the lodge. The family adorned the bear's head with its finest ornaments: bands of silver and wampum, ribbons, and hawk bells. A lump of black tobacco was placed under the nose of the bear.

Early the next morning the family began preparing for a feast to the spirit of "Grandmother Bear." They cleaned and swept the lodge, and they lifted the head of the bear and spread beneath it a new stroud blanket, never before used. I asked Wawatam why such extraordinary gestures were being made to the head of a dead animal. He replied that the Spirit of the Bears had great power—more power than the spirit of any other animal—and so the family was intent on appeasing the spirit of Grandmother Bear.

Try as I might, I could not understand how Wawatam, so wise in some ways, could be so foolish as to honor the spirit of a dead animal. I considered the matter carefully, as I watched preparations being made for the feast. I could understand that the Chippewas saw something human in the bear. I knew that a Chippewa name for the creature was "forest man." (The French as well saw human traits in the bear, for they called it "the shaggy bourgeois.") I too had seen signs of human behavior in the animal. Earlier in the year I had been walking through a grove of trees, when I came upon a bear digging for a type of root, called bear's potatoes. I had no gun with me, so I watched the animal from a distance. The bear worked his potato fields with the zest of a treasure hunter seeking gold, and upon finding his treasure, he sat back on his haunches and relished his roots with the enjoyment of a Virginian chewing tobacco. When the bear noticed me, he went a bit out of his way to sit on a log, where he smacked his lips and yawned, like a man picking his teeth after a grand dinner.

When all was ready for the feast, Wawatam lit his sacred pipe, and blew smoke into the nostrils of the bear's head. He instructed me to do the same, but I, of course, tried to avoid the duty. I argued that the head of the bear no longer had any life in it, and I assured Wawatam that I did not fear the imaginary spirit of a dead animal. Wawatam shook his head at my remarks and replied that he did not agree with my first proposition, and he did not accept my second. To avoid any hard feelings, I finally agreed to blow smoke up the nose of the dead bear.

Wawatam then rose to his feet to offer a prayer to Grandmother Bear. His prayer resembled in many ways his speech to his dead relatives, except that he now lamented the necessity under which men labor to destroy their "friends"—the animals. He reasoned that the tragedy could not be avoided, however, for if humans were to stop killing the animals, humans could not survive. Wawatam assured Grandmother Bear that he and his family loved her and now wished to take her flesh into their bodies.

We proceeded to eat heartily of the bear's flesh—altogether too heartily for my taste. Wawatam placed fifteen or twenty pounds of bear flesh on each dish, and each of us was expected to finish his or her portion, as a sacred offering to the spirit of the bear. I did my best to eat my assigned portion, but all the others were finished with their food before I was half finished with mine. (The Chippewas, it seems, are as well practiced in feasting as they are in fasting.)

Finally, when I thought I could not swallow another morsel, I decided to save part of the cheer of the feast for the next day, when I could better appreciate it. I stealthily slipped strips of Grandmother's flesh under my shirt and hung them from my girdle. When Wawatam concluded the feast with his closing prayer, I made for the door.

I would have escaped the lodge undetected but for a dog at the door, which smelled the meat on me, and in an instant, laid hold of a piece of the bear's flesh and tore it away from me. My family was startled speechless at the sight of my sacrilegious act. Wawatam chased the dog away from the bear meat, but for several minutes he was at a loss as to how to deal with my profane act. Finally he observed that the spirit of Grandmother Bear must have inspired the dog to tear the meat away from me, to keep me from stealing a part of the sacred offering. Wawatam decided that the proper act, under the circumstances, was to burn the uneaten meat, and thus offer up the bear's flesh to the Spirit of the Bears, through a sacrifice by fire.

Embarrassed and shamefaced, I dutifully stayed within the lodge to witness the final sacrifice.

That same day the women proceeded to melt down the fat from the bear's carcass. The oil from the bear filled six porcupine skins. They cut the meat into strips, dried it over a fire, and placed it in the oil within the skins, to be preserved. Even the head of the bear, after three days in its place of honor, finally was dropped into the kettle and was eaten.

Wawatam, however, did not soon forget my sacrilege at the feast of the bear. In the days that followed, he had little to say to me, but he watched me closely.

About a week later, on a sunny, winter morning, Wawatam asked me to accompany him. He led me away from the lodge to a spot next to a stream, where water falling over rocks made a pleasant, splashing sound. He laid two bear skins on the snow and motioned for me to be seated. Wawatam said he wished to know more about me. He asked me about my previous life—the life I once had lived with my true family.

Gradually the conversation turned to spiritual matters, and Wawatam asked me to tell him how I prayed. I did not want to worry my father by telling him that I did not pray, and that I did not believe in God. Instead, I described to him how I had prayed in former times, when my true parents were alive. I told him of how my first family and I had gathered together in silent prayer, to seek the Spirit of Christ, which we believed dwelt within each of us.

At this Wawatam nodded his approval. "It is good to feel the place where words come from," he said.

But Wawatam was too wise to be entirely satisfied with my answer. He asked me a more pointed question: "In the days you have lived with us, Mekawees, have you prayed to the Spirit of Christ?"

I did not lie to Wawatam. I admitted that I no longer prayed at all. Since the deaths of my parents, I said, I no longer believed in God.

Wawatam's misgivings were palpable. He inclined his head toward mine. He seemed to be deeply concerned for me, much like a priest is concerned for a wayward parishioner, or a doctor is concerned for a sick patient. More to the point, Wawatam was concerned for me as a father is concerned for his lost son.

"Mekawees," Wawatam said. "Perhaps it was Machi Manido, the Evil Spirit, who took the lives of your father and mother."

I did not reply, for I saw no reason to enter into a pointless theological discussion with Wawatam. We sat in silence for some minutes.

"Before we met, Mekawees, did you see me in a dream?"

Wawatam's question surprised me. I did not want to hurt my father's feelings, but again I felt compelled to tell him the truth.

"No. I do not remember ever having dreamed of you."

"Do you dream of your true father and mother?"

"Yes. At times my dreams of them are wonderful—at times my dreams of them are frightful and grotesque."

A long period of silence ensued. Wawatam drew forth his pipe and smoked from it. I gazed at the icy water falling over the rocks. From time to time I glanced up at Wawatam's face.

"The time has come," Wawatam finally said, "to tell you of my vision of life. Understand, Mekawees, that my vision of life is my own. It is not yours. But my guardian spirit has instructed me to share my vision of life with you, that it might help you with your own life. My son, you are the only person to whom I have ever told my vision of life."

I understood the importance of what was about to happen. A Chippewa almost never shares his vision of life with another, except perhaps on his death bed. To reveal his vision of life might be considered an act of treason against the spirit that sent him the vision. A Chippewa considers his vision of life to be a mighty mystery, on which he ponders his whole life through.

I knew that most Chippewa youths, when nearing adulthood, went off alone into the depths of the forest, to undertake a great fast. A youth usually built a bed in the branches of a lofty tree, where he lay for six or seven days, without eating or drinking, directing his thoughts to higher matters. The youth sought a vision of his future, a vision that would put him in touch with his *nigouime,* or "guardian spirit." When a guardian spirit finally appeared to him, it might be the sun or the thunder, an animal or some fantastic creature. This guardian spirit was expected to guide the youth through his entire life. I was intrigued by the thought of mere boys and girls subjecting themselves to torments of hunger and thirst for the sake of an idea, a dream, or a question of fate. Few English youths could be convinced to retire to a remote forest, to fast for days on end, to refuse all claims of nature, and to fix their minds so steadfastly on mystical matters that they fall into convulsions and see visions. Such acts of deprivation seemed incredible to me—yet the Chippewas spoke of them as ordinary events.

"I did not attain my dream of life in the same way as do most Chippewa youths," Wawatam said. "I did not enter the forest with the thought of fasting for my dream. Rather, my dream was sent to me, at a time when I greatly needed it.

"My dream of life appeared to me when I was very young, when I stood no taller than my father sitting. The season was autumn. My family was encamped near a broad marsh of wild rice. My sisters and I were hard at work, filling our canoe with wild rice, when we heard the sound of gunshots coming from our camp. The shots were answered by shots from a distant camp, and I recognized the gunshots as sounds of mourning, announcing that someone had died. When I heard the shots, I was overcome with sadness, for I knew in my heart that my mother had died.

"Soon a messenger of sorrow approached our canoe. He told us of what I already knew. Our mother had just died.

"We buried our mother with many tears. But the tears I cried did not wash away my grief. I longed to go off alone, into the forest, to weep out my grief. But my father, my uncle, and my older sisters would not let me go. They watched me closely, for they were worried about my sad and bewildered manner.

"One day, when my father and my uncle left us to go smoke with others, I sprang away from my sisters, and ran so swiftly into the forest that I soon left them behind. I ran farther and farther, not wanting to stop. As I ran, I began to sob and call out for my mother. At last I was exhausted, and I climbed a tall pine tree, where I wept for many hours. Sick with weariness and pain, I stayed in the tree for a long time—I know not how long.

"As I was hanging from branches high in the tree, I heard the voice of a woman, very close to me. I looked about and saw a black form hovering in the air above me. The voice of a woman asked, 'Who are you? Why do you weep?'

"'I am Wawatam,' I said. 'I weep for my mother, who has died.'

"'Come then,' the woman commanded. 'Follow me.' She held out her hand to me, and I took it. Together we stepped away from the tree and into the air. But we did not fall. We glided, as if by magic, through the air. We soared above the forest, till we came to another tall tree, a tamarack, and we alighted atop it. The tamarack trembled and bent, as though it would give way beneath us, but the shadow woman said, 'Fear not, Wawatam. Tread firmly. The tamarack will bear us up.' Without hesitating, she stepped into the air with her other foot, and I followed her. With our second step we glided upward, to the top of a tall birch. The birch tree shook and bent toward the ground, and again I feared that I would fall. 'Fear not,' said the woman. 'The birch will bear us up.' Again we stepped into the air, and our third step carried us to the foot of a mountain.

"'Do you know this mountain?' the shadow woman asked.

"'No,' I said.

"'It is the Mountain of the Stag's Heart.'

"I now understood that what had seemed three steps had in truth been a journey of three days. By day the shadow woman and I had glided through the air. By night we had rested on the treetops. We had soared over vast forests and across broad lakes.

"The shadow woman waved her hand, and a dark rift opened in the mountain before us. We entered the rift and glided ever upward, like hawks soaring up through darkness. Far above us I could see a small light.

"Suddenly we passed into brilliant sunlight. I shaded my eyes with my hand, and I saw that the brilliance was coming from a single lodge.

"'Go into that lodge,' the shadow woman said.

"The door of the lodge opened before me, and I entered. Within the lodge a light was blazing so brilliantly that I had to cover my eyes. I trembled with fear and expectation. At length I heard the voice of a spirit, who spoke to me from the back of the lodge.

"'Wawatam,' the spirit said. 'I saw that you were full of sorrow at the death of your mother, so I sent for you. You are welcome here. Come closer to me. Look about you. You will see how I live, and how things are with me.'

"I grew accustomed to the light, and I looked about. At first I saw nothing but a lantern in the middle of the lodge, which was burning with a fierce light. I understood that the lantern was the sun, and I knew that the Spirit of the Sun was sitting behind the lantern. The Spirit of the Sun again spoke to me.

"'Wawatam. Look beneath you.'

"I looked down, and I saw the earth far below me. I saw trees and grass, tall mountains and great waters. I saw the whole round of the world.

"'Look above you,' said the Spirit of the Sun.

"I looked up, and I saw the vast vault of heaven. The stars were so close that I could touch them.

"'Look before you,' said the Sun. 'Whom do you see? Do you know him?'

"I looked before me, and I was terrified, for I saw myself.

"'You see,' said the Sun, 'you are ever near me. I look upon you each day, and I watch over you. I gaze upon you and know everything you do. I know if you are ill or well. So be of good cheer, Wawatam.

"'Now look to your right and to your left,' said the Sun. 'Do you know the four persons who surround you? They are a gift which I, the great source of life, will make to you. They will be your four children—three sons and one daughter. So you see, Wawatam, your family will be increased. You will live a long life, and your hair will become like mine.'

"I gazed upon the hair of the Spirit of the Sun. It shone like silver. A feeling of great joy came over me, for I knew that I would live a long and happy life.

"'Now look about you,' said the Sun. 'I will give you all the birds and beasts you see fluttering and running about my lodge. You will become a famous hunter, and you will shoot them all.'

"I looked about me in amazement, for I saw a boundless abundance of creatures, running about and flocking within the lodge.

"'In remembrance of your visit to me,' said the Sun, 'and as a good omen for your future, I give you this bird.' The Sun handed me the carved figure of a flying swan. 'This bird travels across the sky and over the waters, ever with his family,' said the Sun. 'This bird will be your guardian spirit.'

"The Spirit of the Sun then told the shadow woman to lead me back to the earth. The woman took me by the hand, and we started to glide downward. I saw that the height we had reached was immense, far greater than the distance it seemed we had climbed. We glided ever downward, and just as the lantern of the Sun was setting in the west, we reached the top of a tall pine tree, that towered high above the others. We spent the entire night climbing down the tree. When my feet at last touched the earth, I looked to the east, and there I saw half the Sun's round lantern, rising above the horizon.

"A black dog ran past us, and the shadow woman said, 'You will sacrifice that dog to me, as a gift for the things I have done for you.'

"This I promised to do.

"'Soon four persons will come for you,' the shadow woman said. 'But do not follow them if they touch you with bare hands. If they hold the leaves of the lime tree in their hands when they touch you, it is good. Follow them. Farewell to you, Wawatam.'

"At that moment I heard voices beneath me. One voice was saying, 'I will go there.' Another voice said, 'I will go there to seek him.' I was too weak to look down to see who was speaking. Suddenly I heard a cry: 'What is up in that tree? Is it a boy? Yes, yes! It is Wawatam! Sisters, we have found him!' The voices belonged to my four sisters, who were searching for me. 'But stay,' I heard one say. 'He dreams deeply. Do not touch him with bare hands. Pick the leaves of the lime tree to cover our fingers, before we take him down.'

"This they did, and they bore me down from out of the tree. They laid me on a bear skin and carried me home. I was so weak that I could not eat food for two days. But gradually I began to eat like the others and to live again among humans.

"Since that time, Mekawees, I have thought often of my vision of life, and of my visit with the Spirit of the Sun. As you can see, all that the Sun promised me has been fulfilled."

Wawatam picked up his pipe, and we smoked from it. I felt honored that Wawatam had shared his vision of life with me, but I could not understand how he thought his vision would help me.

"Have you ever dreamed of your mother?" I asked Wawatam.

"Yes. I dream of her in the autumn, at the time of the wild-rice harvest—the time of the year when I first heard the gunshots that told me of her death. I dream that I travel the Path of Souls, and that I see her and speak with her."

"My father," I asked, "what am I to learn from your dream of life?"

Wawatam again filled his sacred pipe, and we smoked from it. He watched intently as the smoke wafted aloft, carrying his prayers upward. He spoke slowly.

"Mekawees. A man is nothing. The spirit that breathes life into a man is everything. My son, I pray that some day you will feel the breath of your guardian spirit."

24

The principal animals to be hunted on our wintering ground were the elk, bear, deer, beaver, marten, and raccoon. I frequently was assigned the tasks of hunting the beaver and the raccoon, often in the company of Sassaba, my younger brother.

The beaver was of vital importance to our family, both for its precious pelt and its tasty meat. The tail of the beaver was considered a delicacy. To kill the beaver, Sassaba and I sometimes paddled our canoe several miles upriver just before nightfall. When dusk settled over the land, we let our canoe drift quietly with the current. The beavers, which ventured forth during the evening to procure food, were not alarmed by our drifting canoe and often passed within gunshot.

Sassaba taught me that the beaver prefers to eat the wood of the birch, aspen, or poplar, and uses the wood of other trees to build lodges and dams. In broad marshes, where no wood is near at hand, the beaver resorts to eating the roots of rushes and water lilies. It eats great quantities of food, and so is often forced to move to new quarters. The beaver's house is a domed lodge covered with sticks and surrounded by water, but the animal also digs holes or "washes" in the banks of streams and ponds, to which it retreats when threatened.

The female beaver produces two young at a time, sometimes more, and the young ones stay near their parents for two years. The male beaver is a jealous mate. If a strange male approaches a mating pair, a battle ensues, of which the female remains an unconcerned spectator, not caring which party claims her through the law of conquest. I saw scars from such battles on the pelts of many of the beavers we killed. The male is as constant as he is jealous, and never attaches himself to more than one female. Yet the female, for her part, is always fond of strangers. Some of the males live by themselves, build no lodges or dams, and use only washes for shelter. These animals, which Sassaba called "old bachelors," we had to catch in traps formed of logs and baited with poplar branches.

Sassaba said beavers once were endowed with speech, but Gichi Manido took away their speech, lest the animals grow wiser than humans.

Beaver pelts are most valuable when collected in the winter, when the fur is thickest. Sassaba and I often took beavers by approaching a beaver lodge over the ice, and breaking apart the lodge with our hatchets. As we attacked the lodge, of course, the beavers within it were making their escape under water, usually to a wash in a nearby bank. We then had to search for the wash, which we did by striking the ice along the bank. Where the ice returned a hollow sound, we knew there was a wash, and at times we even knew that a beaver was hiding within a wash, for we could see the water moving with the breath of the animal. Our final task in capturing the beaver was often a painful one—we had to pull the animal out of the wash with our hands, and we sometimes were severely bitten.

Sassaba and I preferred the more aristocratic sport of hunting raccoons. This we did in the evening, for the raccoons never left their hiding places till after sunset. We used our dogs to track the raccoons (much like the English use dogs to track foxes, except that we did not have the luxury of riding horseback). When our dogs fell upon a fresh scent, they rushed after the raccoon, all the while serving us notice of their progress by their howling. The raccoon usually made for a tree, where it remained till we came along and shot it.

When snow lay on the ground, nothing more was needed to hunt raccoons than to follow the tracks of a raccoon. We sometimes found as many as six raccoons in the hollow of a single tree.

As we hunted together, Sassaba and I became fast friends, and he taught me his many secrets of the hunt. One day in late autumn, as we approached a small lake surrounded by hills, Sassaba motioned for me to be still. He pointed toward shadowy figures on a hillside overlooking the opposite shore of the lake. The figures were wolves—perhaps six or eight of them. Sassaba pointed toward the lake, where I saw the head of a stag that was swimming toward us, rippling the surface of the water. Sassaba signalled that we should hide behind a log near the lakeshore.

"Mekawees," Sassaba whispered, "the wolves have chased the stag into the water. They are waiting for him to come ashore. The stag is cold and tired, and when he reaches the shore, the wolves will pull him down. But we will take the stag for ourselves. When the stag reaches the shore, he will try to run up this stream. Kill him with one shot."

The stag stumbled to shore and tried to run up the stream bed, just as Sassaba had predicted. I fired my musket and dropped the animal in his tracks. At this Sassaba abruptly stood up, raised his arms, and motioned for me to do the same. His eyes were trained on the ridge overlooking our position. "Brother wolves," Sassaba shouted. "Forgive us for taking your food. But understand that we are only men who face a winter of hunger, while you are wolves, masters of the hunt. You can catch food in every kind of weather. Understand that we are your brothers, for we are Chippewas of the Wolf Clan. We now ask you for your help. Thank you for giving us this food. My family will pray for you."

Sassaba watched the ridge closely as I reloaded my musket. He pointed out to me the pointed ears of a wolf, peering at us from just over the crest of the ridge. He said the animal was probably the leader of the wolves. Sassaba slowly raised his musket and sent a ball flying into a tree trunk just above the wolf's head. The wolf disappeared.

We cut the stag's carcass into several pieces and loaded the venison onto our small sleds, which we pulled back to camp.

When we arrived at camp, Sassaba was quick to tell the family every detail of how we had taken the stag from the wolves. I noticed, however, that he told his story simply and did not boast. I suspected that he did not wish to offend the Spirit of the Wolves. Wawatam said he approved of Sassaba's speech to the wolves, but he also expressed concern, because Sassaba had chased away the wolves with a gunshot. He ordered us to return to the scene of the kill, to leave there the choicest cuts of venison, and to ask the wolves to forgive us for our rudeness. This we did.

During our many hunts together, Sassaba was ever talkative, yet ever attentive to the business at hand. He was an excellent tracker and was forever commenting on the tell-tale signs he saw all about us. Where I saw only faint depressions in the snow, he saw enough evidence to tell him precisely what had happened on that spot days or weeks earlier.

Sassaba was a keen observer of the sky—so much so that I suspected his guardian spirit lived in the sky. (I was never able to confirm this, however, for Sassaba was silent on the subject of guardian spirits.) During the day Sassaba watched the sun and the clouds, and he pointed out cloud formations, for all of which he had particular names. He often foretold the weather by signs he saw in the clouds, but his predictions of the weather, though usually correct, had little to do with science. He often explained a change in the weather in terms of two spirits, Nanibozhu and Paupukeewis, who were forever racing across the sky. When Nanibozhu led in the race, the weather was clear and calm. But sooner or later Nanibozhu grew lazy, lay down in the sunlight, and fell fast asleep. Then Paupukeewis caught up with Nanibozhu, raced past him, and the weather turned gray or stormy.

Sassaba could tell the time by the stars. He recognized the North Star, the planets, and a whole family of constellations, which went by names such as Bear's Head, Bear's Cross, and Man Who Walks Behind a Loon. I sometimes compared Sassaba's Chippewa constellations with the Greek constellations I had learned. He was intrigued by the strange characters and configurations that I saw in the stars. The Pleiades he knew as the Sweating Stones, for he said the seven small stars are arranged in the sky just as the Chippewas arrange stones within their sweat lodges. He pointed out to me the starry trail which the spirits of the dead follow on their journey to heaven. The souls of dead people, he said, pass upward and westward, high above the Milky Way, which Sassaba called *Jibekana*, or "Path of Souls."

Late on a clear winter day, Sassaba and I were following raccoon tracks through the snow, when he pointed to a flock of crows flying eastward. The crows soon were followed by eagles, then more crows. Sassaba observed that there must be a dead or dying animal in that direction. He said if we could find the crows we might find food. So off we went, marching eastward for a time, till we again heard the voices of crows. We found the crows perched high in trees, overlooking a small swamp, raucously calling to one another. The eagles were in attendance as well, perched atop trees on the far side of the swamp, apart from the crows. In the middle of the swamp lay a freshly killed elk, surrounded by wolves.

Unfortunately, the swamp was not frozen over, so there was no easy way for us to retrieve the carcass of the elk. As Sassaba and I hid behind bushes and pondered what to do, a light wind sprang up at our backs. Dried rushes standing at the edge of swamp began to move. The wolves caught our scent and pricked up their ears.

"Nanibozhu is dancing with the rushes," Sassaba whispered.

I turned to Sassaba in surprise. "Nanibozhu is here?" I studied the rushes, which clattered lightly against one another in the breeze. The rushes held the tawny glow of the setting sun. The snow in the shadows held the blue of the darkening sky.

"But Nanibozhu is mistaken," Sassaba said. "He thinks the moving rushes are Chippewa dancers. He has joined them in their dance. When the wind dies, the rushes will stop their dancing, and Nanibozhu will see his mistake."

Sassaba and I watched the rushes for a moment or two, then redirected our attention to the wolves and their freshly killed elk. After devoting some thought to the matter, Sassaba concluded that we could do no better than to make a virtue of necessity. He stood up and raised his arms, as if to address the assembled animals.

"Brother wolves," Sassaba shouted across the swamp. The wolves looked up. The crows fell silent. "We have hunted all this day, and still we have no food. But we will not bother you, my brothers. We will not chase you from your meal. You may eat your food in peace. We ask only that the Spirit of the Wolves be kind to our family. We ask that the Spirit of the Wolves send the animals to us."

25

During the winter evenings my family spent together within our lodge, Old Mother sat in her honored place to the left of the lodge door; Wawatam sat in his honored place to the right. We all sat on animal skins, with our legs toward the fire, our backs toward the cold, and our shoulders covered with blankets. We men busied ourselves repairing traps and weapons, while the women wove fish nets of twine, made from the fiber of the wood nettle, spun on their thighs. Old Mother claimed that the Chippewas once learned the art of making fish nets from the spiders.

Through these times of winter darkness, Wawatam and Old Mother entertained us with countless tales and fables.

"Winter is the safe season for storytelling," Old Mother assured me. "This is the time of the year when many creatures are asleep or far away. The evil snakes and the toads are under the ground. There are fewer ears to take offense at the stories we tell."

Wawatam and Old Mother told their tales simply and fluently, without inflection or affectation. The life was in the story itself. Listening to their stories was like listening to the steady splashing of a stream, or the murmur of the wind. Characters in their tales included men, women, children, spirits, animals, and monsters, which changed form so often that it was difficult for me to comprehend just what sort of human, creature, or demon was being described.

Sassaba sometimes provided the inspiration for a story, when he boasted of his hunting exploits. Upon hearing such a boast from Sassaba, Wawatam rolled his eyes, raised his hand, and announced, "Iagoo is among us." We all smiled at this, for Iagoo was a fabled braggart. Wawatam invariably followed his announcement by recalling one of Iagoo's great lies.

"One evening Iagoo was sitting in his lodge by the bank of a river when he heard the voices of ducks on the river. He was too lazy to rise from his mat, so he lifted his musket to his shoulder and shot through the side of the lodge. His bullet struck a swan that was flying past, twenty brace of ducks on the river, two loons swimming beneath the water, and a masquinonge lying at the bottom of the river."

When a gust of wind blew a flurry of snow into the smoke hole of our lodge, Old Mother sometimes remarked, "Ah! Paupukeewis is gathering up his nets." Paupukeewis was a trickster spirit who knew the secret of changing snow and ice into fish.

The most popular hero of our winter tales was Nanibozhu—a legendary figure among the Chippewas. Nanibozhu was half man and half spirit. His mother was a mortal. His father was the sun. His brothers were the four winds. No challenge was too high or too difficult for him to attempt, yet no mischief was too low or too trivial for him to engage in. It was Nanibozhu who saved the earth after the great flood, by breathing life into the drowned animals and by burying seeds and bits of root to resurrect the plants. It was Nanibozhu who brought the gift of Indian corn to the earth, by defeating the Spirit of the Corn in a wrestling match. Nanibozhu was able to leap across vast distances and to glide swiftly across the water in his magical canoe, without so much as lifting a paddle. He was able to speak to the animals, and he called each of them "brother." He could take the form of a human, an animal, a plant, or a rock. He once lived with the beavers, and he built an enormous dam for them. Another time he lived with the wolves, and he ranged freely across the countryside with them. Nanibozhu was admired for his strength and his wisdom—yet he could just as easily be foolish, or petty, or cruel. He was never wiser or better than the people whom he visited.

Wawatam sometimes told the story of Nanibozhu and the dance of the animals.

"Nanibozhu once captured a great fish—so large that its oil filled a small lake. Nanibozhu invited all the animals to come to the lake, to feast on the oil. The bear arrived early and jumped head-first into the lake. He swam about in the oil, drinking great gulps as he swam. This is why the bear has so much fat on his body. The moose arrived late, and the partridge nervously watched the feast from behind a bush, till the oil was almost gone. This is why the moose and the partridge have so little fat. The hare and the marten were last to arrive, and this is why they have no fat at all.

"When the animals had finished feasting on the oil, Nanibozhu invited them to dance. Picking up his drum, he cried out, 'New songs from the south wind! Come, my brothers, dance for me!' He urged the animals to shut their eyes, and to dance about him in a circle. This they readily did. But when a fat goose passed near Nanibozhu, he grabbed the goose and twisted off its head, all the while singing and beating his drum to cover the noise of the fluttering goose. In a tone of admiration, he shouted to the animals, 'That is it, my brothers! That is the way! You dance splendidly!' He killed several more animals, till at last the loon, suspecting that something was amiss, opened one eye. 'Ha-ha-aha-aha-aha!' cried the loon. 'Nanibozhu is killing us!' All the animals sprang away from Nanibozhu—running, flying, hopping, crawling, squirming. The loon ran toward the water, but Nanibozhu was right behind the bird. Nanibozhu was furious with the loon, and he kicked at the bird, just as the loon reached the water's edge. This is why the loon's back is flat, its tail feathers are few, and its legs are bent straight back from his body. This is why the loon is not able to walk on the land."

Old Mother told us a story of Nanibozhu and a baby. "Nanibozhu once visited a Chippewa camp on the south coast of Lake Superior. There he saw a baby girl, lying on a mat, carelessly sucking her toe. Nanibozhu was fascinated by the baby, for he had never seen anyone—human or spirit—suck her own toe. Nanibozhu sat down, took off a moccasin, and pulled his foot toward his mouth, to see if he cared for toe sucking. But the effort sent him sprawling backward, and he struck his head on a rock. At this the baby laughed with glee, thinking that the stranger was entertaining her with his foolishness. Nanibozhu became furious. He was determined to suck his own toe. He prepared himself for a great effort. He put his back to the edge of the lake, in case he should fall over again. He jerked his foot with all his might toward his mouth, but before his toe reached his mouth, he flipped himself violently into the lake. With a great splash he landed atop a water lizard, which was lying under the water, and he flattened the back of the creature. Seeing what he had done, Nanibozhu felt sorry for the lizard. He collected two clam shells, and he covered the lizard with them, putting one shell on the top and the other on the bottom of the lizard's body. 'There, brother turtle,' Nanibozhu said. 'Your body will be protected from this day forward.'"

One evening, while Old Mother was telling us a story, a kettle that was hanging over the fire moved, as if by itself. This seemingly insignificant event cut short Old Mother's story in an instant, and the entire family remained strangely silent for the rest of the night. The next day Old Mother explained to me that the moving kettle was a sign that a "windigo," an evil, man-eating spirit, was in the neighborhood.

The members of my family believed that all nature was alive with spirits and full of "medicine," or magic. They believed that lakes, swamps, islands, waterfalls, mountains, and even rocks had their own spirits. Where I saw only a lump of shining copper, they saw something mysterious and wonderful. Where I saw only a field of flowers, they saw myriad fairy spirits.

Wawatam sometimes spoke of his encounters with the spiritual forces of nature. He received my particular attention one evening when he mentioned an island in Lake Superior, which he said was covered with shining, yellow sand. I was credulous enough to think that the yellow sand might be gold dust, and I eagerly asked Wawatam just where the island was located. He said it lay near Isle de Maurepas, but he went on to warn me that I should stay away from the island, for fear of angering an evil spirit who lived there, and who guarded the island with monstrous snakes.

Wawatam said he had visited the enchanted island only once, as a young man.

"I went to the island alone," Wawatam said, "for I had been instructed in a vision that I should visit the island, and that I would be protected there by my guardian spirit. I approached the island from the windward side, and as I neared the island, I blew smoke of the kinnikinnick into the air, as an offering to the evil spirit that lived there. My offering must have appeased the evil spirit, for when I landed, I saw no monstrous serpents and no yellow sand. Instead of serpents, there were hawks, which hovered over my head and screamed at me in anger. They dove at my face and tried to claw out my eyes. This made me think that the spirit of the island had changed the serpents into hawks, and that he had changed the yellow sand into white sand.

"I entered a grove of trees, where I came upon three caribou that behaved strangely, as if a spell had been cast over them. They did not run away from me, but instead, they turned to stare at me, as if they did not know what to think of me. I fired my musket and killed one caribou. The other two ran off a short distance, but then they returned. I recharged my musket, and I killed a second caribou. The third then took to running about, from one place to another, in great confusion.

"I walked farther into the woods, all the while wondering at the strange behavior of the caribou. Suddenly I came upon the bones of many caribou, lying all about. I thought there was something strange about the bones, for they lay together in whole skeletons, as if none of the caribou had ever been torn apart by wolves or butchered by Indians. One skeleton lay buried in the earth, with only its skull and antlers above the ground. The sight of the mysterious bones frightened me, and made me realize that the caribou of the island belonged to the evil spirit who guarded the island. I recalled that I had killed two of his creatures, and I feared that the evil spirit would now kill me. I ran with all my speed back to the two caribou I had killed. I built a great fire on the sand, and in the fire I burned the carcasses of the two creatures. I did not eat a bit of their flesh. I then laid my sacred pipe in the fire, as an offering to the evil spirit, so that he would allow me to leave the island without killing me."

Wawatam said he had never in his life visited a more mysterious place than the Isle of Yellow Sand. I, however, lost all interest in the place, once I learned that its guardian spirit had the power to transform its shining, yellow sand into merely white sand.

From time to time my family asked me to tell them stories of the English. I could not think of any English myths or legends worth telling, so I translated stories from my Bible.

Wawatam favored certain Psalms, passages from which he carefully recorded in hieroglyphic drawings on birchbark. But he was deeply puzzled by a few Bible passages. He was astonished by Abraham's willingness to sacrifice the life of his son on the altar of God. Wawatam said he was suspicious of any god that would call for such a cruel sacrifice. "Perhaps it was Machi Manido, the Evil Spirit, who imitated the voice of Gichi

Manido, so that he might fool the father into making a terrible mistake."

Wawatam was more certain in his conclusions regarding the story of Noah and the ark. "It was Nanibozhu who disguised himself as Noah," Wawatam asserted. "But Nanibozhu did not save the animals by building a boat. Rather, he breathed life into the animals after they drowned."

Old Mother was equally certain about the true identities of Jonah and the whale. "It was Nanibozhu," she declared. "And the fish that ate him was a sturgeon."

At times it was all I that could do to keep from laughing at such thoughtful discussions of theology.

One evening I read to my family the story of Moses and the Ten Commandments.

And Mount Sinai was altogether on a smoke, because the Lord descended upon it in fire: and the smoke thereof ascended as the smoke of a furnace, and the whole mount quaked greatly.

The story of God's visitation upon the children of Israel inspired Wawatam to tell me the story of the Great Spirit's visitation upon the Indians. He said the story was told by the Sioux, but nevertheless, he believed that it was true.

"Gichi Manido once spoke to the Indians from atop a high ground. This happened in ancient times, at a place called 'Fountain of the Pipe'—a place that holds powerful medicine for all Indians. The place lies far to the west of here, on a high plain which the French call *Coteau des Prairies*, which separates the waters of River Saint Pierre from the waters of River of the Missouris.

"At the time of the great flood, all the Indians gathered together at Fountain of the Pipe, to escape the rising water. But the water continued to rise, and it drowned the people. The flesh of the Indians was transformed into a mass of red stone. The only Indian to survive the flood was a young woman, who caught hold of the foot of an eagle as it flew past. The eagle carried her to the top of a high cliff, where the bird and the woman mated. From this union the woman bore twins, and from the twins sprang many children, who peopled the earth with Indians.

"But it was not long before the Indians separated into nations. They created new languages, and they started warring against one another. The Sioux took for themselves the lands that surround Fountain of the Pipe, and they killed all strangers who wished to take medicine from Fountain of the Pipe.

"Gichi Manido was saddened to see his people fighting with one another, so he sent runners to all the nations, summoning them together at Fountain of the Pipe. From the east came the Iroquois. From the west came the Crows and the Blackfeet. From the south came the Cherokees. From the north came the Crees. We Chippewas attended the grand council in great numbers. All the nations came together in peace.

"Gichi Manido stood atop a high rock and looked down upon his people, who spread across the plains below him in numbers like the grass. He reached beneath his foot and pulled from the earth a piece of red stone. He showed the red stone to the people, and he told them it was their flesh—the flesh of all Indians. He turned the stone around in his hands and shaped it into a great pipe. He drew smoke from the pipe, and he blew the smoke into the air. The smoke rolled across the land and settled over the heads of the people. Gichi Manido told the Indians that henceforth they should make their sacred pipes from the red stone, and that they should smoke their pipes whenever they wished to pray to him. He commanded that whenever the Indians visited Fountain of the Pipe, they should come together in peace.

"Gichi Manido again drew smoke from his great pipe, and he enshrouded himself in it. A fierce wind sprang up from off the prairie and blew away the smoke. When the smoke had cleared, Gichi Manido was gone. The wind fanned a great flame, that rose from out of the red stone, and the people stood in awe before it. The flame melted the stone and glazed it to a lustrous shine. A dark oven opened in the earth, and two women entered the oven in a blaze of fire. To this day the two women remain at Fountain of the Pipe, where they live beneath five great boulders. The women are the guardian spirits of the place. All who would take the sacred stone from Fountain of the Pipe must first invoke the spirits of the two women who guard the stone, to gain their permission.

"From that day to this, Fountain of the Pipe has been a place of peace, and a place of powerful medicine. It belongs to all the Indian nations."

Wawatam held his pipe next to his arm. "See, Mekawees. The pipestone is our flesh."

One evening Wawatam surprised me by asserting that a long-departed ancestor of his, a man named Makwa, had witnessed the arrival of the first Frenchmen in America. The story told by Makwa had been passed down through generations of Chippewas, and Wawatam said he would now tell it to me. (I could not believe that Wawatam knew such ancient history. Yet the more he told me of the story, the more I thought it had the ring of truth to it. Perhaps the story was true, I reasoned, for the chronicles of the Chippewas are their collective memories.)

"The grandfather of my father's grandmother was a great prophet," Wawatam said. "He was of the Bear Clan, and his name was Makwa. Late one night, many years ago, Makwa saw a startling vision. He was visited in a dream by strange beings, who had hair on their faces, and who wore strange clothing. The dream worried Makwa greatly, so without telling anyone of it, he sought a further vision that might show him the meaning of the dream. Makwa shut himself up in his prophet lodge, apart from the others, and there he chanted sacred medicine songs and beat his drum. He fasted in solitude for days on end. He took many sweat baths, all alone. His actions excited others in his village, who wondered what would be the end of it all. Would Makwa see good hunting or a famine, a war with the Sioux, or something else just as grand?

"At length Makwa came forth from his prophet lodge and called together the midays, the chiefs, and the prophets of the village. He told them that something astonishing had happened. In his visions he had seen beings of a strange race, who arrived from the east, from across the great water. The strange beings came in monstrous, wooden canoes, with posts as tall as full-grown trees. From the posts were hung pale skins, each larger than twenty moose skins sewn together. The strange beings halted their monstrous canoes in the middle of the River Saint Lawrence, and paddled ashore backwards. The faces of the strange beings were pale, and were surrounded by bushy hair. They had long knives tied to their waists. They carried long stems, from which there came fire and smoke, and sudden thunder that made the earth quake.

"It took Makwa half a day to tell of all he had seen in his visions. The people of Makwa's village listened to him in amazement. When Makwa finished his story, the people discussed the matter carefully and agreed that they should send envoys across the lakes and rivers, toward the east, to see for themselves the strange beings.

"The envoys embarked, with Makwa as their leader. They traveled for a month, through the countries of other nations. None of the nations they met knew anything of the strange beings, for no other nation had so great a prophet as Makwa. The Chippewa envoys at length came to the lower regions of the River Saint Lawrence. There they came upon a clearing in the forest, where they saw that the trees, even the largest trees, had been cut to the ground. They saw that the trees had been cut with smooth, level cuts, such that they had never seen before. Makwa said the trees must have been cut by the long knives he had seen in his vision. Near the tree stumps they found shavings of wood, rolled into ringlets. They found pieces of worsted cloth and brightly colored calico. These things were strange and new, and altogether wondrous. The envoys fastened pieces of cloth about their heads and put wood shavings in their hair and in their ears, thinking that the objects held powerful medicine.

"The envoys continued their search, and suddenly, at a bend in the river, they came upon the strange beings themselves. The strangers had bushy beards and pale faces, long knives, and fire-stems—just as Makwa had seen in his vision. On the river floated monstrous canoes, built like wooden baskets. Miracles were everywhere.

"The strangers were Frenchmen, who announced themselves to the Chippewas, by speaking through an Indian. The Frenchmen and the Chippewas behaved kindly toward one another.

"Makwa sent the best of his hunters into the forest and told them to return with meat, so that he might give a feast to the strange beings. Makwa bent to light a fire, by rubbing a cord on a stick. But before Makwa could make a flame, the leader of the French drew forth a fire-steel and started a blaze with a single spark. At seeing the sudden fire, Makwa uttered loud cries about the iron. The French leader raised his musket and shot it into the air. Makwa heard the sudden thunder and felt the earth quake. Makwa was speechless.

"When Makwa recovered his wits, he drew forth his sacred pipe and lit it. He presented the stem of the pipe to each of the four winds, then to the sun, then to the leader of the French. He blew smoke on the French leader and his miraculous possessions. Makwa believed that the stranger and his possessions were powerful spirits.

"The Chippewa hunters returned with venison and berries for a feast. Makwa drew forth his medicine bag and made ready to pray to it, to thank the Spirit of the Sun for lighting Makwa's way in his search for the strange beings. But the French leader stopped Makwa, saying that he did not approve of the medicine bag. The French leader said his God forbade him from eating food sacrificed to evil spirits, or to the skins of animals. He said that the one true God—the God worshiped by the

French—did not live in any animal skin. He said the true God lived above, in heaven. He pointed to the sky.

"Makwa agreed to shut up his medicine bag, and he asked the French leader to help him see the God of the French. Makwa said the God of the French must be the greatest spirit of all the spirits—for no other spirit could give such wondrous things as guns and fire-steels.

"Everyone, Frenchmen and Chippewas alike, shared in the feast, and in the smoking of pipes. When the feast was ended, the French leader made a speech.

"'Chippewas,' the French leader said. 'I see that the young men of your nation are handsome and strong. From their births they have lived only in shadows, yet they are as handsome as men born in countries where the light of God always shines. Your people will become another nation when they know the light of the French. I am the dawn of that light, which soon will appear in your country, which will shine more and more brightly, till it causes you to be born again. If the young men of your nation will carry French weapons, they will never again fear their enemies. To your young men I give my musket, to honor their courage. My musket will serve them better than all their spears and arrows. To the old men of your nation I give my kettle. They will carry it everywhere without fear of breaking it. They will cook in it the food which they will offer to Frenchmen, who soon will visit your country. To the women of your nation I give this colored cloth and these awls and knives, which will serve them better than all the pieces of stone and bone they now use. To the children of your nation I give these colored beads, more beautiful than the brightest stones to be found in your country. Soon other Frenchmen will bring other precious things to your country. They will give precious things to your people, if your people will give them beaver skins in return.'

"Makwa thanked the French leader for the wondrous gifts, and he said he was sorry for not having beaver skins to give in return. Before that time, Makwa said, the Chippewas had roasted their beaver skins.

"The envoys returned home with their treasures, which caused great excitement among the Chippewas. People from all parts of the country came together at the Sault de Sainte Marie, to see the miraculous objects. The calico and the worsted cloth were torn into a thousand pieces, to be shared by all. Strips of calico were tied to the tops of poles, and were carried by runners from one village to another. The wood shavings were given to hunters, who wore them as talismans. The musket and the kettle remained in the hands of Makwa, to be revered as sacred objects by the entire nation.

"In those days," Wawatam said, "the Chippewas believed that all things received from the French were full of goodness."

26

The Chippewas call February the Moon of Hard Snow. True to its name, the month brought sunny days and cold nights, which left a brittle shell of ice on the snow. The weather favored our hunting, for the crusted snow could bear up a hunter, or at least his dogs, but the deer and the elk broke through with every step, and the ice cut their legs to the very bone. We sometimes killed as many as twelve deer in just two hours. For the entire month we put up four thousand weight of venison.

Wawatam announced in March that the time was drawing near for us to leave our winter grounds, and return to Michilimackinac. He was concerned, however, that the followers of Pontiac might threaten my safety. He asked if I had noticed any ill omens during the winter, or if I had seen any visions of Michilimackinac in my dreams. I confessed that I had not. The question of my safety was of such great concern to Wawatam, that he insisted on going off into the forest by himself, to fast and to seek of a vision of my future.

Four days later Wawatam returned to us with welcome news. He had indeed seen a vision, foretelling him that it would be safe for me to return to Michilimackinac. Thus reassured, my family and I gathered together our dried venison and skins, and prepared our bundles for the march. The distance to Lake Michigan was just seventy miles, but over this distance we had to carry all our earthly belongings on our backs. We set off at dawn on the day of our departure and marched till midafternoon, when we stopped to build a scaffold. On the scaffold we placed our bundles, to keep them from the wolves, then we doubled back to our camp, which we reached by nightfall. The next morning we carried fresh loads, which we again deposited atop the scaffold, and again we returned to camp. In this fashion we continued to march back and forth, over a single leg of our journey, till we had advanced all our wealth to the scaffold. We then moved our lodge to the site of the scaffold, and we began the next day to carry our bundles over the next leg of our journey. So we continued, shuttling back and forth, till we were not far from the shore of Lake Michigan.

At a thick grove of maple trees we rendezvoused with one of Wawatam's sisters, her husband, and their children, who had already set up camp. Soon we were joined by other families, all returning from their wintering grounds, and all related in some way to our family. As each new family arrived at the camp, each was welcomed affectionately by the others. The women kissed one another, and they kissed their little nieces and nephews, whom they had not seen for four or five months. The little ones, in turn, hugged one another and ran off to play. The men shook hands, smoked their pipes, and shared news and rumors of the war against the English.

The reunion of the families occurred early in the month of April, which the Chippewas call the Moon of Boiling, for it is in early April that the Chippewas boil the sap they gather from maple trees, to make sugar. (The French have their own name for this time of the year—they call it *les temps des sucres*, or "time of sugar.") Indeed, the Moon of Boiling was a sweet season for us all. It was a time of promise, when new life appeared on the land. It was a time of merriment, when our families came together again.

The first order of business at the sugar camp was to build a lodge, some twenty feet long and fourteen feet wide, open at the top, with a door at each end, and with fires in the middle that ran the entire length. The women built the structure in a single day. The next day they made buckets of birchbark, which they hung from wooden spouts inserted into cuts in the tree trunks. From the spouts dripped flowing sap, which slowly filled the buckets. The sap then was poured from buckets into moose-skin vats, which in turn were emptied into boilers hung over the fires.

The trees produced the greatest quantities of sap on sunny mornings when the ice lay as thick as a dollar on the puddles.

The women worked hard at the sugar camp, but they seemed delighted to be there. Through all their toil, they gossiped with one another constantly. They often looked tenderly upon their nieces and nephews, or took time to run and kiss a child, or put straight a shirt, or sit down for a moment to admire a little one. They threw thick-boiled sap into the snow, transforming it into sticky globules of sugar, for the children to twist and chew. While the women collected sap and rendered sugar, we men cut wood and kept the fires burning. We also hunted and fished.

One fine day in early April seemed to announce the very arrival of spring. Ardent sunlight melted the last of the snow from the shadows. Trickling meltwater soaked into the soft earth. The shrill voices of frogs and the trills of blackbirds resounded from the river bank. A warm breeze blew from out of the south, full of the fresh aroma of life.

Wawatam and I were busy collecting firewood for the sugar lodge, when Wawatam abruptly shaded his eyes with his hand, and looked toward the southern sky. I soon heard what he heard—the high-pitched murmur of a flock of swans. Then I saw the swans—a brilliant ribbon of white against the blue of the sky. The swans passed overhead, their long necks pointing northward. Wawatam raised a hand in the air, as if to wave to an old friend.

The return of the swans on such a fine spring morning inspired Wawatam to tell me a story of the seasons.

"An old man was sitting in his lodge, by the side of a frozen stream," Wawatam said. "He was old and desolate. His hair was white with age. His body trembled in every joint. The time of the year was late winter. The old man had passed all that winter, day after day, alone within his lodge, listening to the low whistle of the wind as it swept before it the snow.

"Late one night, as the old man's fire was dying out, a stranger approached the lodge. In the stranger's eyes was a sparkle. His cheeks were red with the blood of youth, and a smile played upon his lips. He walked with a light step. On his head he wore a wreath of sweet grass, and in one hand he carried a bunch of flowers.

"'Ah, my son,' said the old man. 'I am happy to see you. Come in. Come in and tell me of your adventures, and what distant lands you have seen. We will pass this night together. I will tell you of my powers and exploits, and you will do the same. We will amuse one another.'

"The old man drew from his sack an ancient pipe, filled it with tobacco, and handed it to the young man. They smoked together. When they were finished, the old man spoke.

"'I blow my breath,' said the old man, 'and the streams stand still. The very water turns hard as stone.'

"'I breathe,' said the young man, 'and flowers spring up in the meadows.'

"'I breathe,' said the old man, 'and the leaves change their colors. My breath blows the leaves from the trees. The birds feel my breath, and they rise up from the water and fly southward. The animals hide from my breath. The ground becomes hard as flint. I shake my hair, and snow covers the land.'

"'I shake my hair,' replied the young man, 'and warm showers of rain fall upon the land. The plants lift their heads up out of the earth, like the eyes of little children. My voice recalls the birds. The warmth of my breath unlocks the streams. I walk through the woods, and the woods are filled with music. The earth rejoices. For I am Seegwun—Spirit of the Spring.'

"At length the sun began to rise over the old man's lodge. A gentle warmth settled over the place. The tongue of the old man fell silent. His head drooped with weariness. A robin began to sing from the top of the old man's lodge. A stream broke forth from its shell of ice and began to murmur beside the door of the lodge. A ray of sunlight entered the door and shone upon the old man. It was then that the young man recognized the old man as Peboan—Spirit of the Winter. Tears of meltwater began to flow from the old man's eyes. The sunlight grew warmer and warmer, and the old man became smaller and smaller, till at last he melted entirely away. Nothing remained on the spot where the old man's fire had burned but the *miskodeed*—a small white flower that blooms in the early spring."

Wawatam and I sat side by side on a log and basked in the warmth of the sunlight. We smoked from our pipes and watched the young children play in the puddles.

Suddenly the peace of our sugar camp was pierced by a cry of horror.

We rushed to the sugar lodge, where it was all too obvious what had happened—an infant girl had fallen into a vat of boiling syrup. The little girl was snatched from the vat instantly, but she was scalded terribly. Her face was skewed in a grimace of pain, and her skin was bright red. She was not breathing. An old woman bent over the girl and blew breath into her mouth. The old woman's breath brought forth from the young child a thin and tortured scream, followed by another, then another. Each breath the child took became a rasping cry of agony.

The girl's mother struggled franticly to embrace her daughter, but others held the mother back, saying that her touch would only hurt the daughter.

A miday arrived to treat the little girl. Others began a feast, at which they offered up songs and prayers, and beseeched the Great Spirit to save and heal the child. Everyone at the feast was expected to eat great piles of food as a sacrifice to Gichi Manido. Dogs were sacrificed as well, and were hung from the tops of poles.

I dutifully attended the feast, but my heart was not in the eating. As we feasted, I could hear the screams of the child coming from the sugar lodge. It seemed to me that her screams were growing ever fainter. I was beside myself with anguish.

As night approached, I felt compelled to leave the feast. I asked Wawatam if I could go off by myself, to pray for the child in my own way. He readily consented. I walked out alone, among the trees, to a spot where I could no longer hear the cries of the child or the beat of the miday's medicine drum. The night was cold and clear. The sky was full of stars.

I dropped to my knees in humble supplication. I opened my heart to the Lord, and I was overcome with prayer. I felt the Light of Christ shining through me. For much of the night I prayed to God, begging that he save the little girl's life.

When I returned to the camp, shortly before dawn, I did not hear the voice of the little girl. The silence made me hope that she was recovering.

In the end, however, all our prayers, all our incantations and sacrifices—all went for naught. As the sun rose, the little girl died.

At word of her death, the Chippewas gave vent to the most violent grief. The men blackened their faces and stuck knives and needles through their arms and breasts. The women shrieked and moaned. They loosened their hair and poured ashes over their heads.

I retreated once again into the woods, where I was bewildered by my disappointment and sorrow.

Late that morning the body of the little girl was passed through a hole cut in the back of her family's lodge. The lodge fire was put out, and the lodge was torn down and destroyed.

The child's body was placed atop a scaffold, where it would be safe from the wolves till it could be carried to the family's burial ground on the shore of Lake Michigan.

Several days later we set off for Lake Michigan. The forlorn father of the dead child carried his daughter's body the entire distance, without once putting it down. Upon reaching the lakeshore, the father bore the small body straight to the burial ground, which was situated on a hill overlooking the lake. Relatives set about digging a grave and lining it with birchbark. Within the grave they placed an axe, a pair of snowshoes, a small kettle filled with meat, several pairs of moccasins, a string of beads, a carrying belt, and a small paddle. Above the grave they erected a board, on which they painted a white semicircle, with a black crescent above it. I recognized the semicircle as the Chippewa symbol for the day, and I easily guessed the meaning of the blackness that covered the day.

The last act before the burial was performed by the mother. She placed her finger within her baby's tiny hand and wept over the body. She kissed her daughter's cold face, and she cut from her daughter's head a lock of hair.

The body was taken from the mother, was lowered into the ground, and was buried beneath the earth.

For some time after the burial, the young mother refused to leave her daughter's grave. Seeing her doubled over with grief, I was moved to try to comfort her. I knelt beside her and placed my hands on her shoulders. I offered her the usual arguments: that her daughter was fortunate to be released from the miseries of this life, and that some day the little girl would join her in a new life—a life happy and everlasting.

The mother nodded to me through her tears. She said she knew it was true. Some day she would travel the Path of Souls in search of her daughter. Some day she would find her daughter, using the lock of hair she now clutched so tightly in her hand. Some day a relative would place in her own grave the same lock of hair—a small relic hallowed by a mother's tears.

27

While we were camped on the shore of Lake Michigan, my Chippewa kinsmen kept a strict watch, day and night, for they expected their English enemies to exact a cruel revenge for the attack on Fort Michilimackinac. Their fears were based on the dreams of the old women, who saw visions in their sleep of a swift and bloody assault. I tried to assure my kin that the English would not bother to attack such a small band of Indians, on such a remote corner of the earth. But try as I might, I could not calm their fears.

Amidst the general state of alarm, there came a report of a real but less formidable enemy. A young hunter said he had spotted a mountain cat in the woods nearby. The camp was placed on the alert, for such an animal had been known to attack and carry off small children. Twenty hunters, myself included, set off in search of the fearsome animal.

We had gone less than a mile when our dogs caught the scent of the cat. We followed the howling dogs, and soon we found the big cat, perched on a branch of a large pine tree. We shot several bullets into the cat, but he clung tenaciously to his branch. When the cat finally fell from the tree, he was dead by the time his body hit the ground. The Chippewas paid their respects to the creature with tobacco smoke and prayers. Then the young hunter who first saw the cat claimed its skin as a trophy.

Wawatam spoke with awe of the animal we had just killed. He said a mountain cat was able to catch and kill any animal it wished. He said if there were as many mountain cats as there were wolves, there would be no deer.

In late April our fleet of canoes embarked for Michilimackinac. At Le Grande Traverse we came upon a large encampment of Chippewas, who said they dared not proceed any farther, lest they be destroyed, for they feared an attack by the English. A council was held, at which I was repeatedly asked if I knew of any English plans to attack the Chippewas. The Chippewas believed that I could see distant events in my dreams, and that I could predict the future. I claimed complete ignorance of any such matters, but my lack of vision only aroused their suspicions. Some warriors thought I was hiding information from them, and a few muttered darkly that I must be an English spy.

For several mornings running, the old women awoke from their sleep to report terrible dreams of an attack, in which even their grandchildren were cruelly slaughtered by English soldiers. The women were tormented by fears founded on nothing more than their imaginations.

Finally, to lay all such anxiety to rest, I awoke one morning to announce that I had indeed visited Fort Michilimackinac in my dreams and that I had seen no English soldiers there. (Of course, I had made no such visit.) The women were relieved to hear of my peaceful dreams—particularly Old Mother, who vouched for my honesty and good character. (Having made my announcement, I could only hope that in fact there were no British soldiers at the fort.) I went on to assure the Chippewas, this time with complete confidence, that if ever the English were to return to Michilimackinac, I would speak strongly on behalf of my Chippewa brothers and sisters, for the kind treatment I had received from them.

Reassured by my alleged dreams, the Chippewas gathered up their belongings and embarked for Michilimackinac the same day.

In crossing Le Grande Traverse we were overtaken by a sudden deluge of rain, accompanied by fearsome lightning and tall waves, which dashed water into our canoes so rapidly that we could not bail it out as fast as it came in. We sacrificed several dogs to the tempestuous spirit of the lake, and we managed to reach the far shore without loss of human life.

When we arrived at the Ottawa village at L'Arbre Croche, the Chippewas asked the Ottawas for news of the English. An Ottawa, who had just returned from the fort, confirmed my earlier report that no English were present at the fort. Thus reassured, my tribe made the rest of its journey to Michilimackinac with complete confidence.

On the afternoon of April 27, 1764, Fort Michilimackinac appeared on our horizon. The sight of the fort made my heart rise in my breast, for I expected to find my partner, Etienne Campion, waiting there for me. I soon was disappointed, however, for I found only a few Indian families camped near the fort, and a few French families living within it. The Indians and the French treated me kindly, and I had complete freedom of both the camp and the fort. But no one at Michilimackinac had heard any word of Campion, which concerned me greatly. I feared that my partner had been injured or killed, for I believed that nothing short of injury or death could keep him from coming to my aid.

Shortly after we arrived at the fort, Wawatam returned from the Indian camp with a remarkable story. It seemed that the previous winter a lone Sioux warrior, a young man named Narrhetoba, had visited the camps of the Chippewas on the south coast of Lake Superior. His boldness in coming alone among his blood enemies had astonished the Chippewas. Some had wanted to kill the Sioux warrior—but others had protected him, had praised his boldness, and had even called him an *odgidjida*, or "hero." Narrhetoba passed the whole winter among the Chippewas, and when spring came, he took leave of them as an honored friend.

Wawatam remarked that the young Sioux warrior was much like me. "Each of you bravely visited the country of the Chippewas," Wawatam said. "Each of you tried to bring peace to the country of your enemies." This was lofty praise indeed, and it embarrassed me, for Wawatam had a far higher opinion of me than I had of myself.

Within the fort we found two Frenchmen trading with the Indians. My family turned over to them much of our wealth in furs, to pay off our old debts. This done, my share of what was left included a hundred beaver skins, sixty raccoon, and six otter—all together worth one hundred sixty dollars. With my earnings from an entire season of toil, I tried to buy new clothes, of which I was in great need, for I had gone six months without a shirt. But on learning the prices of goods, I realized that my money would not go far. I was able to buy just two shirts, at ten pounds of beaver skin each; a pair of scarlet leggings, fashionably garnished with ribbon, at fifteen pounds of beaver skin; and a blanket, at twenty pounds of beaver skin. In paying such high prices, I quickly depleted my wealth, but not before I had bought ammunition and laid in an ample supply of tobacco, of which I had grown quite fond.

I asked a Frenchman about the British soldiers who had been taken prisoner at the fort the year before. He informed me that Major Etherington and the others had been freed from captivity the previous autumn. Their freedom had been won by a lieutenant named William Gorrell, who had been commandant of the fort at Green Bay. Lieutenant Gorrell, it seems, had inspired a war party of loyal Sauks, Foxes, Menominees, and Winnebagos to accompany him to Michilimackinac, where he had demanded that the Chippewas turn over their British captives. In this he had been assisted by several Frenchmen, including Father Jaunay, the Jesuit priest, and Charles Michel de Langlade, the half-breed war hero, each of whom had helped persuade the Chippewas to release their prisoners. The freed British soldiers had retreated in canoes to Montreal.

I was pleased to learn that my countrymen were safe—but I envied them as well. It seemed that I was now the only Englishman still alive in all the Upper Country.

28

My family and I soon left Fort Michilimackinac, to build our lodge within the Chippewa village that was taking shape on the Isle of Michilimackinac. Eight days passed uneventfully, but on the ninth day there arrived a war party of twelve Chippewas, fresh from fighting the English at Detroit. This turbulent band of angry, young men hailed from Bay of Saguenaum. They had come to Michilimackinac to convince their brethren to join Pontiac, in his siege of the English fort at Detroit. One of the young warriors chose a spot in the middle of the village, and there he sat, day and night, beating his war drum, muttering wild songs, and seeking a vision of victory in battle.

Wawatam soon brought me the disagreeable news that the Saguenaum warriors had recognized me as an Englishman and that they intended to kill me. They planned to make of me "a mess of English broth" to serve to the village, in order to bolster the courage of the warriors of Michilimackinac.

Wawatam was quick to exert himself in my defense. He called together the chiefs and warriors of Michilimackinac, who discussed the matter for but a short time. Chief Minavavana then summoned the Saguenaum warriors to council, and he surprised them by having me sit by his side. He declared that I was under his protection and that he would personally avenge any harm I might suffer. He told the warriors of Saguenaum to return to Detroit, saying that the young men of Michilimackinac would not be so foolish as to join them in the war.

The Saguenaum warriors departed angrily, without a word.

A few hours later we were surprised to hear that a canoe of Iroquois from Niagara had just arrived at Fort Michilimackinac. We crowded into our canoes to cross the strait, eager as we were for news from the east.

On the beach next to the fort we found six Iroquois warriors of the Seneca nation, accompanied by two Frenchmen. The faces of the Senecas were painted blue and white, the colors of peace. Their heads were close-shaven, but for feathered scalp locks at the crowns. Two or three of them wore British medallions on their breasts. The Chippewas greeted the Senecas peacefully, with the obligatory smoking of pipes. Then one of the Senecas, taking up a thick belt of wampum, delivered a short but pointed speech.

"Chippewas. We are men of the Seneca nation. We visit your country in peace, and we bring you this belt of peace. We come here as envoys of Sir William Johnson. We come here to tell you that Sir William Johnson is preparing a grand feast at Fort Niagara. His kettles are full. His fires are lit. His face is painted white. He is sending envoys to all the Indian nations of the Upper Country. He is inviting all to partake in the feast.

"Sir William Johnson has sent us here to ask that you join in a new friendship with the English. We ask that you join in a new friendship with us as well, and with our brothers among the Six Nations. By joining in a new friendship with us, you will also join in friendship with the English, for the Six Nations have made peace with the English.

"Chippewas. Think carefully of what I say to you. The English and the Six Nations are on the march with a grand army. Before the fall of the leaf, their boats and their canoes will appear on these waters, in numbers like the waves. Each boat will be full of English soldiers. Each canoe will be full of Iroquois warriors.

"Chippewas. Sir William Johnson urges you to seize this opportunity for peace, for if you fail to do so, he promises that he will destroy you utterly. When your enemies appear before you, it will be too late to talk of peace."

The Seneca orator drew forth a war hatchet, and held it aloft in his right hand. In his left hand he raised the belt of wampum.

"Chippewas. You see before you your choice. You may choose this belt of peace, and it will serve as a chain of friendship to join your nation with the English. Or you may choose this war hatchet, and we will see which nation will make it the bloodier.

"These are the words of Sir William Johnson. I will await your reply."

The tenor of the Seneca's speech raised great concern among the Chippewas, who met among themselves to discuss whether they should send envoys to Fort Niagara. They knew that little time could be lost, but they considered the matter to be of such great importance that they thought it called for more than merely human knowledge. Accordingly they began preparations for invoking the Great Turtle—the all-knowing, all-seeing messenger of the Chippewa spirit world.

The women set to work building a large temple lodge of poles and birchbark. Inside the lodge they erected a narrow tent, within which a prophet was to conjure and to summon the Great Turtle. The frame of the prophet's tent was built of five sturdy posts, each ten feet long, and each from a different type of tree. The posts were firmly planted two feet in the ground and were bound together at the top by a hoop, forming a structure in the shape of a chimney. Over the structure were spread moose skins, fastened together by thongs of moose hide. On one side of the tent a flap was left hanging loose, to allow for the prophet's entry.

When the temple lodge and the prophet's tent were finished, there was nothing more to do but await the approach of night. I was vitally interested in the outcome of the ceremony, for I knew that a Chippewa voyage to Fort Niagara might provide me with a means of escaping the Upper Country. (I did not allow myself too much hope, however, for my hopes had been dashed too many times before by unexpected turns of fate.)

As night fell, the entire village gathered within the temple lodge. Fires were kindled in a circle about the prophet's tent. The flames cast unearthly shadows on the walls and the ceiling. Soon the prophet appeared, nearly naked, his entire body painted green, his face painted red. A hush fell over the audience. As the prophet approached the tent, he muttered incantations and rattled his shishiquoi. He was a shriveled old man, yet he seemed strangely animated and powerful. A flap of the tent was opened for the prophet, and he crawled beneath it.

No sooner was the prophet's head within the tent than the entire structure began to tremble. (I was startled by this, for I had watched the tent being built, and I knew its framing was sound.) The prophet within the tent began to sing and beat his drum, and the tent began to sway back and forth like the mast of a ship caught in a tempest on the open sea. The more the prophet sang, the more violently the tent swayed to and fro.

Suddenly the singing stopped.

Strange voices came from within the tent—some yelling, some barking like dogs, some howling like wolves—and within the horrible concert were mingled sobs of anguish and screams of the sharpest pain. Articulate speech was uttered as well, as if from human lips, but in a tongue entirely foreign to either Chippewa or Englishman. The audience hissed at the terrible voices, recognizing them as belonging to evil spirits that deceive mankind. The frightful noises continued for some time, then abruptly stopped.

Faintly at first, a feeble voice, like the cry of a young puppy, seemed to announce the arrival of a new character within the tent. No sooner was the new voice heard than the Chippewas all clapped their hands for joy and declared the voice to be that of the Great Turtle—the Spirit that Never Lies.

The arrival of the Great Turtle inspired new sounds from within the tent. During the next half hour we were entertained with a succession of fine songs, each sung in a different voice, none in the voice of the prophet. Finally the prophet himself addressed the assembled multitude. From within the tent he formally announced the presence of the Great Turtle, and he declared that the spirit was ready and willing to answer all questions put to it.

The questions were to be posed by Chief Minavavana. But before the chief spoke, he placed a rope of black tobacco under the flap of the tent, as an offering to the Great Turtle. Chief Minavavana then asked the prophet to inquire whether the English were preparing for war, and whether there were many English soldiers at Fort Niagara. The prophet, in turn, posed these questions to the spirit, and the prophet's tent began to rock so violently that I expected it to fall to the ground. I presumed that all the shaking was a prelude to the spirit's answers, but instead of answers, a terrific cry suddenly resounded throughout the temple.

The Great Turtle had departed.

A quarter of an hour passed in silence, as I waited impatiently for the next scene in the imposture. At last the return of the Great Turtle was announced by the sound of his voice coming from within the prophet's tent. The Great Turtle commenced to deliver a speech, in a language wholly unintelligible to everyone but the prophet. The prophet informed us that the spirit, during its brief absence, had soared across Lake Huron and the Country of the Hurons, had paused for a few moments above Fort Niagara, and then had sailed onward, over Lake Ontario and the River Saint Lawrence, as far east as Montreal. At Fort Niagara the Great Turtle had seen no great number of soldiers, but on flying over the River Saint Lawrence, the spirit had seen the water covered with boats. Each boat was filled with redcoated soldiers, in numbers like the leaves on the trees. The soldiers were coming up the river, the spirit said, to make war on the Chippewas.

Chief Minavavana posed a third question to the prophet. "If our young men visit Sir William Johnson, will they be welcomed in peace?"

I listened intently for the answer.

The Great Turtle, this time without a fresh trip to Niagara, responded immediately with the most gratifying news: "Sir William Johnson will fill their canoes with gifts—kettles, guns, lead, powder, and large casks of rum, such that the strongest Chippewa cannot lift. Every Chippewa will return safely to his family."

At this the joy within the temple was universal. Amidst a general clapping of hands, a hundred voices cried, "I will go! I will go!" I shared strongly in the sentiment.

With questions of public interest resolved, individuals now took the opportunity to ask the Great Turtle personal questions, such as the condition of an absent friend, or the fate of an ill relative. I stayed at the temple lodge to watch the prophet's show, while the others in my family retired to their lodge to sleep.

As I listened to the visions and predictions of the Great Turtle, I noticed that the spirit's answers allowed for great freedom of interpretation. And yet I must confess that I, too, yielded to my anxiety for the future. When it was my turn, I placed an offering of tobacco under the flap of the tent, and I asked the spirit whether I would ever again see my native land. My question was put to the spirit by the prophet, and the tent trembled and swayed as usual. The spirit's answer came back quickly: "Take courage and fear no danger, for nothing will harm you. In the end, you will return safely to your country."

The Great Turtle's assurances wrought so strongly on my gratitude that I placed a second offering of tobacco within the flap of the tent.

That night the assembled Chippewas chose twenty men to make the long journey to Niagara. The chosen twenty set to work preparing their equipage, for their voyage was to begin early the next morning. I asked Chief Minavavana if I might accompany the Chippewa envoys on their voyage to Niagara. He readily agreed. I assured him that I would do everything in my power to help the envoys make peace with the English.

I now was faced with the difficult task of telling my family that I wished to leave them. I dreaded the task, for I did not want to hurt anyone's feelings.

It was late at night, and a cold fog was rising off the lake, when I finally made my way back to my family's lodge. Within the lodge I found Wawatam and Old Mother, still awake, sitting over the embers of a dying fire. The others were asleep.

"Father, Old Mother," I whispered, "the canoes soon will be ready to depart for Niagara. Their departure may be the last chance that ever I have to return to my homeland. It pains me to think of leaving you, but I must go."

Wawatam and Old Mother showed no surprise at my announcement. Wawatam calmly filled his pipe, and the three of us smoked from it. I watched my parents' faces, as they watched the smoke rise into the air.

Wawatam spoke slowly. "I am glad, my son, that you have this chance to return to your country. Though you are my son, I have not forgotten that you are a prisoner here." He looked out across the dark lake, where a streak of gray light heralded the coming dawn. "This will be a fine day, Alexander Henry. It will be the day of your freedom."

Old Mother awoke the others and told them of my plans to leave. We all smoked together in silence. No one tried to convince me to stay.

I packed my wardrobe, which consisted of just two shirts, leggings, a blanket, and a musket. I left the rest of my belongings for my family, including the silver armbands with which they had adorned me the summer before. Wawatam, however, insisted that I keep the collars of wampum he had placed around my neck when first he adopted me into his family.

All but Sassaba were silent, as I prepared for my departure. Sassaba, however, posed dozens of questions to me: "When you live among the English, Mekawees, will you buy a horse and a carriage? Will you hire a servant, who will dress you in the morning? Will you ride on a sailing ship? Will you fish in the ocean? Will you hunt for whales? Will you marry? Will you have children?"

I responded to Sassaba's questions with what few answers I knew. To most of his questions I simply replied, "I do not know."

And when Sassaba asked the inevitable question—"Will you ever return to us?"—I again said, "I do not know."

The time for my departure came quickly. Wawatam filled his pipe and handed it to me. "My son. This may be the last time that ever we smoke from the same pipe. I am sorry to part with you. You know the affection I hold for you. You know the dangers to which I have exposed myself and my family, to save you from your enemies. I am happy that my efforts have not been in vain."

My family walked with me to the lakeshore to wish me farewell. I realized that I was as sorry to leave them as they were sorry to see me go. One by one, I thanked each of them for the many acts of goodness shown me.

To Sassaba I gave my clay pipe, asking that he remember our adventures together whenever he smoked from it. He, in turn, gave me his gaily decorated, three-cornered hat, which he fancied would serve me well among the English.

Old Mother embraced me. "How happy I am, Mekawees, that you can return to the country of your people." She smiled broadly as she bid me farewell, but tears marked her cheeks.

Finally I stood before Wawatam. My heart was in my throat, and I resorted to quoting scripture. "Father, there is a sacred saying among the English:

> *'He who pursues righteousness and kindness will find honor and life.'*

The two of us clasped hands. I looked into Wawatam's eyes, perhaps for the last time, and I knew what needed to be said. "My father, nothing can break the cord that binds us together. I will remember you always. Thank you for saving my life."

I walked to the water's edge and took my place in a canoe. I lifted my paddle and pulled it back through the water, in unison with the strokes of my fellow canoe men. Our canoes glided swiftly away from shore.

Suddenly I heard Wawatam's powerful voice open into prayer, and I turned to look back at him. He was looking upward. His arms were raised to the sky. He was beseeching Gichi Manido to care for me—his son—till the time we should meet again.

I fixed my gaze on the horizon before me and tried to contain my emotions.

My canoe mates fell silent, perhaps out of respect for the prayer that resounded at their backs. We paddled onward, into a brilliant sunrise. Wawatam's voice faded into the distance behind us. The lake was calm. The air was still. Our canoes were encompassed by silence.

After a time I turned to look back upon the Isle of Michilimackinac. I again saw my family—a small knot of people on a distant horizon. I again saw my father—his arms raised in a prayer I could not hear.

I knew my father's prayers would serve me all my life.

Sources

Literary sources used in writing *Enemies* are listed below, in order of descending importance.

Travels and Adventures in Canada and the Indian Territories Between the Years 1760 and 1776
By Alexander Henry
   Much of the plot of *Enemies* was drawn from Alexander Henry's own true story. Henry's memoirs of his youth, committed to paper when he was in his late sixties, were first published in 1809, and were reprinted in 1901. Henry's memoirs are exceptional among frontier narratives, for they tell a story in which compassion prevails over racial hatred and violence.

Kitchi-Gami: Life Among the Lake Superior Ojibway
By Johann Kohl
   Johann Kohl, a German ethnologist, lived among the Ojibway (or Chippewas) for four months in 1855. Unlike other writers of his time, Kohl saw admirable qualities in the culture of the Chippewas. He wrote, "When I was in Europe, and knew them [the Indians] only from books, I must own I considered them rude, cold-blooded, rather uninteresting people. But when I had once shaken hands with them, I felt that they were men and brothers, and had a good portion of warm

blood and sound understanding." Kohl's book served as a rich source of cultural detail.

Jesuit Relations and Allied Documents; Vols. 48 and 50
Edited by Reuben Thwaites
   The letters of early Jesuit missionaries in the wilderness—in particular the letters of Father Claude Allouez and Father Claude Dablon—provided *Enemies* with the lamentations voiced by Father Louis Jaunay.

Voyages of Pierre Esprit Radisson
By Pierre Esprit Radisson
   Radisson was the first European to write in any detail of the Great Lakes wilderness. In the winter of 1658-59 he suffered through a famine among Indians living near Lac Courte Oreilles, in what is now northern Wisconsin. Much of Radisson's account of that famine appears in the words of Etienne Campion in *Enemies*.

Algic Researches, Comprising Inquiries Respecting the Mental Characteristics of the North American Indians
By Henry Rowe Schoolcraft
   Schoolcraft recorded a number of Chippewa legends while working as Indian agent among the Chippewas in the early 1800's. His writings inspired the poem "Song of Hiawatha," by Henry Wadsworth Longfellow, as well as some of the winter tales told by Wawatam and Old Mother in *Enemies*.

Description of Louisiana
By Louis Hennepin
   Hennepin, a Franciscan priest, served under Robert Cavelier de La Salle in the voyage of 1680. In his account of that ill-fated voyage, Hennepin described in splendid detail the prairies of the Illinois Country and recalled his own captivity at the hands of the Issati Sioux.

Indian Tribes of the Upper Mississippi Valley
Edited by Emma Blair
   Blair's book contains a speech delivered by French explorer Nicolas Perrot in 1668, when Perrot made first contact with Potawatomis, Mascoutins, and Miamis living on the west coast of Lake Michigan. Perrot's words were echoed in *Enemies*, in the French explorer's speech as recalled by Makwa.

Letters from North America
By Antoine Silvy
   Silvy, a Jesuit priest, recorded his observations of the Illinois Country in the years 1710-12.

Travels Through the Interior Parts of North America in the Years 1766, 1767, and 1768
By Jonathan Carver
   Carver, a young Englishman, toured the Great Lakes wilderness in the years 1766-68. He fancied himself an explorer, working on behalf of the King of England, although Frenchmen had explored the Upper Country more than a century before Carver's time.

Sir William Johnson Papers; Vol. 10
Edited by Milton Hamilton
   The letters of Sir William Johnson, superintendent of Indian affairs in North America in the years preceding Pontiac's Rebellion, provide insights into the failings of British policy toward the Indians.

Letters and Notes on the Manners, Customs, and Condition of the North American Indian; Vol. 2
By George Catlin
   A frontier artist, Catlin was the first white man to write of the Pipestone Quarry, in what is now southwestern Minnesota. His description of that site was the source of the legend of "Fountain of the Pipe," as related by Wawatam in *Enemies*.

Collections of the State Historical Society of Wisconsin; **Vols. 3 and 18**
   The Wisconsin collections contain extensive writings by French and English frontiersmen. In particular, the journal of fur trader Peter Pond provided for *Enemies* the details of a summer fur fair, and the recollections of Augustin Grignon provided insights into the character of Grignon's grandfather, Charles Michel de Langlade.

Michigan Pioneer and Historical Collections; **Vol. 8**
   The Michigan collections enriched *Enemies* with the vision of the Wolf prophet, as recited by Pontiac in 1763. The prophet's vision served as a call to arms for the Indians of the Upper Country.

Louisiana Historical Collections; **Vol. 2**
   This volume contains a narrative written by Father Jacques Marquette, a Jesuit priest, describing the exploration of the Mississippi River in 1673 by Louis Jolliet.

Other Readings

The author recommends the following books, for further reading on related topics.

Up Country: Voices from the Great Lakes Wilderness
Edited by William Seno
    A compilation of vividly written chronicles from the Great Lakes wilderness. Excerpts from many of the sources listed above appear in *Up Country*.

Black Elk Speaks
By Black Elk and John Neihardt
    The recollections and visions of an American Indian—a Sioux medicine man—who fought in the Battle of the Little Big Horn, and who saw white soldiers and settlers take his people's lands.

The Voyageur
By Grace Lee Nute
    A well-researched description of the colorful lives of French voyageurs who served the Canadian fur trade.

France and England in North America
By Francis Parkman
    The classic history of the struggle for the North American continent.

The Conquerors
By Allan Eckert
   A history, in novel format, of Pontiac's Rebellion.

The French Regime in Wisconsin and the Northwest
By Louise Phelps Kellogg
   The definitive history of French efforts in the Great Lakes region, between the years 1603 and 1761.

The British Regime in Wisconsin and the Northwest
By Louise Phelps Kellogg
   A chronicle of the British presence in the Great Lakes region, from the end of the French and Indian War to the end of the War of 1812.

Places

Bay of Boutchitaouy: Saint Martin Bay, north of Mackinac Island, at the northwest end of Lake Huron.

Bay of Saguenaum: Saginaw Bay, on the west coast of Lake Huron.

Cape Saint Ignace: a point of land on the north coast of the Straits of Mackinac, formerly the site of the Jesuit Mission of Saint Ignace.

Chekagou: now the site of Chicago, Illinois; formerly the site of a canoe portage linking the Chicago River, which flows into Lake Michigan, with the Des Plaines River, which flows into the Illinois River.

Coteau des Prairies: "hill of the prairies;" high land in Pipestone County, southwest Minnesota; the present site of Pipestone National Monument.

Fond du Lac: "bottom of the lake;" at the west end of Lake Superior.

Fort de Chartres: a French fort on the Mississippi River, fifty miles below the present site of East Saint Louis, Illinois.

Fort Lévis: a French fort on Isle Royal (now Chimney Island), on the Saint Lawrence River, seventy-five miles below the outlet of Lake Ontario.

Fort Duquesne: a French fort at the present site of Pittsburgh, Pennsylvania.

Fort Edward Augustus: a British fort at the present site of Green Bay, Wisconsin.

Fort Le Boeuf: a British fort near the present site of Edinboro, northwest Pennsylvania.

Fort Miamis: a British fort on the Maumee River, at the present site of Fort Wayne, Indiana.

Fort Michilimackinac: a French fort that was captured by the British, on the south shore of the Straits of Mackinac, Michigan.

Fort Niagara: a British fort located where the Niagara River empties into Lake Ontario.

Fort Ouiatenon: a British fort on the Wabash River, near the present site of Lafayette, Indiana

Fort Pontchartrain: a French fort that was captured by the British, at the present site of Detroit, Michigan.

Fort Presque Isle: a British fort at the present site of Presque Isle State Park, Pennsylvania, on the south coast of Lake Erie.

Fort Saint Joseph: a British fort at the present site of Niles, southwest Michigan.

Fort Sandusky: a British fort at the present site of Sandusky, Ohio, on the south coast of Lake Erie.

Fort Venango: a British fort near the present site of Venango, northwest Pennsylvania.

Fountain of the Pipe: an Indian pipestone quarry, revered as a sacred place by many tribes; now Pipestone National Monument in southwest Minnesota.

Grand Portage: A trading post and canoe portage linking the north coast of Lake Superior with the Pigeon River; located at the northeast tip of Minnesota.

Grand Village of the Illinois: a populous village of Illinois Indians located on the Illinois River, near the present site of Starved Rock State Park, in central Illinois.

Grande Traverse: Grand Traverse Bay, on the east coast of Lake Michigan, a hundred fifty miles southwest of the Straits of Mackinac.

Hampton docks: a colonial seaport at the present site of Hampton, Virginia.

Isle de Maurepas: a large island off the east coast of Lake Superior.

Isle de Montreal: a large island on the Saint Lawrence River, on which the City of Montreal is located.

Isle de Perrot: an island on the Saint Lawrence River, located just west of Isle de Montreal.

Isle du Castor: Beaver Island, a large island at the north end of Lake Michigan, forty miles west of the Straits of Mackinac.

Isle of Michilimackinac: Mackinac Island, located just northeast of the Straits of Mackinac.

Isle of Saint Martin: Saint Martin Island, lying off the east coast of Point Saint Ignace, ten miles northeast of the Straits of Mackinac.

L'Arbre Croche: "crooked tree;" an Ottawa village near the present site of Cross Village, Michigan, fifteen miles southwest of the Straits of Mackinac.

L'Oiseau: a rocky promontory overlooking the Ottawa River, near the present site of Deep River, southeast Ontario Province, Canada.

La Cloche: "the bell;" Great Cloche Island in the North Channel of Lake Huron, north of Manitoulin Island.

Lac à la Pluie: Rainy Lake, just north of International Falls, Minnesota, in southwest Ontario Province, Canada.

Lac de Saint Louis: Lac Saint Louis; a wide stretch of the Saint Lawrence River, just above Montreal.

Lac des Deux-Montagnes: a wide stretch of the Ottawa River just above Montreal, where the Ottawa River joins the Saint Lawrence River.

Lac des Isles: a lake in south central Ontario Province, Canada, north of Lake Nipigon.

Lac Nipigon: a large lake in south central Ontario Province, Canada, fifty miles north of Lake Superior.

Lac Nipisingue: Lake Nipissing, northeast of Georgian Bay in southeast Ontario Province, Canada; part of the Ottawa River trade route.

Lachine: a rapid on the Saint Lawrence River, just above Montreal; so named because French explorer Cavalier de la Salle outfitted his expeditions here, and skeptics scoffed at La Salle for seeking a trade route to China.

Lake of the Sorcerers: Lake Nipissing; see above.

Longue Sault: Long Sault, a stretch of rapids on the Ottawa River, just below Hawkesbury, Ontario Province, Canada.

Matawa Sipi: Mattawa River of southeast Ontario Province, Canada; enters the Ottawa River at Mattawa; part of the Ottawa River trade route.

Mission of Saint Ignace: a Jesuit mission to the Indians of the Upper Great Lakes; founded in 1670 on Cheguamegon Bay on the south coast of Lake Superior, and later moved to the Mackinac area.

Oswegatchi: a settlement on the Saint Lawrence River below Lake Ontario, now the site of Ogdensburg, New York.

Oswego: a settlement on the southeast coast of Lake Ontario, now the site of Oswego, New York..

Pays d'en Haut: the "Upper Country," a name the French gave to the region surrounding the Upper Great Lakes.

Point de Grondeur: a rocky promontory on the north coast of Georgian Bay, in Humboldt Township, south Ontario Province, Canada.

Portages à la Vase: formerly a series of canoe portages, linking the Ottawa River trade route with the French River and Lake Huron; located at North Bay in southeast Ontario Province, Canada.

River Aux Sables: Big Sable River, Manistee County, Michigan; empties into Lake Michigan just north of Ludington.

River of the Foxes: Fox River of east central Wisconsin; empties into Green Bay at the City of Green Bay.

River of the Missouris: Missouri River.

River Saint Joseph: Saint Joseph River; empties into Lake Michigan at Benton Harbor, southwest Michigan.
River Saint Pierre: Minnesota River.

Rivière des Francais: French River of Ontario Province, Canada; drains Lake Nipissing and empties into Georgian Bay; a part of the Ottawa River trade route.

Rivière du Moine: a river in southwest Quebec Province, Canada; joins the Ottawa River sixty miles east of Mattawa.

Rivière Petite: Mattawa River; see above.

Sault de Parisienne: one of a series of rapids on the French River between Lake Nipissing and Georgian Bay; located in southeast Quebec Province, Canada.

Sault de Rideau: a waterfall at the mouth of the Rideau River, at the present site of Ottawa, Canada.

Sault de Sainte Anne: a rapid at Montreal, where the Ottawa River joins the Saint Lawrence River.

Sault de Sainte Marie: a rapid at the present site of Sault Ste. Marie, Michigan, now the site of the Soo Locks.

Sleeping Bears: tall hills of sand overlooking Lake Michigan at the present site of Sleeping Bear Dunes National Lakeshore, west of Traverse City, Michigan.

Trois Rivières: an early French settlement on the Saint Lawrence River, midway between the cities of Quebec and Montreal.

Upper Country: the region surrounding the Upper Great Lakes.

Upper Lakes: the Upper Great Lakes.

Wagoshense: Waugoshance Point, a point of land extending westward into Lake Michigan, fifteen miles west of the Straits of Mackinac.

Fort Sault de Sainte Marie

Lac Nipisingue

Rivière des Francais

Fort Michilimackinac

Lake Huron

Bay of Saguenaum

Fort Pontchartrain

Lake Erie

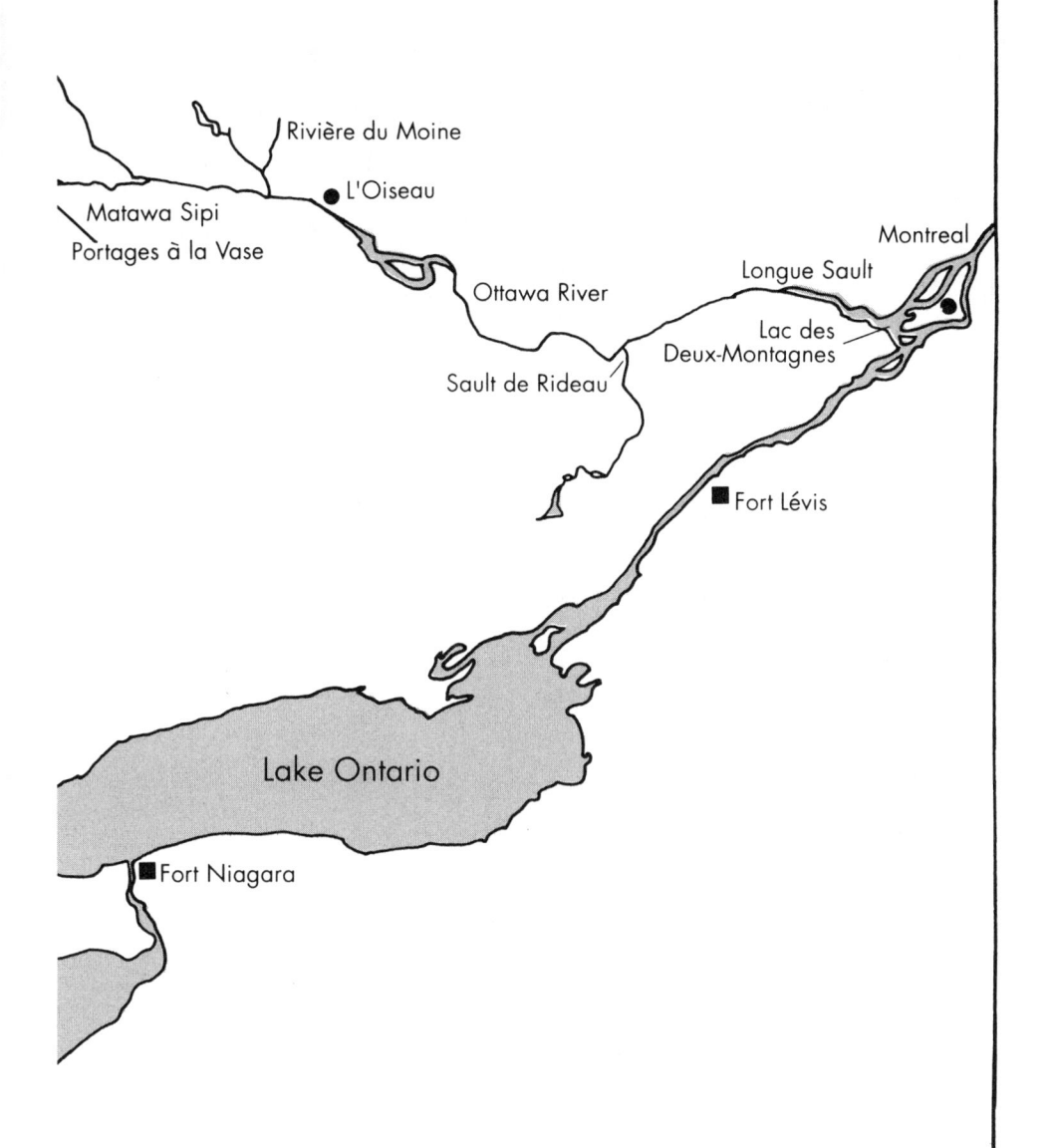

Locations and modern place names are identified in an appendix

Map of Lake Michigan

- Fort Michilimackinac
- Isle du Castor
- Sleeping Bears
- Le Grande Traverse
- River of the Foxes
- Fort Edward Augustus
- River Aux Sables
- Lake Michigan
- Chekagou Portage
- Fort Saint Joseph

Locations and modern place names are identified in an appendix

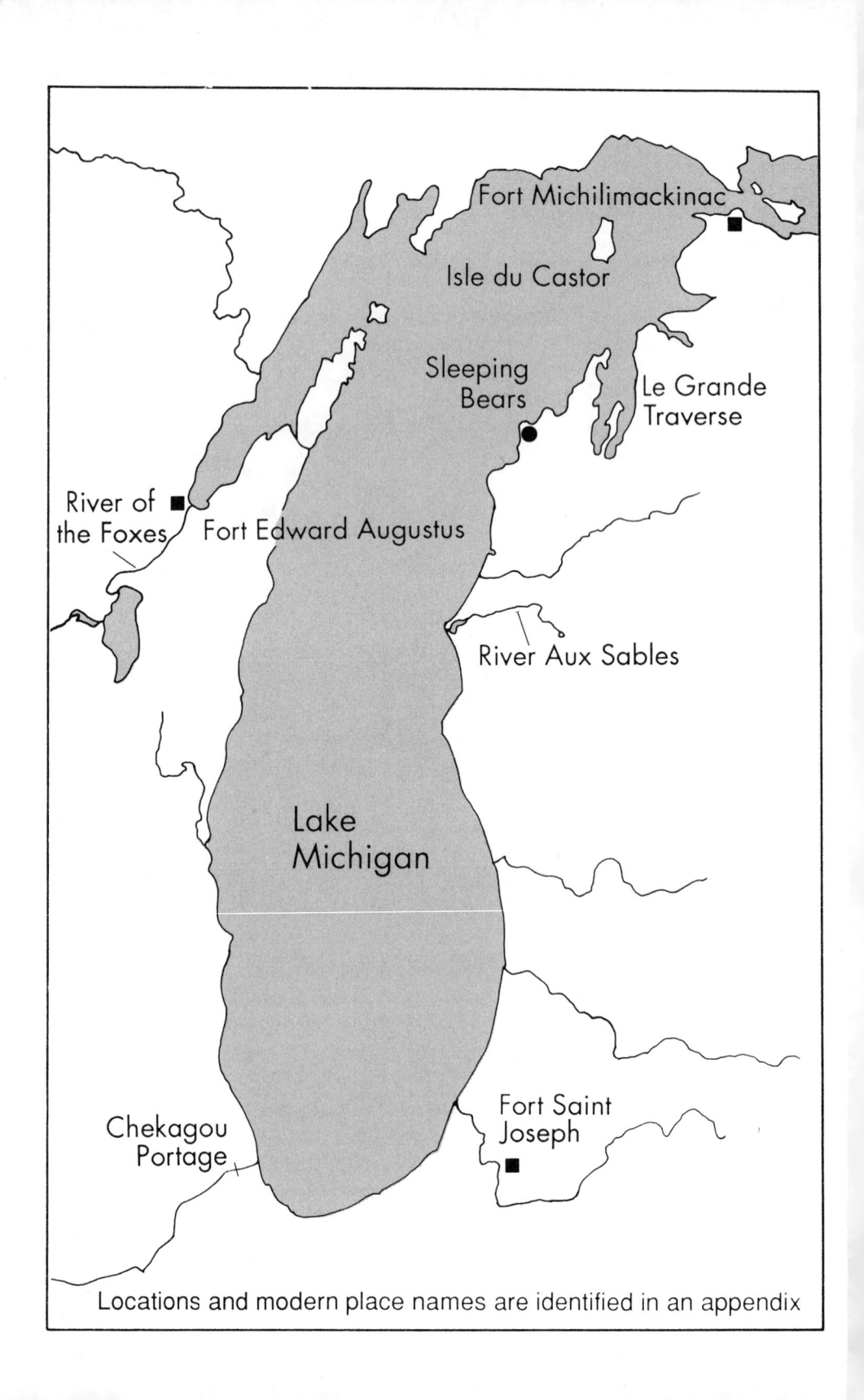

Lake Superior

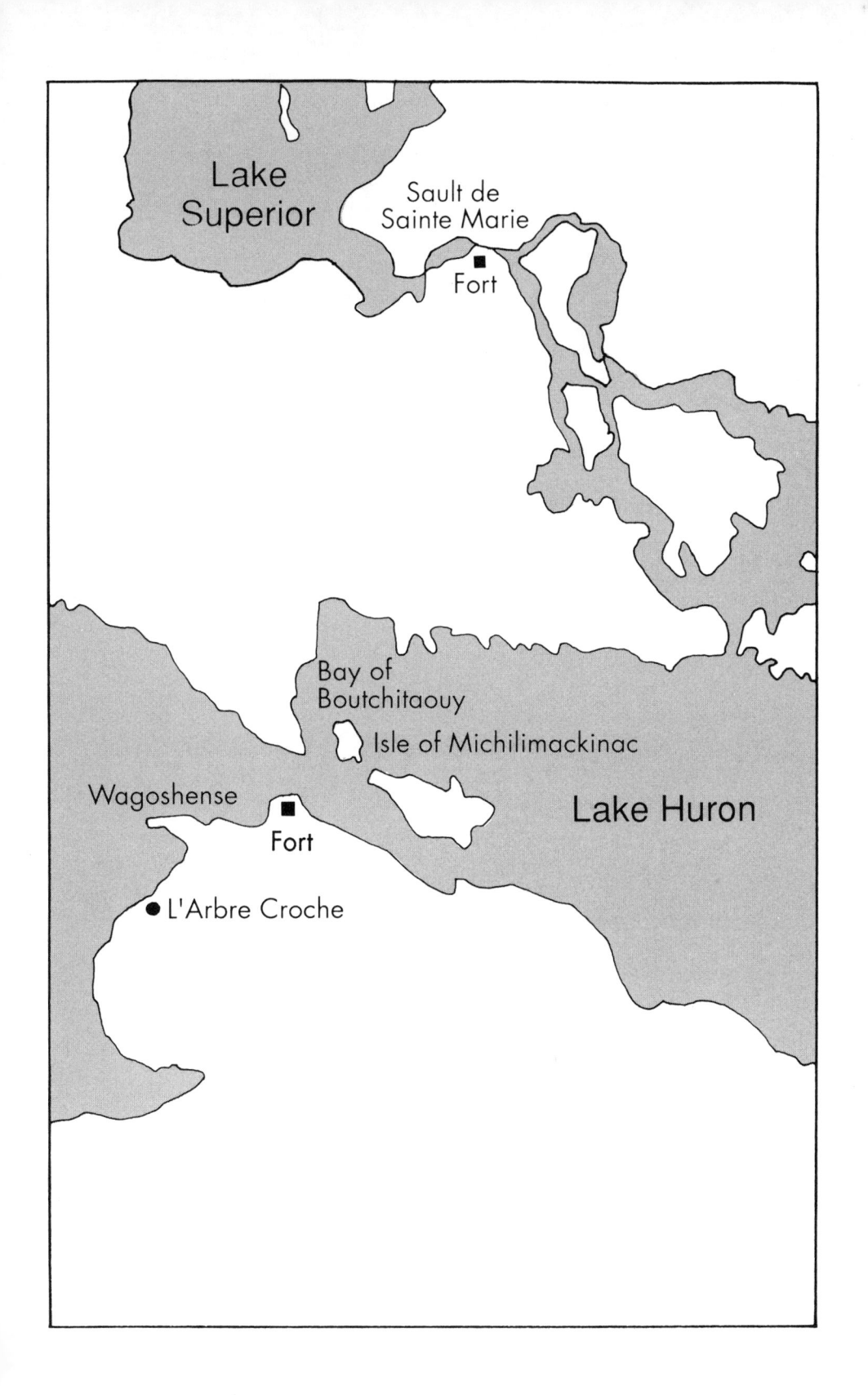

Sault de Sainte Marie
■ Fort

Bay of Boutchitaouy

Isle of Michilimackinac

Wagoshense
■ Fort

• L'Arbre Croche

Lake Huron